TIGER ISLAND

SGT. HAWK BOOK FOUR

PATRICK CLAY

ROUGH
EDGES
PRESS

Tiger Island
Paperback Edition

Rough Edges Press
An Imprint of Wolfpack Publishing
5130 S. Fort Apache Rd. 215-380
Las Vegas, NV 89148

roughedgespress.com

This book is a work of fiction. Any references to historical events, real people or real places are used fictitiously. Other names, characters, places and events are products of the author's imagination, and any resemblance to actual events, places or persons, living or dead, is entirely coincidental.

Paperback ISBN 978-1-68549-125-3
eBook ISBN 978-1-68549-124-6

TIGER ISLAND

THE SERGEANT OF DEATH!

"Them no good sons of bitches," Hawk snarled. Anger quelled any fear Hawk might have had. He snatched a frag grenade from his web belt and straightened its cotter pin on the fore-sight of his Thompson. He pulled the ring and the pin slid grudgingly through the two holes that held down the spoon. Holding his hand around the body of the pineapple, he gripped the safety lever down. Hawk threw an elbow out and pulled himself toward the unchallenged Nambu machine guns.

His eyes were nearly closed as he pulled himself forward, an inch at a time. His mouth was jammed shut, drooping defiantly at the corners. He thought of nothing. The sight and sound of the lightning spewing from the conical flash guards prevented his brain from functioning.

He looked into the two mouths of the spitting guns.

The sergeant opened his hand, and the safety lever flew off. Hawk's arm lashed stiffly up from the earth. The grenade turned end over end. As the grenade went off, Hawk jumped to his feet.

1

"They say that there is a man out there. Sergeant Hawk is his name. But...I don't know." That was what the colonel had said.

The Japanese guns were quiet that night. None of the men facing them knew why. Other men, far away in the regions of safety reserved for superiors, knew why. There was a problem. It was a big one, and both sides were momentarily confused by it. And now both sides were quiet.

Captain Clinton Jordan ducked beneath the low doorway of his bunker. His grimy clothing creaked as he did. It was a Japanese pillbox, deep and safe; it had recently been converted into the company command post. It smelled safe, close and cozy, with that Japanese smell of fish and rice. The smell had first withstood American artillery, and later that of the Japanese. Inside lolled the sparse staff common to a Marine Corps command post. The night was clear and warm, and Jordan could hear men talking. Other smells blew in from the forest. Smells of death crept through the little doorway. It was a sickening odor that never passed and yet you never got used to. It was meant to be smelled and hurried away from. It was nature's way of warning you. Even if you could do that, it would linger in your nostrils and tease your throat with a gag.

Jordan had been here for four days. He hadn't seen the nearby front. Marine front lines seldom stayed in one place for four days. These hadn't moved in ten. Because of the problem. Jordan didn't know the details yet. He did know that marine officers led—and leading meant from the front. He knew he had to go up there. He had to see this Sergeant Hawk. Colonel Hulmore had to be sure that Hawk was still alive. He couldn't put it off any longer. He had to be the one to do it. Well, maybe he *could* send someone.

The executive officer, Lieutenant Szerch, walked to Jordan's side. His lumbering bulk blocked the light of the lantern. He knew something was bothering the captain. "Well," said Jordan, conscious of the fact that he could still change his mind at this point, "I think I'll go have a look at the front."

"Yes, sir," Szerch encouraged. "It's been pretty quiet, so this is probably the best time."

"Yes. I'll go to first platoon's positions." First platoon was in the center of the company line. They took most of the casualties, during both the attack and the counterattack. Not that that was an accomplishment.

He had to go see them. He could do no less. One couldn't reach their position in the daylight. Enemy artillery, of an intensity never before experienced, kept them cut off by day. Constant mortar fire dropped straight from the sky and severed the telephone wires. But at night, men would take ammunition and supplies up to them. Tonight, Jordan would go with them. And he was beside himself with fear. The front line: the closest thing to hell that man could devise, a place so horrible that only night creatures dared slither into it.

He had to face the men that lived there. What would they think of him? Would they laugh in his face? He couldn't hold it against them if they did. What business did a twenty-three-year-old have in such a position? But now was the best time to go. He hadn't had the opportunity to do anything to make them hate him. If he waited any longer, they would distrust him, simply because of that fact.

Slipping outside, they walked through the damp island night, listening to the idle, distant conversations of the men. They were men whose words were at some distance from their brains. Shock and emotional numbness were lodged comfortably, somewhere between their minds and their tongues. Corporal Stinson, from supply, led the way. He went up there nearly every night. He liked it. He had put in for a transfer to a line company. That was easy to get. He was a short, skinny boy, who smiled every time he said something. The insects played their boring music.

"Watch your step, sir," Stinson advised, as they left the road. Szerch followed him across the muddy earth that lay before the jungle. Jordan took up the rear. Stinson carried no supplies tonight. The captain was his cargo. Stinson glanced back at them and smiled. The corporal's rifle was slung haphazardly across a narrow shoulder. The officers carried theirs. "Dead Jap, here, sir," the corporal smiled as they passed into the oppressive forest. It wasn't a wicked smile.

Jordan saw a dark, bloated shape in the shadows. It

was probably two to three times the size of a normal human body. The odor took his breath away. "What's the body doing here?" Jordan snapped, the outrage of it making him temporarily forget his fears.

"Hell, sir, we ain't seen no GR for our own guys, we sure as hell ain't gettin' together no burial detail for those bastards."

Jordan didn't answer. He would do what he could about it when he got back. He knew he couldn't change the organization and customs of the whole war. No sense in making a scene over it until he knew as a practical matter what could be done. A minute later he was glad that he had said no more about it. The three marines passed row upon row of slain enemy soldiers, lying in a clearing. They had fallen like stacks of dominoes, each slightly overlapping the next. Jordan flinched slightly, thinking for a microsecond that the corpses posed a danger. There would be no threat, however, barring a mass resurrection. It was incredible being among them. So many, so harmless. Too real to be real. Precision death. Death baffles the young. It all stops. How can it all stop?

Stinson walked on silently, his boots thudding against the damp earth with a calm rhythm. When will he stop? Jordan thought. My God, I couldn't have been this far behind the lines. He could feel the sense of foreboding with each step. The muscles around his neck bunched tighter and tighter until they began clawing at the muscles in his chest and restricting his breathing. In spite of his brain's constant warnings, his boots carried him closer and closer to a horror he had never experienced. They could see a shallow foxhole in the scraggly brush ahead. Thank God, Jordan sighed to himself. He wondered how far ahead of the hole the Japanese might lurk.

Stinson's stride never slowed. Jordan hadn't been under fire before, but he thought it wise to at least crouch a bit. Szerch and the corporal didn't see him bent over his rifle, taking his cautious steps. "Hey, Lennie," Stinson shouted in a bold and unmilitary manner, "I got the new skipper and Lieutenant Szerch."

A voice replied, "Come on, Stinson." Jordan stood erect and walked toward the hole. The man below stood up and saluted him. Jordan returned the salute before remembering that you don't salute on the front line. It makes you a target. He was about to jump into the hole, when Stinson lit a cigarette and shifted his weight casually to one leg. "This here's the second line of defense, sir," the corporal said. He said it just in time. Jordan had taken a step toward him. He intended to slap the cigarette out of his hand and push him into the hole. He had mistaken this rear area position for the front.

He remembered the map. They had to have a second line of defense due to infiltration—and in case the front suddenly collapsed. It all looked different from this perspective. It was an incoherent jumble. It felt different. But, yes, two squads of third platoon were in support positions.

"Seen anything?" Jordan croaked to the shadowy man in the hole.

"Sir? Oh, no, sir, not this far back. Not for a few days or so. I don't know what's goin' on out there. Just some shellin'. Damnedest thing."

"Uh...yeah. Well, that's good, isn't it? Let's go, Corporal," Jordan said. Stinson waved to Lennie and took up the march again. Jordan forced a nervous sigh. He had to remain quiet. He had almost made a fool of himself several times already. Quiet and humble, that's the ticket. Don't throw orders around. What the hell do you know about any of it?

They continued the walk until the tension mounted to a screaming peak. The captain was ready to admit that he had made a mistake. He had had the good fortune to be thrown into one of the few easy campaigns and had taken to pushing his luck. He considered slipping and twisting his ankle. No. He would see the front lines. My God, he had joined the Marine Corps, he could do that much. It was quiet tonight, everybody said so. It had been quiet.

The trees began to thin out. Their black bodies were denuded by violent white stripes. Palm, ficus, and rain trees changed into unidentifiable shards of twisted wood. The splintered stumps increased in frequency until the forest disappeared altogether. Craters and debris stretched far out into the night. The landscape looked like the underside of the planet Jupiter. The forest that once seemed oppressive, concealing and threatening was warm, protective and comforting in comparison to this.

"It's a good idea to stay low here, sir," Stinson said. "Sometimes we crawl it. People get killed on quiet nights, too, you know, sir."

"Thank you, Corporal," the captain replied, "I think we'll skip the crawling until it becomes necessary." That sounded good, Jordan thought. Sort of brave; not brave, tough. That was it. Tough.

"Yessir." Stinson kept his rifle slung over his shoulder. He harbored no misconceptions of being able to return any fire that might rake the open ground. If the shooting started, you had to save your ass and run like hell. Let the riflemen take care of the revenge department.

American dead rotted in the ragged craters. Others lay decomposing across the splintered stumps. The open sky was a dark purple. Disgusting, Jordan thought. Unheard of, for marines. They could at least recover the bodies in the darkness. "These are Americans, Corporal," Jordan called to Stinson.

The corporal went to one knee and spun around. His helmet straps swayed. Jordan swallowed hard when he saw the expression on Stinson's sweat-pocked face. "Better...better hold up on the conversation, sir," the corporal whispered urgently. The whites of his eyes glowed with a greenish tint beneath his helmet. "This... is it, you know, Captain, the Japs are out there. Those bodies ain't goin' nowhere."

Jordan flushed with embarrassment. He realized that the corpses were none of Stinson's affair. Still, it wasn't right. The Corps was touchy about those things. "What sort of men are these," Jordan whispered to Szerch. He meant it derogatorily.

Szerch, a bit of a dimwit, tried to be profound. "Live ones, sir," the exec whispered, "all they got left is their lives."

They reached the front line without incident, as so many had done before them. A thrill of excitement and accomplishment rippled through Jordan's vibrating intestines. He dropped into a slit trench. This was it. The ultimate. The front. And he was here.

A T-shaped hole was cut into the soft soil behind the slit trench. The smell of human waste billowed over it. That was where the animals that lived up here went to relieve themselves. There was nowhere else to go. They were supposed to bury it with shovels. After ten days, they were burying shit with shit. They probably didn't notice it anymore. It was the least of their inconveniences. Jordan saw a man at the end of the trench he had jumped into.

He was a small, wasted man, perched beneath a massive helmet. His rotted clothing seemed oversized for his disintegrating little body. His hair was long, his beard was filthy. Two eyes shimmered in his narrow head. "Hi, Eddie," Stinson said. "How come you didn't challenge us?"

"Either I kill you or I don't. No need talking it over," Eddie lowered his rifle muzzle. "You bring something to eat?" The voice was thin and hollow, weak and vicious.

"Not yet," Stinson answered. Jordan noticed that Stinson now looked like a perfectly normal human being, next to Eddie. Eddie was one of *them.* "I brung the new skipper to see you. I'll bring some stuff later. I got a few more trips to make."

"Hope you don't get killed, Stinson," Eddie said. His lips rolled back in slow motion in what could loosely be described as a smile. Teeth gleamed beneath the dirty beard. "I'd sure hate that."

Jordan stared with morbid fascination at Eddie. The rifleman hadn't acknowledged his presence. Captain's bars weren't as impressive here as in a rear area.

"Yeah, don't forget the thirty calibers next time, Stinson. You know, the kind that everybody uses?"

Stinson smiled. "This Eddie guy has a real sense of humor, Captain. I brought a bunch of forty-five caliber ammunition up one night and I ain't never heard the end of it."

"Six men got killed that night. Men, that is," Eddie said in his peculiar voice, too bitter to sound angry. "We didn't have no bullets. It was us and our bayonets and a lot of Japs."

"I know," Stinson nodded. He had heard this a hundred times.

"Then why'd you do it, Stinson?"

"I did what I's told, Eddie."

"You're gonna get killed crossin' that open space, Stinson." Eddie laughed a desolate, pleading whine of a laugh. "I'm sure gonna hate that."

"I'm Captain Jordan," the officer interrupted. He thought that the two men were preparing to fight one another. He didn't know that this was one of Eddie's good moods. The rifleman was too tired and weak to fight, no matter what impression was given off by the corroded shell of his twisted being.

"Yeah? What are you doin' here, Captain? Officers get killed just as quick as the rest of us up here." Eddie looked away from Jordan as he said this. It was the first indication of any normal inhibitions. He was intimidated by the officer. Officers can get you killed.

"Where's Hawk?" Stinson asked, taking none of it seriously.

"Hawk's a son of a bitch," Eddie said. He nodded his head. "One of these days they'll get him. We'll all be a lot safer when they do."

"Where is he?" Stinson asked again.

"In the listening post, right out there with them, like a dumb shithead."

They sat quietly looking in different directions. "I

guess you won't get to meet Sergeant Hawk, sir. We can't go way out there," Stinson commented. A wind puffed across the silent black void in front of the trenches.

"I'll go to him," Jordan heard himself say. He had to do it. "How far is it?"

"Only about seventy yards—straight ahead, Captain," Eddie laughed.

Stinson smiled. "Hell, Captain, it won't do no good to go see Hawk, anyways. He ain't got nothin' to say. You'll wanta get a little more time under your belt before you go out into something like that."

It got quiet. Eddie was the next to speak. "Nah," he drawled. "Leave Hawk alone. All he's good for is gettin' somebody killed."

"He's the platoon leader of the foremost unit." Jordan justified himself to them. "I've been ordered to give him a message."

"A message for Hawk?" Eddie shook his head. "That means an attack. That's the only message he ever gets. Don't worry, I'll give him the message, if he comes back. You go on back and take it easy, Captain."

Jordan considered it. He didn't let it show in his face. He only said, "No."

Stinson rubbed his palm across his mouth. "I'll go with you, sir, if you want," he said, his tone failing to disguise his misgivings.

"One of us should stay here, Captain," Lieutenant Szerch spoke up. He had no intentions of going. No one laughed at him. They all looked at him.

"Of course," said Jordan. "I'll go alone." That put a strange end to the conversation. It was too dangerous to open your mouth at that point.

Jordan felt a sour bag languishing in his stomach. It

swirled and lurched, clutching to get up and through his tightened throat. It was that pure and repulsive hell-born fear that few ever experience. It was cold and mocking. Like Eddie. He confronted it for the same reason that so many other Marines—and other men—had confronted it. The others were watching him.

Jordan looked over to the trench to his right. Shadowy, ratlike creatures crawled about over there. Other Eddies. He assumed that Stinson would see to it that they didn't shoot him in the back. He climbed over the sandbags without another word. Eddie looked over the bags at the officer's departing shadow. He smiled at Stinson.

His soggy stomach turned to dry ice as Jordan snaked across the open ground. Up and down, he clambered over the irregular earth, braced for a collision with a bullet on the higher folds of dirt. The ice turned into razor sharp steel. The steel cut into his nerves and his blood vessels. He couldn't think. Blood stayed out of his extremities. Air wouldn't go into his lungs. Still, he crawled forward, tasting all of the backed-up impurities in that burning and sour fear.

He saw the listening post. The haven was nothing more than a little hole behind a rot-papery log. He wriggled closer, his breath coming in metallic gasps. He could see himself squirming on the ground. He clenched his teeth like an actor performing for an imaginary camera. The grunt of a challenge came from the hole. The password escaped him. He paged through his memory. It wasn't there. The most important word in the vocabulary and it wasn't there. The more he thought about it, the greater was the blank he drew, until he found himself thinking of nothing at all. Then the aroma of the overturned earth took him back to his childhood in Wisconsin. Warm summers and safety. Happy friends and no school. Digging caves out by the road. Again, the harsh grunt came from the listening post. This time it meant business.

"It's...Captain Jordan, your company commander," he whispered urgently. "I forgot the...uh..." Jordan swallowed. "Hawk? Are you there?" An eternal silence followed. Would the creatures in the hole shoot him?

"Come on in, Captain," said a relaxed voice. Jordan recognized a heavy southern accent. He remembered that the sergeant was from Mississippi, an odd thing to remember when he was having trouble remembering his own name. Jordan crawled into the hole. His tensed body moved without a sound.

"Hello, Cap'n," another voice said with a New York accent. "I'm Corporal Canlon. Nearly plugged you, sir. You oughta make a noise or something." The voice sounded like a boxer's, and it was a little loud.

"I forgot the password," Jordan admitted. He took a deep breath. "I guess I'm a little nervous."

"Well, you're better off than me then. I'm scared shitless. Hell, nobody can remember them damn passwords. They pick these big words with R's in them. Japs are supposed to have trouble with them words. I have trouble with 'em, too, though, you know. They're from famous books and shit..." Joe Canlon laughed self-consciously and consoled the officer.

"Why don't you keep your goddamn voice down?" a shadow on the other side of the hole said to Canlon.

"Are you Sergeant Hawk?"

"Yessir."

"Pleased to meet you. Clinton Jordan. How far away are they?"

"They got positions thirty yards off. They come in closer sometimes," Hawk replied. "They could hear that foghorn a mile away," the sergeant nodded his helmet at Canlon. Their faces were invisible to one another beneath the ponderous steel domes. Jordan hopefully thought that Hawk was exaggerating the proximity of the Japanese.

"They come in closer, all right," Joe said in a lower tone. "They go behind us a lot, in between us and the lines. One night, one of 'em stepped in our hole. Had his whole leg in it. I musta pissed for a half hour. He cussed a little in Jap, pulled his leg out and kept goin'. Hawk just sat there watchin' him."

"It looked to me like you was doing the same thing," Hawk said. "Why don't you shut up, Joe, you talk too goddamn loud."

"Have you heard any indications of an attack?" Jordan asked.

"Well, no, sir," Hawk answered. "You hear a lot of noise. They don't try to be quiet up here. After a week or so it all sounds about the same. I'd have to say that we ain't heard nothin' outa the ordinary, no, sir."

"I have a message for you, Sergeant. An order." Jordan's lips were trembling. "You're not to tell anyone why our advance halted or why we've set up these positions for the last week and a half." Hawk didn't say anything. Jordan heard what sounded like quiet spitting. He guessed that Hawk was chewing tobacco. It was a common habit near the front, where smoking was a problem. "There are supposed to be some non-Marine war correspondents in the area. You are free to talk to them on any subject, except that one. And that won't be easy, because that will be the only subject that they are interested in. Make no references to why we've stopped."

"Well, sir, that *will* be pretty easy. I ain't got the faintest idea of why we stopped."

"You're not even to speculate."

"Yessir. Okay, not that any reporters'll make it up here."

"Why *did* we stop, Captain?" Joe asked in a rough whisper, so as not to anger Hawk.

"I...hell, I don't know. No one knows. Everybody thinks you know because you're on the front line. I was hoping maybe you could tell me," Jordan said.

"Against orders, sir," Canlon quipped. Nobody got the joke.

"No, sir," Hawk said. "We was just told to stop one day. You can bet your ass somebody up there knows why."

"I heard something," Joe began, "I heard we had to stop on account of there being a—"

"I reckon I told you to keep your goddamn voice down enough times already," Hawk interrupted. "If the goddamn Japs is too stupid to shoot you, I'm gonna do it myself." Hawk and Canlon looked past Jordan at one another. "Hear me?" Jordan saw an unspoken communication between them.

"Yeah, Hawk."

"What was he saying?" Jordan leaned closer to Joe.

"Shit," Hawk answered for him, "Who knows. He's fulla shit, sir. You'd be surprised at how ignorant some of these people up here are."

"What did you hear, Corporal?" Hawk looked

anxiously out toward the Japanese. The prolonged conversation was starting to worry him.

"Oh, uh, nothin', sir."

"Well, what the hell was it?"

"Oh, you know, just that there were a lot of Japs out there and all. A lot more than we expected."

"Yes," Jordan sighed, "that is true. More of them than there are of us. I know that to be a fact. But listen, Canlon, that goes against the general order forbidding the spreading of rumors. So you can't even say things like that. Understand?"

"Yessir," Joe mumbled. He was getting a little tired of being preached at like a two-year-old. It's no fun being in a foxhole with two men who outrank you.

The silver moonrise topped the edge of the forest containing the Japanese. A gigantic half of the sphere was visible. One could clearly see the lunar landscape. Jordan exhaled cautiously and looked over at Hawk. He could see the foxhole better in the ethereal light. All was highlighted in shades of powdery gray. The sergeant's eyes were a ferocious blue, smoldering beneath the cloth-covered helmet. They were the eyes of a powerful predatory beast, merciless, and yet somehow sad. Jordan shuddered when he saw them. A sad killer.

"I just wanted you to know who was in charge, now," said Jordan. "Our company is the most forward unit, and you're stuck out in front. Whatever happens, you'll be on the cutting edge."

"Typical shit," said Canlon.

"Uh, yes," Jordan agreed. "You're doing a great job. I know it sounds trite, but you are. I'm going to try and get more food and ammunition sent up. I'll do something about the dead, too."

"Send us some live ones," said Joe.

"Okay." The captain slapped Joe's shoulder. "I'll be going now."

"Nice to meet you, sir," said Hawk.

"Yeah," said Canlon, "don't see too many officers out here. They don't last long." Jordan crawled out of the hole and winced when he saw the moonlight on the open ground. "Yes, I know. Field-grade Marine officer is about the most hazardous profession there is." The captain looked over the well-lit battleground. He knew it was dangerous to leave under the stark illumination. But he couldn't stay any longer. The tension was unbearable. He felt only relief as he crossed the deadly open space. Dying was better than staying.

"Bein' a corporal's pretty damn hazardous," Joe said as he listened to Jordan scramble away.

"Yeah," said Hawk.

"Nice guy, though," Joe said, "don't you think?"

"Yeah."

"At least he came out here. That means something to a guy, you know."

"Yeah, a stupid guy."

"No, really, he was a nice guy."

"Yeah, me and the whole Jap Army had to sit here and listen to two shitasses talk their guts out. Now he's gone and our ass is still here. Nice guy," Hawk spat. "You nearly showed your ass off. You started to tell that screwy story about the two platoons in C Company."

"Well, he wanted to know what we heard. That's what we heard. Everybody's sayin' that them two platoons just disappeared into thin air."

"Joe, you think a goddamn captain wouldn't know if two whole platoons disappeared?"

"I guess so. I guess he would know something. I hope that story is just a buncha shit."

"It is."

"I mean, if it's true, the Japs got a secret weapon. You know?"

"That's exactly why you can't have no rumors. Some dumb shitbag like you goes to spreadin' the horseshit."

"You know what's wrong with you, Hawk? You just don't care about nothin'."

"I care. I broke my ass gettin' Swede Jansen transferred into one of them platoons the day before they... turned up missin'. He *had* to be with his buddy over there. Where is the son of a bitch now? That's what goddamn carin' does for you."

Joe rubbed his nose. "Well, ain't it true? Ain't they got some kind of secret weapon? Unless...it wasn't the Japs what got 'em."

Hawk looked casually along the moonlit edge of the forest. "If they're gone," he said, "the Japs either got 'em or they were withdrawn. They sure as *hell* didn't disappear. Ain't nothin' but a paycheck disappears. They woulda had to surrender and been marched off, and you know damn good and well two marine rifle platoons didn't do that."

"Yeah," Joe agreed. He pushed back his helmet and puffed out his cheeks. "Maybe it was one of them rocket ships. You know—like from Mars? They coulda had giants on it and just swept 'em up; or...or shot 'em with them disintegrator ray guns."

Hawk frowned and continued watching the forest. "I'm sure glad you said that, Joe. I was kind of afraid you were goin' nuts. Now I ain't got nothin' to worry about anymore."

"I don't see what else it could be."

"No damn shittin' doubt about that."

"Could be ghosts. Plenty of those around. Maybe devils. What could it be? What do you think?"

Hawk clenched his teeth and snorted. He didn't think very often. When he did, it was about the realm of reality. Reality was harsh and his job was to outwit it. That didn't let him be very indulgent toward fancy, or the fanciful. "I gotta secret weapon." He raised his Thompson. "I'll match mine with theirs any time their ass is ready. Now why don't you shut that crap up and give us a chance of lastin' through the night?"

"Hey! Do you hear something?"

2

Hauptmann Mittelstadt took off his crisp black uniform and stretched it across the foot of his bed. Black wasn't meant for the tropics. But he was damned sure going to wear it. He looked with unjaded pride at the red, white, and black swastika on the exposed sleeve. He sat on the edge of the bed and sighed. He would never get used to this humid climate.

The tropics were hot, bug-infested, and filthy. He had liked Manila. It was a city, with all of the benefits of civilization. It had once been American—and that made it an exciting place to be. Rechnung, this miserable little island, was another matter. His was a two-part mission, however, and he would see it through. His mission in Manila had ostensibly been a social visit. He was the Reich's goodwill ambassador to their Japanese allies. There had been lots of dinners, with reporters and photographers. His true objective had been to make a study on the feasibility of Nazi designs on the Pacific, and the Japanese Empire itself. The possibilities looked good.

That part of the mission was enjoyable. The second part involved this rat hole and nearby Verhangen Island, site of old Verhangen Prison. Verhangen had once been German, before being abandoned in 1918. This island, Rechnung, had been abandoned by God before the dawn of time. Just such a location was required. The place was remote, totally isolated. It was the sort of place idiots would fortify and fight over—Japanese and Americans. It was testing ground for the German *Vergeltungswaffe Orient.*

Mittelstadt's only companion on Rechnung was Sergeant Pechmann. Pechmann had been stationed here, a thousand years ago, and he loved the place. He was reliving his youth.

Mittelstadt looked up. Flies darted across the ceiling, challenging the synchronization of the blades of the overhead fans. The quarters were cramped. The Japanese were not generous with space. Mittelstadt had nothing but contempt for them. That was why the Nazi regime, true to its code of charm in fostering foreign relations, had chosen him. But Rechnung was more than unhealthy and uncomfortable for Mittelstadt. It was dangerous.

American marines held the southern half of Rechnung. The front was aimed in this direction. Mittelstadt considered himself more suited to political intrigue than to fighting. He didn't like being this close to the United States Marine Corps. Even the Japanese were afraid of them. Americans were, generally, a childish people, who worshipped movie stars and baseball players. But Mittelstadt had read a propaganda leaflet that described the Marine Corps as refuse from prisons, asylums, gangster mobs, and remote rural areas. A rap at the door startled him.

"Enter," he said in Japanese. He had studied the tongue for only three months, but he was able to communicate. A Japanese corporal in an oversized cap stepped into the opening. He bowed, his shadow leaping back and forth on the bare floor. The corporal brought word that Mittelstadt was to join General Kawamoto for an evening of entertainment. An Australian coast-watcher, a British pilot, and an American underwater demolition man were being prepared for execution. Mittelstadt assured the corporal that he would be there.

The German made his appearance at Kawamoto's HQ before dark. He found the preparations for the festivities nearly complete. A canvas awning had been strung across posts of palmwood. Colorful banners of elite Japanese units hung from the canvas. General Kawamoto knew of the German love for military insignia. It made war arty and clean—exciting, like a child's newly painted toy.

General Kawamoto was neither newly painted nor arty. He was the man Tokyo felt most suited to this dirty and desperate battle with the fanatical American marines. When Corporal Omato told him that Mittelstadt had arrived, he jammed the cork into his bottle of nipa juice and slammed it on the desk. He had no regrets. Fine sake awaited him outside. He strutted to the low doorway and out into the orange twilight. He stopped at the door and put his hands on his hips. He always did that. He was tall, a fraction over six feet, and his great bulk made him look taller still. He liked to stand in the little doorway, with his head grazing the top, for all the lesser men to see. He was more than other men, and not only because of his rank.

Kawamoto saw the German visitor under the awning. He was taller than the German. He smiled. The grimacing expression pushed the round shape of his shaved head into an oval. His wicked mustache became more wicked as it drooped on either side of his little teeth. It was exhilarating to look so wicked, to feel so wicked, to be so much more of a man than any other man.

Kawamoto stomped down the halved log steps and walked over to the lantern-lit shade of the awning. He greeted the German and they sat close together in the dreamy mixture of waning sunlight and wavering lamplight. Kawamoto had to force himself to be sociable. His maturing process had left him unscathed by traditional Japanese politeness. His had been a military background and he had long been at the top of the pecking order. No need to be nice up there.

Their conversation began awkwardly. Each inexplicably disliked the other. Soon, however, they stumbled onto a topic of common interest—the art of killing. It was quite a science, after all. Yes, the Japanese rifles were by and large of small caliber, but many were fixed with telescopic sights, Kawamoto noted. Stopping power was the important thing, Mittelstadt countered. If you don't hit them they don't stop, Kawamoto replied. The German saw that Kawamoto was a true expert of the craft. He had devoted years to practice with weapons and the martial arts. Mittelstadt was confident of German power in the military field. For example, he knew German eyesight was superior to Japanese. Germans didn't need scopes. He left this un-mentioned.

Like a true boor, Kawamoto left no point conceded. His thick-headedness made even the arrogant German appear gracious. The Germans were weak in the area of bladed weapons, Kawamoto insisted. Bayonets must be long to reach the heart. Such warfare was a thing of the past, Mittelstadt said.

The executions were delayed as the discussion lengthened. They covered all of it: the quickest way to dispatch a man with the bare hands, the importance of a bullet's length versus its diameter, the maiming radius of the various artillery shells—they finally spoke of the secret weapon. But this left them solemn and businesslike. Soon they reverted back to the more romantic ways of killing.

* * *

In the southern part of Rechnung Island, Sergeant Hawk drank a cup of coffee. He had made it through another night in the LP without an enemy probe. Killing was neither art, science, nor pastime for Sergeant Hawk. It was his reason for being. He had no need to study it, to talk of it, or think of it. It was in him. His ways weren't always neat, and they were seldom accomplished without great risk, but he did a lot of it. He understood it and he was good at it. He knew he had to do it. Grief, anger, hatred, love, sadness—they all churned within the dark recesses of Sergeant Hawk and came out as revenge. He lit a welcome cigar and sighed a thanks to the breaking daylight. He was back in the front lines and alive. That's all he asked of life. Front lines were rear areas for him.

Jordan was coming up to see him again. He knew

that meant trouble. Something bad must have happened between last night and this morning. His reaction to the news bothered him more than any fear of what was to come. He had always craved action, thrived on combat. It was his pride and his passion. This morning he felt tired. The eleven nights of tense calm had had a hypnotizing effect on him. He felt that he would be content in doing this forever. This was all right. In fact, he was beginning to have that terrible and fatal affliction that signals the downward onslaught of old age: he felt *entitled* to go on doing this. The thought of again crashing through a jungle blanketed with enemy artillery held no appeal for him. Losing another twenty-five to fifty percent of his men in casualties seemed foolish. Which ones would die next time? He was pretty good at guessing that. Perhaps he saw his own name on the imaginary list. He was developing a reflectiveness that was unbecoming a killer.

He wasn't afraid. The odd structure of his nerves and hormones had designed that out. Fear was the source of mental illness. Crazy people were afraid. He had seen enough of fear and insanity to know that. Crazy people worried, crazy people panicked, and crazy people died. The crazy people thought that he was crazy. But he was still here, unafraid, still doing this after all these years, and the others, or what was left of them, had been put under the ground—or rotted on top of it.

What was left of Sergeant Hawk stared out across the open ground to the LP he had spent the night in. He drew on his cigar and took a swallow of the watery coffee. He didn't like coffee. His jaw muscles tensed under the blond growth of beard. No, he wasn't afraid.

He just didn't want to do it. Not today. Probably tomorrow. The fiery eyes seethed over the top of the tarnished folding cup. He heard his breath inside. No, he wasn't afraid.

Joe Canlon sat beside him. Joe smiled a nervous, gap-toothed grin. Hawk looked back at him without expression. "Hello, windbag," the sergeant mumbled.

"Brought you something. Want to heat it up?" Joe handed him a tin of "food," its bottom third corroded green with spoilage. Hawk opened it slowly. "This don't look like it's worth wasting a match on," said the sergeant.

"Nah. I'd sure like to have a can of dog food right now."

"Or a bowl of hog swill."

"Did you see the captain crossing the break?"

"No. I knew he was comin', though." Hawk chewed sleepily on the ration of garbage. He carefully took another spoonful off the top of the tin. "Wonder what this is?" he said, looking intensely into the package.

Distant thumps tickled along the line of forest hiding the Japanese. Enemy mortar shells soon made their characteristic sucking noise as they arced overhead. The air crackled with streaking vibrations. Joe didn't get up. He raised his shoulders to his ears and grimaced. The shells hit in loud black flowerings along the open ground behind the trenches of first platoon. Joe raised up a bit to see if the captain, crawling through the break, had been hit. Jordan and two others had stopped and were hugging the earth. "I don't think he'll make it," Joe said disinterestedly.

"He'll make it. Captains are useless. The useless ones always make it." Hawk shook his head. "Take C

Company. Best in the world, them boys was. Swede Jansen...Billy Ray Harkrider...Pogue Gist. Old salts. Don't get men like that now. Just get a bunch of windbags and loud talkers. From New York or some such place." Joe smiled.

Jordan got up and ran. The intensity of the mortar fire increased. Observers were after Jordan. Hot shrapnel swished over Hawk's head. He gingerly put the nondescript mash of food into his mouth and began studying the next spoonful. He skillfully avoided the lethal bottom third of the container. He shook his head again. "Can't figure out what the hell this is. I don't want the men eatin' this shit."

"No. Stinson said he'd bring up some more stuff. I figured you and me could polish the rest of this off. Some of them young kids get sick too easy."

Hawk nodded in agreement as Jordan and another man dove into the trench amidst a flurry of dust. The captain's face was ashen, and he was shaking.

"Stinson was hit," Jordan gasped.

Hawk looked out over the field of exploding mortars. He saw only hot furrows of smoke. "You don't leave a man that's hit, Captain."

"There was nothing to leave," said Lieutenant Szerch, the other man. "He took a direct hit. It's crazy coming up here in the daytime," said the breathless exec. Hawk's radioman dove into his trench with the others.

"Get everything you can on TA355," Hawk muttered to the radio operator. He pointed out toward the jungle with his spoon. "We'll shut 'em up for you, Lieutenant," he told Szerch. Within minutes the horizon behind the treeline leapt up to mid-sky with black-capped red explosions. "One fifty-fives," Hawk commented. "Good deal. We ain't got much, but we goddamn sure got artillery." He munched calmly on his interrupted brunch. The 155's screamed overhead, tearing out little portions of Jordan's eardrums. First platoon loved that sound. It was falling on the Japanese. The enemy mortars stopped, and after a while, so did the American barrage. "Prompt." Hawk winked at the captain. "They musta knowed you was comin', sir."

"They did," said Jordan. "They should have done that before I walked out here."

"Damn right. Ain't nobody gonna tell you what to do or look out for you in the rear, sir," Canlon said. "You gotta spell everything out for them assholes." Joe had finished his meal. He threw the half-filled tin toward the Japanese. "There you go, Tojo!"

Hawk looked down at his tin. "I know it's a sin to waste food, but I'm a high liver." He tossed the tin at the forest.

"We're going on the attack," Jordan said suddenly.

"I figured," Hawk said, relighting his cigar. Anguished cries of men hit during the barrage could be heard in the following silence. An aid station was about a hundred feet away and corpsmen were scurrying in and out of it. Joe looked in that direction.

"But not here. They want us to pull out and hit the beach behind the Japs, open another front. A place called Stocken Bay," Jordan said. He took off his helmet. He was still shaking. Two stretcher bearers carried a wailing marine within twenty feet of them.

"Hey, that's old Zarko," said Joe. "Hey, Zark!" But the man didn't answer. He kept screaming. The stretcher bearer looked at Joe with an odd expression. Red strings hung out of Zarko's pants where a right leg had been. "That's gonna kill his brother," Joe said with a worried look.

"Who takes our position, sir?" Hawk asked.

"They've put together a new company, made out of HQ men and cannon cockers. They'll come up and then we'll withdraw."

"That's dangerous. They need a line company up here," said Hawk.

"I know it. But there aren't any. They've stopped sending in the men. We're not even getting replacements."

"What's going on?" Hawk scowled. He wasn't used to his rear echelon drying up behind him. He thought that part of the war had ended at Guadalcanal. Of course, the food had been bad lately. Just like the Canal. Somebody was scared of something. They didn't want to waste men on this sector. He didn't know what it could be, though. The Japanese were a little tough, but they had always been tough. No one hesitated because of that.

Joe was still looking at the aid station. "I'm gonna go see who all got it," he said. "Some of our guys is hurt."

"Stay put," Hawk snapped.

Joe stood. "They hit a bunch of our guys."

"Visiting the wounded area is against orders," Szerch said. Joe put a boot out of the hole.

"I told you to sit your ass down," said Hawk. "You can't do nothin'."

Joe climbed out. "Maybe they need blood or something. I got a rare type, you know, somebody might need some."

"All right, Joe, don't come back here blubberin'

about who got hit. I'm warnin' you, I'll kick your goddamn teeth in. We'll know soon enough who got it. You're just gonna get spooked," Hawk shouted. Joe stopped. He turned around and came back, sitting quietly next to Hawk. The sergeant turned back to Jordan. "I don't see why we stopped here, sir. Why don't we just go on with what we got here?"

Jordan looked down. "I'll...fill you and the others in at the CP. This is a problem area. Something came up. We're really going to get the wrong end of the stick where we're going, too."

"Oh, good," Joe mumbled.

"We pull out as soon as the others arrive and are positioned. Smooth transition, you know. Don't leave any of our weapons, captured or otherwise for them," said Jordan.

"Aye, aye, sir," said Hawk. "You can bet on it. Spread the word, Joe."

Joe looked up. The desperate cries of the wounded and dying became louder, both on the inside and outside of Joe Canlon's head.

* * *

THE BEARDED AND emaciated Australian had a Christ like appearance. The Japanese soldiers gathered under the blazing torches in front of Kawamoto's headquarters. The general got to his feet. He strutted up to the Australian coastwatcher, smiled at his men and took a deep breath. He then leapt off the ground, snapping his leg out sideways with a roaring shout. The knife edge of Kawamoto's boot caught the man in the throat, and he fell to all fours on the ground. The general looked displeased with the results of his kick. He was a perfectionist. The man was still alive. The crowd cheered. They knew they had to praise the general, or else end up his victim themselves. Kawamoto took a deep breath and bowed to them. He always took their forced cheering seriously. He looked angrily at the prisoner and returned to his seat.

He called for his corporal. The men had nicknamed Corporal Omato "The Ghoul." The aide carried a samurai sword. "One blow, Omato, or your head will be the next to fall," Kawamoto instructed him. Omato bowed solemnly. A studious expression was on his face as he aimed at the prisoner kneeling before him. He brandished the sword in all manner of preparatory maneuverings. He was confident, the blade Was of the finest steel. His eye fixed firmly on the scrawny and wrinkled neck of the Australian. He raised the sword with both hands, high over his head. Decorum was preserved when he did it with one blow. The crowd appeared ecstatic when the head slid heavily to the dusty earth.

General Kawamoto laughed until he nearly fell off his chair. "Well done, well done," he managed to choke to the executioner. He jumped with little convulsions of glee, his chair creaking as if it might break under the strain. Pechmann was quiet. Mittelstadt didn't seem pleased. The Hauptmann had only a sickly smile on his face. This irked Kawamoto, he had gone to a lot of trouble for this party. All of his men were watching, and watching the reactions of the foreigners with particular interest.

Tamatsu Taniguchi put his hand on the back of one of the young men in his unit. The young man could not look at the gory scene. Taniguchi steered him away from the crowd. Taniguchi's lieutenant gave him a dirty look. All were supposed to look upon Kawamoto's antics with great pleasure. Taniguchi ignored the officer, for he did as he pleased. He had been an NCO a long time. No one told Taniguchi what to do.

Mittelstadt realized that everyone was looking at him and so he forced a laugh. The Japanese, who had quieted down by now, began again to laugh when they heard him. This seemed to please Kawamoto. The general ordered another round of sake. "I was embarrassed that my kick did not kill him," Kawamoto confessed amidst tears of joy, "until I saw what pleasure came from the sword."

"Yes," Mittelstadt agreed. He looked uncomfortably around the crowd of cheering men. He felt very vulnerable. Kawamoto summoned the British pilot. The general turned him over to Mittelstadt, suggesting that the German halve his skull with the sword. Mittelstadt apologized. He had studied fencing, but this particular use of the sword was beyond him. He knew he had to act quickly. All faces were turned toward him. The German unsnapped his pistol and walked up to the pilot. The pilot struck an apathetic pose, a sneer of defiance on his face. Mittelstadt had trouble looking at him.

Kawamoto's greatest thrill was watching the eyes of the condemned victims. You could see their terror there. Mittelstadt watched the ground. He raised his arm quickly, leveled the pistol at the space between the man's eyes and pulled the trigger without a pause. In spite of the strong supporting bone, the entry hole of the 9 millimeter slug was far from neat. The exit was worse. The crowd had been instructed to cheer just as enthusiastically for the Hauptmann as it had for its own general. Many were disappointed with the abrupt efficiency of Mittelstadt's method, but they obeyed orders. Mittelstadt bowed to the crowd and returned to his seat. Taniguchi watched solemnly and lit a cigarette.

Kawamoto knew that his tough troopers were let down by the simple pistol execution. He saved the day, however, when the last prisoner, the American, was brought to him. He was hanged, with a handle being placed on the rope to allow him to save himself for as long as his arms could hold out. Mittelstadt and Kawamoto talked of the secret weapon as the man died. After it was over, most of the men were thoroughly satisfied with the evening. Taniguchi was ordered to bury the dead prisoners. He threw down his cigarette and walked away.

3

Hawk watched the rugged shoreline sprawled before his landing craft. It was quiet. They were already well within mortar range. We might hit the dry ground unopposed, he thought. He cupped his hands over the end of a long thin cigar. The wind was high. After twelve days of inactivity, they had every reason to catch the enemy by surprise. So, they told him at the briefing. The opposite seemed more logical to him. And yet, air reconnaissance showed no enemy movement toward the western beaches of Rechnung, off of which lay the marine invasion force. The Japanese remained firmly entrenched in their jungle lines across the middle of the island. This second beachhead, at a place called Stocken Bay, would allow the Americans to open a front in the Japanese rear. That was to be the official version of the operation, if word of it leaked out. And that's what most of the men thought they were doing.

A lip of white sand stretched before a purple ledge of rock along the shoreline. Growing atop the ledge was a fence of palm trees. Their brilliant green foliage waved a friendly greeting to the approaching LCVP's. The water was absolutely blue, unusually serene. The sky matched its scintillating beauty in a mirror image.

Hawk's eyes narrowed as he surveyed the gorgeous scene. It was a rotten place for a landing. The enemy could shoot down on the exposed beach from the perpendicular cliff that fronted it. The palms gave them added concealment. You would never get them off that rock. It was the sort of place a Japanese machine gunner would have chosen for an American landing. The trees were unmarred by any signs of prep fire. This was a surprise. It was supposed to be unconventional. Only a company, Dog Company, would be invested at this time.

The inner tips of Hawk's eyebrows raised high over the bridge of his nose. He knew a little bit more of this operation than the other mute green creatures gathered around him. He had attended the briefing for platoon leaders at Jordan's CP. Jordan said that he was telling them all that he knew. The Japanese had a secret weapon. He said it just like that. They had used it once. The rumors were true. Two platoons of C Company were the victims. The exact nature of the weapon was still somewhat vague. It wasn't to be mentioned until some more concrete evidence came in. They were landing Dog at Stocken Bay to provoke the enemy. They were inviting a second use of the weapon. The briefing ended there. The platoon leaders left scratching their heads. Hawk overheard Jordan tell a lieutenant in third platoon that they knew what the weapon was, that they had a defense against it, but that they weren't going to use it. That sounded a little strange to the sergeant. He figured they didn't really know what it was. Otherwise, he wouldn't be here.

Hawk had a working idea of what it was. He knew what it had to be. He knew what they thought it was. Beads of sweat were on his forehead, although it was quite cool out in the barges. He put a thick hand on the gunwales. It had to be gas. He would have been sure of that had another piece of the puzzle not been added.

All of the survivors of C Company had been shipped out to prevent the spreading of rumors. But a supply sergeant had been transferred out of the company the day of the withdrawal. He was put into a rifle platoon—Hawk's. Miller was his name, and he had been the first man on the scene after the disappearance of the two C Company platoons. He found no sign of a struggle. The phone wires were cut, and the gear had vanished with the men. They had reported in only fifteen minutes before. Hawk told Miller not to retell the story if he cared to stay in the platoon.

The problem was, even if gas had been used, a struggle would have ensued. Traces of the horrible conflict could hardly have been erased. And were there a danger of chemical warfare, it would seem that Jordan would have issued masks. The Japanese were always shouting threats of gas, but Hawk had never heard of it happening. That didn't mean that it hadn't. Vanishing, disappearing—those were strong words to a man bobbing in the surf off Rechnung Island. If this thing wasn't gas, it was something worse. Something that some bespectacled idiot in a white frock coat had devised to kill Sergeant Hawk. What could be worse? The coxswain shouted.

Third platoon dashed into the surf when the ramp

dropped open. Hawk took his men in behind them. The cold water rose to his chest, he held his Thompson overhead with one hand. The enveloping water pressed against his lungs and made it more difficult to breathe. He looked back at the concerned faces of the boys jumping into the water. "The bottom's solid, men. Don't worry, come on," he encouraged. A wave rolled up to his chin, spitting white bubbles in his face.

Carter Spence, an enormous fellow with eyes like a rhinoceros, said, "If I drown I'm gonna kick your ass, Hawk."

"It'll be the last ass you kick, shitbag," Hawk answered. He stood to one side and let some of his men pass him. The ungainly Spence was negotiating each step as he came out of the ramp. This aroused the never long dormant ire of the sergeant. "Get movin'. If you're a goddamn cripple, join the Army." Spence waded by without comment. Canlon struggled to Hawk's side. He was shorter and having a tough time against the heavy waves.

"They could've got us a damn sight closer," Canlon wheezed.

"Yeah. Sons of bitches," said Hawk.

"Sure quiet up there."

Hawk tasted the salty wind. "Yeah. It is."

The landing came off like a training exercise. Better —not a shot was fired. Someone usually felt obligated to blast a few rounds at the trees in these types of operations. Orders were strict; no bullshit. It was better to get set up quietly before the Japanese knew they were intruded upon. Since everyone knew that they were a part of a lone company, invading the rear of a Japanese division, the order did not go unnoticed. The possibilities of enemy retaliation from the cliffs above sobered even the nervous and the silly fellows. Joe Canlon kept his safety on. He knew that he was a little too quick on the draw.

The company formed an orderly line along the beach. Hawk felt good about it. Other landings had caught him in some gruesome situations, before ever setting foot on dry ground.

Instead of moving toward the cliff in a skirmish line, Jordan ordered an approach march formation. Several of the NCOs, Hawk among them, thought that maybe Jordan had fallen heir to a company before he was ready. Predictions of tragedy proved premature. Without incident, the company mounted the thirty-foot ledge by the convenient use of a rockslide. Had enemy troops been in position, the marines would have been bowled over like tenpins. Jordan trusted his reconnaissance reports implicitly, a mistake that far more experienced commanders have made. This time he was lucky. He gave the order to dig in at the top of the ridge.

That order brought protests. The officers wanted to proceed until they were stopped. Hawk knew then that Jordan was all right. He stuck to the order and the advance halted. Hawk knew what Jordan's orders were: provoke the secret weapon. The officers also knew the order. Hawk figured they were afraid. They wanted to provoke instead a general attack, and be withdrawn or replaced, or at worst reinforced. Jordan did it right. He ignored his pale-faced advisors and did exactly what he was told. He dug in and waited. He would give the Japanese every opportunity to exterminate his command with their weapon.

Hawk's platoon was placed on a flank against a

blind wall of stone. A rectangular rock jutted up out of the earth at his right hand. This made him uncomfortable. A howling contingent of the enemy could round this formation and present themselves to him with only twenty yards notice. He had his LP and his patrols, but sometimes they didn't come back. He tried to cut the odds further against his unfavorable position by propping up sheets of tin found on the beach. They served as murky mirrors reflecting on the back side of the rock formation. Anything approaching from that direction cast a shadow on the tin.

Rumors began to fly before the day was over. Some of the men thought that the Japanese had collapsed. Otherwise, they wouldn't have been placed here in such a vulnerable position. Hawk wondered about that himself. They were too vulnerable. The Japanese didn't need a secret weapon to wipe them out. He wondered what the brass had for an answer to that. The answer was that that was okay. Part of the risk. Hawk suspected as much.

Canlon noticed Hawk's uneasiness during the day. It was easy to spot. He had seen the sergeant wake up from a sound sleep, join in the repulsion of a terrifying night attack, and doze off contentedly again once it was over. He wasn't the nervous type. Canlon had heard Miller's story. He figured Hawk knew more than he was telling. He stepped down into Hawk's foxhole and they watched the jungle darkening below them. Another war night was approaching.

Joe slung himself down and rubbed his nose. "What do you think, Hawk?"

"If I did any thinking, I sure as *hell* wouldn't be here."

Joe sighed. He didn't like this. The tension he had felt all day eased into a nice cold fear. A trapped feeling caused perspiration to sprout in patches across his face. "That was true. About them two platoons, wasn't it, Hawk?"

The sergeant didn't say anything for a while. "Yeah," he finally answered in a low voice. "A lot of it, I guess." He bit off a piece of chewing tobacco. He offered Joe some, but he refused it.

"What do the Japs got?"

"I don't know. Nobody's sayin'."

"What are you sayin'?"

Hawk spat and shrugged. He looked down at the skein of foliage surrounding the base of the cliff. "I ain't. If I had to guess, I'd say gas."

A bolt of razor-edged lightning shot up Joe's gullet. "Jesus. Gas?" Hawk faced away from him with a stoic expression. Joe swallowed and aimed his eyes at the grim jungle. "You know, I don't really want to die, yet. I got a few things I'd like to do before I go."

"Everybody does. Everybody goes, though."

"That's easy to say."

"That's the way it is. You might as well understand it. You *have* to die. You're wet shit in a bag. The bag rips and you're gone."

"Yeah. But not tonight."

Hawk pushed back his helmet and ran a sleeve across his forehead. "Tonight, tomorrow, thirty years—what's the goddamn difference? You have to do it. Cryin' don't make it not so."

"Like I say, I got some things to do."

"Ain't nothin' you'll ever do gonna amount to a pile of shit. What's a shitass like you gonna do? Feel good for five minutes, or an hour, then feel bad the rest of the time."

Joe laughed. "Yeah."

"Think of all the great people there's been. None of 'em meant shit. The world didn't need their ass. This right here is the biggest thing you'll ever do. What are you gonna do anyways? Turn out ball bearings in a plant ten hours a day? Nobody's ever ready to go. People a hundred years old think life's too short. People are always whining, always so scared they're missing out on something. They're too goddamn stupid to see that there ain't nothin' to miss out on."

"You make life sound great, Hawk. No wonder you don't care about nothin'."

"I ain't in no hurry to die. When I go, I'll try to make it count. Just don't go shittin' yourself that you can't bear to part with this world—because one way or the other, you're going to."

"Yeah," Joe whispered. "I know it. I don't know if I really knew that before tonight." His glazed eyes stared at the forest for a minute. "But I want to put it off every minute I can."

"You will."

* * *

KAWAMOTO GRUNTED approval when he read the message off the teletype machine. It was exactly what Mittelstadt had predicted. The spineless Americans were cautioning against spreading rumors about the secret weapon. They feared an outcry for countermeasures, countermeasures that would eventually spread to Europe. The Americans were always worried about

Europe. Their war was here. It had begun here. They were the only defending power in the Pacific, and still they worried about Europe. That preoccupation would spell their doom. Japan was no part-time adversary.

They were hoping that the Japanese would not use the weapon again. They didn't know that Kawamoto and Mittelstadt had been given a free hand in the use of the weapon. Had they been aware of that, they would have been assured of future grief. The general read of their bait, Dog Company, landed to the rear on Stocken Bay. The message ended with a rhetorical question. Would the enemy be reckless enough to strike another time? Kawamoto cocked his head and smiled. What fun. It was like torturing an animal. He considered the possibilities.

He would let the marines stay awhile. He would encourage a strengthening of their forces. No American could resist the thought of a second front. Even the toughest American military minds were trained in seeking the easy way out. Shortcuts, quick finishes, that was the American way. They were too timid and soft a people to slug it out, strength for strength. They may have planned to use Dog as bait, but if they thought that their second front really had a chance, they would reinforce it. He would let their confidence increase, let them multiply their resources on Stocken Bay, and then one night, quietly annihilate them.

Kawamoto tore up the message. He didn't want Mittelstadt to see it yet. He didn't know why. He was just a secretive man, an irritating man, in almost every respect.

Enough of work, he thought. Now for today's entertainment. He went into his office and took out his map of Verhangen Island. He had been designing a concentration camp for the impoverished natives of Rechnung and Verhangen. He put an elbow on the map and placed his chin in his hand. He drew a little square for the adult facilities and another for the children's.

* * *

THE DAYS DRAGGED ON. Hawk and Canlon forgot their tensions. The electric feelings of that first night were replaced by boredom. But the passing of the time only increased Jordan's fears. He realized that, by now, the Japanese had to know that he was there on Stocken Bay. He also knew that they were debating whether or not to use the weapon again. He didn't know Kawamoto. He had his own ideas of the Japanese character, and while in the. abstract he imagined all of the enemy were men like Kawamoto, he probably would have been shocked to know that such a creature really did exist. Jordan was fresh from a boyhood of going to church on Sundays and the boy scouts on Tuesdays. He still thought that good and noble intentions ruled most men's lives. How then could there be wars? Well, war was man's noblest adventure. But he was scared. He knew what the weapon was.

Hawk and Canlon operated on a more elementary level. They weren't concerned with the functioning of the enemy mind. They were concerned with such things as the rain, the food, and of late, the beer rations. During the last three days, they had started getting beer rations. It was almost as good as being in the Army. They got only three cans per man per day, but that was three more than before.

Other signs of civilization also had appeared. A regular base was going up on the edges of Stocken Bay. Jordan first had officers' quarters constructed. The men had plenty of free time. The quarters improved daily, from lean-tos, to sheds and then into perfectly habitable sheet metal buildings. After that, the barracks for the enlisted men went up. It was all quite unusual, and intentionally so. Colonel Hulmore confided in Jordan that command was angry over the Japanese failure to exterminate Dog Company. Hulmore wanted to see just how strong the enemy's resolve to not use their weapon was. He wanted to create an inviting target.

One sunny morning, the colonel took another dramatic step. He sent in Navy nurses. The presence of the ten nurses meant that the area was absolutely safe. Given the ratio of nurses to men in the Pacific, there should have been several marine battalions on Stocken Bay instead of one company. Jordan didn't like the idea. He gave up protesting the move when he was told that Colonel Hulmore didn't like women, and the move was probably well thought out. The young captain didn't believe the colonel actually meant for harm to come to the women, in spite of what he was told. Had Jordan understood about Hulmores and Kawamotos, he might have understood war.

No one seemed to notice that there was no need for nurses. There were no casualties. But the attractiveness of the bait continued to be enhanced. A tank was put ashore on the bay. It was left on the beach in full view of the cliffs above. The crew that unloaded it left with the delivering LST. It sat there, motionless, like some great monument to stupidity.

Comfort and supplies increased, but one thing

didn't increase: fighting men. Hawk felt that that was the one thing that would make the beach safe. He suspected that even that wouldn't make it truly safe. That was why the brass wasn't willing to spend any more lives on the project. Fighting men, a nuisance under normal peacetime conditions, were a precious commodity in war. No expense would be spared on the window dressings at Stocken Bay—just so there would be no real loss. Being set up and played for a sucker was a part of Sergeant Hawk's life, so he didn't worry much about any of it. He worried about the same things the other men worried about: the rain, the food, the beer, and lately, the ten nurses.

Hawk didn't think about women very much. No need to out here. He had never done well with them when he had the opportunity. They were harmless creatures, but best left alone. You couldn't knock the hell out of them, and that was the only satisfaction you could get from them. So to hell with them. No one waited at home for Sergeant Hawk. That was fine. He needed no whining, self-indulgent creature hanging on him in order to feel part of a whole. He admitted that he might be a little uncivilized about them, and maybe he was wrong. But he had enough trouble staying alive. He was no kid looking for someone to coo at him and smooth his curls. Women weren't important.

He was up on the cliff the first time he saw her. Tall, blond, piercing eyes, a little nose and wide mouth. Her name was Ivania Broeder. Everyone knew that. He didn't have to ask her name, he finally overheard it. He didn't think about her a lot. He was no adolescent seeking a fantasy world in which to dwell. But he noticed her. Often. On this particular morning, he watched her radiant smile as she crossed the beach with another nurse and went into Jordan's CP.

Hawk looked over at Canlon. It was daylight. Joe was asleep. "Wake up, shitass," he growled. Joe didn't stir. Hawk kicked him. "Don't you know you're supposed to be on watch? Goddamn bastard, you're gonna get me killed yet."

Joe moaned and sat up. He watched Hawk climb wordlessly out of the hole. Joe was a practical man. The only reason he had to stay awake was to keep from getting kicked. When Hawk was out of sight, his eyes closed, and his mouth opened again. He was dreaming of nurses.

Hawk didn't see Ivania Broeder that day. Other things were going on. Seabees landed in the afternoon. Hawk was glad to see this. Technically they should have been considered noncombatants. The Navy construction men were no pencil pushers, however, and their presence may have been due to a misunderstanding of this by Colonel Hulmore. They had contributed to the fighting when situations warranted it. They were on the average older than the marines and their crustiness made up for any deficiencies in training. They weren't marines, of course, but neither were they nurses. The old salts in the Marine Corps had a fondness for Seabees, and their landing pulled up morale considerably. No doubt the construction men had been put aboard to make Stocken Bay an even more ripe plum for the Japanese picking. Hawk didn't think that was the case. He was wrong. He didn't know Kawamoto.

On the day following their arrival, the Seabees were sent out in front of the marine lines. They didn't seem aware of this or of the danger they were in. In the valley that lay beneath Hawk's perimeter, they were blasting and bulldozing the stubborn jungle trees. It sounded like a full scale battle. A little spotter plane, a Widgeon, hovered above them, its droning motors unheard amidst the ripping noises and chaos below. Hawk watched the scene for a while. The Seabees were being used not as mere bait, but more like a red cape. They were clearing an airfield—in front of the American lines. Hawk shrugged as he watched the mud-churning bulldozers. He bit a mouthful of tobacco from a plug. Plenty of marines had died on this island. Why not a few Seabees? He spat.

He watched for a long time, chewing quietly and making critical observations on how the men operated the heavy equipment. Finally, the cruelty of it sank through to even his barnacled conscience. Perhaps it was the remembrance of himself driving piling in far off Mississippi that struck a sympathetic chord. How could they put those men out there like that? Those fellows probably had families. They weren't youngsters. The Japanese *had* to attack them, and they sure as hell didn't need a secret weapon. He watched and waited and still nothing happened. The work progressed at a speed that freeway drivers in America would have thought miraculous. Hawk got up at last. He had to talk to Jordan about it. Shit. It was getting under his skin. Somebody might have made a mistake. Those men ought to be pulled back. He slouched down the cliff, across the beach and into the CP.

Jordan was there. Fans whirred wildly in the impossible to cool building. Ivania Broeder was there, too. Jordan introduced her to Hawk. They smiled at one another, exchanged greetings and an awkward silence followed. Hawk filled it with a preliminary comment upon his concern for the safety of the Seabees. By the time he and Jordan exchanged a couple of sentences, Ivania Broeder was gone. This probably irritated Jordan. It also irritated Hawk, but by that time he was caught up in making his point. Both of the men grew short of temper. The girl's empty chair often fell under their gaze.

"Do you think it's my idea, Hawk? Do I look crazy to you?" Jordan sat on the edge of his makeshift desk. Hawk stood before him.

"No, sir. But we could cover 'em a little better. They really got their ass stuck on the block out there."

"*They* go right where they are, down in that valley. *You* go right where you are, up on the ridge. Those are the orders. Now—you tell me how I can protect them any more than I already am and still obey those orders."

Hawk squinted at the captain. The kid wasn't being a wise guy. He was just stating the facts, the facts as he perceived them. Hawk's voice relaxed a bit. "I'd feel better with an OP up ahead of 'em, sir. Maybe a squad for observing. Maybe even a little recon patrol every now and then during the day. Anything to give 'em a little warnin' if anything happens. You know...sometimes them orders ain't carved in rock, sir. A man can do a little bit here and there without breaking orders."

Jordan didn't relax. "We have air recon."

"Not much."

"It doesn't take much. A squad is a lot of men. I only have a company."

"Well, they're all supposed to get killed, one way or the other anyway, ain't they, sir?"

Jordan looked down nervously. His face was a

greenish white. He could no longer hide the fluttering in his chest. His voice became less argumentative in tone. It sounded muffled, fearful. "I...we...need you here, Hawk. We need to get along. Okay, maybe a patrol. Maybe a squad. Do you want to take it?"

"Well, yessir. Like I say, we oughta have several patrols goin' on around the clock. I'd be glad to take my share."

Jordan nodded, rounded his desk and sat in his chair. "You take a squad up the valley. Regiment wants contact, you can probably deliver. It might be a good idea. We might see what those slimy bastards are up to. Go today. Whenever you want. Let me know. After you're gone, I'll tell regiment and see how they take it. I'm going to approve of just this one patrol, and you're taking it."

"Yes, sir." Hawk swaggered toward the door and then stopped and turned around. "I reckon it's a good idea, sir."

Jordan didn't look up. "Probably." Hawk left.

The captain watched him climb the cliff. Hawk got on his nerves. The sergeant didn't like this setup, and that meant it had to be bad. Hawk didn't know what he knew, he just sensed the trap. Jordan found it difficult to meet the challenging eyes that had seen so much more of the war than he had. One could see right down into the fiery eyes, right through to the back wall of Hawk's head. What strange and cruel things went on behind those eyes? Jordan didn't want to know. He only wanted to survive this and somehow make an adequate showing. Not a good showing, mind you, adequate would do. He wanted his small town life in Wisconsin. He wanted to be free of men like Sergeant Hawk and their way of life. But he had to make an adequate showing. He was still deep in the throes of misgiving a young man has about manhood. He picked a bad place to have those throes. Real men were a dime a dozen in the South Pacific. Their standards were tough, and they buried them by the truckload, every hour of every day.

And now Jordan had to worry about Ivania Broeder. He could think of her and forget all about this misery. But he couldn't forget that she was here and that that was dangerous, for both of them. He suffered it all without complaint. He still respected age and rank and thought for some reason that someone somewhere knew what was best to do with his life. War would change that.

Hawk picked his way through the positions of first platoon. Remaining stationary had cluttered the area with unnecessary debris. The sight of this excess baggage aroused his anger. He was a believer in traveling light. To make the situation worse, the nurses were up on the line handing out atabrine, sulfa, and wound tablets. Men were milling about and chattering at the women. He glared at the jolly scene with an unsympathetic eye. He had been thinking of asking for volunteers for the patrol. The state of disorganization that he found made him choose a more efficient method. He would take Cavell's squad.

It would be easier to work with a squad. They wouldn't have to work with personnel with whom they were unfamiliar. Besides that, Cavell's squad was doing most of the lollygagging. This was usually the case. The best fighters usually made the best lollygaggers.

He dispersed the knots of idle marines in a restrained way. He was angry, but one develops a certain affection for people about to die. He saw that Ivania Broeder wasn't there. He told Joe to get Cavell.

One thing Hawk didn't notice, but it noticed him. Belva Cook was one of the nurses distributing the medical supplies. She was *the* nurse as far as most of the men were concerned. She wasn't aloof like the beautiful Lieutenant Ivania Broeder. She was a friendly Texan, able to laugh and joke with the men in complete security. She wasn't afraid of them, and she didn't think herself better than they. They appreciated this, probably even more than her full figure and ant waist. Hawk had seen her before. Black hair, blue eyes, never without a pixie smile. He made the required appraisal of her body. That was about all.

Women made him uncomfortable. He had to control himself around them. At least when he was around men, all he had to control was his desire to kill someone every now and then. He wasn't even especially good at that. His attitude therefore left him pretty much a denizen of the male environment, unless approached. After being approached, he invariably remained a denizen of all the male society, the speed of his return to this status depending upon how tender were the sensibilities of the approaching female. He was handsome. But he was kind of rough.

Belva Cook had watched him in much the same manner he had watched Ivania. The eyes that men feared, she found irresistible. She knew he was a vicious frontline killer. Just the sort of man a girl from Texas liked. She saw a gentleness, however, in the tragic eyes that no one else saw. She saw a strength in the cruel mouth that needed caring to grow and survive.

None of this was accurate, of course. Gentleness had

long ago been beaten out of Sergeant Hawk. He was through growing, and a little air and water were all he required to survive. He wasn't looking for a girl from Texas. He had been infatuated by a fancier type. He didn't blush or stutter when Belva Cook walked up to him, as he would have in the case of Ivania Broeder.

"Have you had your atabrine, Sergeant?" she asked.

"Yes, ma'am. Every day at chow. You don't think I'm always this color, do you?"

She laughed at the rebuff. "You aren't as yellow as some of us. You have to have the right dosage, you know."

"Well...I get enough. Anything that turns you yellow is bad for your liver." Hawk looked down. He finally realized he was talking to a woman. She had a way of sneaking up on you. "Joe—get some bandoliers, you're comin' with us."

Joe walked over. "What are we doin'?" he asked.

"Goin' up the valley."

"I been sick at my stomach here lately, Hawk...you don't think..."

"Get some bandoliers and go over there with Cavell." Joe slunk away.

"There's been a lot of sickness here," Belva said to Hawk, ignoring the interruption. "You should take care of yourself."

He looked directly at her for the first time. She smiled. She was very good-looking, he thought. "I ain't sick."

"You've heard of the skin condition the Seabees have come down with?"

"Uh...no, ma'am."

"It's mostly on their arms, but it gets on any exposed

area. Terrible sores eat their way right down to the bone. You should put your sleeves down and button your blouse. We don't know exactly where they're getting it."

Hawk looked blankly at her. She smiled another flattered smile. But he wasn't thinking of her. He was thinking of gas, of chemical warfare. "I'd like to hear more about that," he said, unconsciously scratching his vein-encircled arm.

"Come down to the hospital and I'll show you some when they come in. You can talk to Dr. Wilson about it, too. Come any time. I'd be glad to show you around."

"I will. Thanks." He forced a smile out of his dead facial muscles, winked at her and turned away. Enough was going on around them for this to not seem rude. Sergeant Cavell had finally made an appearance and Hawk had to get him squared away.

Joe Canlon came back to Hawk's side after Belva left. "Hey, Hawk," he said, "Hey, there." Hawk turned to face him.

"What the hell is it? And it better not be your goddamn stomach."

"Naw, I was just wonderin'. What'd the captain say? I mean, about where we're goin'."

"He said take the squad up the valley. Ain't we had this little talk before?" Hawk walked off.

Joe looked down the ridge at the evil, haunted jungle below him. It was quiet now. The vegetation was vivid green beneath solemn gray clouds. "Take a squad up the valley," Joe growled.

4

THE *HANCHO* TANIGUCHI ORDERED HIS POINT MAN forward. A flanker was motioned forward to cover him. The patrol had few expectations of meeting any resistance. The *hancho* took no chances. It wasn't his job to take chances. It was his job to reduce the odds, to somehow bring them all back alive. Taniguchi had been in the army for twenty years. He had been in China when all of this began in the early thirties. He was still here, here being the planet earth. That was no easy accomplishment. One of the ironies of being a soldier is that the better you are at your job, the more dangerous it becomes. They send you on the bad ones. They keep you in the bad ones. They need your experience, as well as your blood.

Today the *hancho* wasn't worried. His prominent jaw muscles tensed as he surveyed the close jungle ahead of him. His eyes, the eyes of a caring father wolf, did not have that sorrowful alertness today. His assignment was an easy one. General Kawamoto was going on a patrol near the American construction battalion. The foolish general wanted to see how many of the noncombatants he could kill. Taniguchi knew there would be little or no resistance. He had led a half dozen patrols into the area. His only concern was that Kawamoto would enjoy the slaughter too much and remain in the vicinity too long. If he did that, the marines on the ridge might come down and let their presence be known. The *hancho* respected marines.

There weren't many of the American devils on the ridge, but then there weren't many in Taniguchi's patrol either. The irresponsible Kawamoto, an exalted general officer, was going personally on the little sortie. He treated it as if it were some grand safari. He was bringing a photographer, as well as the two Germans with him. It spoke well of the general's confidence in Taniguchi.

The *hancho* had nothing but contempt for Kawamoto. Taniguchi could kill, no one questioned that, but he didn't like it. He conceded that it had to be done, and then he did it. An operation such as this was more than frivolous, it was a sin. One didn't play with death. One might beat the odds, but never tempt them. This same reasoning forbade Taniguchi from letting his objections to the patrol be known. Kawamoto was a man to be feared. Not because of his considerable personal prowess, or his obvious madness, but because of his position. Society had put Kawamoto in control of Taniguchi.

Generals wielded massive power. That was frightening. It was also infuriating to know that a perfect idiot could surface upon any rung of society. Someday, should the opportunity present itself, the *hancho* might dispose of the general. He wanted this done, not out of any bloodthirstiness, but out of his own sense of justice. He also realized that it would hardly be possible for a lowly sergeant to do such a thing: nevertheless, a sergeant might play a part in it.

He had been forced into doing brutal things, but not into being a brutal man. As well as making him into a virtually perfect soldier, decades of war had made him tolerant—some would even say gentle. He had learned that violence and brutality took only repulsive seconds. A man could be gentle and relaxed and happy for most of his life—so long as he was ready for those few seconds when they came. Kawamoto had not learned this. He had fought his wars from the rear areas. He felt insulated from the brutality; it was something to enjoy, something that happened to other men. Death was his hobby. It was Taniguchi's vocation.

An almost imperceptible smile spread the deep lines on Taniguchi's face. Today, death may come closer, he thought. The general was bringing himself very close to the enemy and reality. This enemy wasn't chained for the execution. It was all supposed to be very safe— by Taniguchi's own reconnaissance reports. But the odds on getting killed were much better here than they were in the safety of Verhangen Prison where Kawamoto spent most of his time.

One didn't play with the odds. Kawamoto played too much, especially with men's lives. Now he was accidentally playing with his own. When one flies from reality, one eventually comes to harm oneself. Taniguchi liked that, because his wily old senses of doom were acting up this morning. Yes, today something would happen. You couldn't fool Taniguchi. For some unpredicted reason, there would be trouble today.

Taniguchi would be ready for it, because he was always ready. But would Kawamoto be ready?

* * *

CAVELL GAVE a hand signal from down on the trail. Hawk ordered the others down through the furrow in the rock. Lichen covered the stone walls of the passage. A handful of mournful fronds that hung out over the rock served as each man's turnstile into the unknown. A gang of Seabees silently watched them. One or two of the men waved to them. Hawk stood high on a promontory and studied Cavell. The pitted face made the young man look much older. Cavell had been a good scout. He was tall, strong and psychotically brave. He hardly ever spoke. His senses were unerring, like the proverbial bird's in flight. But Cavell was no longer a scout. He was a squad leader. He had been promoted out of the job he was best suited for, and into one for which he had no qualifications. There was Cavell, down at the front of the patrol, just like a scout.

Hawk understood this and he understood Cavell. The military wasn't a corporate ladder to climb to glory. The purpose of the military was war, and war was a disgust-ting tragedy to be dispatched as quickly and as efficiently as possible. Taking yourself out of the danger wasn't efficient. There were rules in life, and they involved ambition and success. But this wasn't life. Kill them. That was the rule here. Everything else was nonsense.

Heat undulated beneath the enveloping trees. The trail ceased its downward lilt and twisted on a level course through the natural hothouse. Hawk felt the heat breathing and swirling beneath his helmet, sinking into the flesh behind his ears and under his hair. Sinking and sinking endlessly, as if the flesh was an insatiable sponge. His fatigues welded to him, black with sweat. The humid atmosphere vibrated all around the men, bouncing against their faces, worming its way into their insides. Such heat worried the sergeant. Depending upon how long they were out in it, and how much exertion was required of them, it would weaken them proportionately. It slowed their reflexes. It could also of its own power kill them. A lifetime in the southern climate made Hawk a slow talker and a slow walker. Here it made him a survivor.

The trail was wide and dry. The frequent rains drained from the gravelly soil. Trails made the travel easier. A wide one kept the insects and leeches off. Hawk ordered them into the underbrush. They were only a few miles from the enemy. He preferred a few leech bites to the mines and ambushes that accompanied trails. Ulcers healed, but legs didn't grow back. Grumbles followed the order.

The undergrowth wasn't as dense as it looked. The leafy foliage yielded calmly to them. The soil wasn't quite right for the thorny hold-him-fast, or the other barbed briars. Hawk ordered a straight course through the jungle, roughly parallel to the trail, and veering only a few degrees from it. Lyles, a gawky New Englander, was sent to the point. He tracked some sort of joke that went unheard by anyone before he disappeared into the greenery. A light wind blew among the higher leaves. The ground was still.

Cavell stayed near the front. Hawk let the men walk closer together than he should have. They felt more comfortable that way. The sergeant stayed in the middle of the single file. Trouble could erupt at any point, and he wanted to be within striking distance of it. He became a sort of roving flanker, and there were no others.

The beautiful forest closed tightly about them, the plant life growing thicker. Each man felt lonely with his thoughts. Leaves hung from above like fuzzy, long-fingered hands. The hand waved before their eyes, hypnotizing them with their graceful movement and gentle color. Hawk impatiently brushed a trumpeting yellow flower from in front of his eyes. The ground was a double-folded blanket with the softness of the moldy leaves. The still air was filled with feathery spores, floating busily back and forth. The decay smelled fresh and sweet in the choking heat.

Hawk glanced down occasionally to avoid the huge knots of roots and the ever-present adders. The killer snakes had chosen this isolated wood as their homeland. One had to expect to see at least one in every thousand square feet.

The thrashing of the men drowned the calm hush of the wind through the leaves. A bird or two would scream angrily as Lyles made his way deeper into the trackless jungle. Hawk didn't believe in a sixth sense. He believed a man better count on the five that he knew he had. And yet something about the palpable quiet was threatening. The squeaking of the helmet and rifle straps was too complacent. The patrol went deeper in forest, unopposed. Just when he had assured himself that he was only being grandmotherly, he heard the shots. They were followed by the sounds of vigorous running near the point. Joe Canlon leapt an inch off the ground when he heard the sudden noise. Hawk ran quickly to the head of the column.

Lyles burst through the weeds, dragging his rifle and a dripping red arm. "I think it was a Jap scout," he said breathlessly. "I ran smack into him, and we shot each other." Lyles wasn't in shock. His expression was steady, his words matter-of-fact. He had found Taniguchi's point man. Hawk had the wound tied off, rinsed and sprinkled with sulfa before the corpsman could come up from the rear. He also had Cavell swing the column into a triangular defense perimeter, with the long side of the triangle facing north. Lyles had come from the north. The sergeant kept himself and Canlon in the middle of the triangle as reserves.

Cavell was sent out to see what was going on. He was chomping at the bit. No one else was. The men could hear nothing from the forest ahead of them. Everyone hoped it was a lone enemy sniper. Everyone knew better. No need for a sniper out here. Their lungs were paralyzed, and the breath came in gasps. Joe's heart bubbled beneath his breastbone. A dirty little fight was shaping up. No way out. Kill or die. Cavell came back shortly with a report of seeing two of them crawling toward the Americans.

"How far apart?" Hawk asked his squad leader.

"Wide. Fifty, seventy-five feet. Looks like an attack, a little one, or they'd be closer together." Cavell spoke in a low voice charged with a strange restrained emotion. His face was pitiable, covered with jungle ulcers and discoloration. Hawk felt sorry that he had to be here for some reason.

"Radio," Hawk snapped. He soon had Jordan. "Contact, sir. Looks like a small party. Not sure yet. Nicked

Lyles. He's okay. I'd appreciate some rockets in Sector 187, Captain, to head off whatever it is."

"You're putting me on a spot, Hawk. Over."

"I'm on a spot, Captain."

"I'd have to bring in the LCI's. Over."

"Uh...yeah. Over."

"All right, don't count on it."

"No, sir. Out." Hawk waved the radio away. He rocked his helmet back and ran a finger up and down his straight narrow nose. "I hope they get some shit out here," he told Canlon, "to let them Japs know they care."

"But they don't," Joe said.

"That's gonna be the problem with this one. We best figure on weaselin' out of it ourselves."

"Let's move fast and pull back. Get the goddamn hell outa here."

Movement could be heard in the brush now. The unknown was rustling quickly and surely toward them. "Nah. Might get into something worse if we start runnin'. We're set and ready here." Hawk bit off a crescent of tobacco. "We're okay, I expect." Joe looked over at Hawk's expressionless face. Sometimes he hated his friend. Cold and slow as a glacier. Business as usual. Trapped in a blood-hungry jungle wasteland. Hawk spat.

"Let 'em start it," Hawk called to the line of prone men. "We might take the attack after we see how strong they are."

When Hawk said "might," it meant he had every intention of charging the underbrush. Under these circumstances, few men would order such a thing. But they knew Hawk's style. Their uncomfortable anxiety degenerated into hard, cold fear. Real, body-shaking fear pulsated through the group like a current. Wild individual emotion bridged the small gaps between their bodies and became a joint fear, larger and worse than the fear of a lone man. It was the type of emotion best described as lightly controlled panic.

They were marines. They had been prepared for it. They had done it before. They were still human beings.

***

General Kawamoto shuddered with excitement. This was as close as he'd been to a small party action in his thirty years as a solider. Taniguchi assured him that there weren't many marines. The Japanese force would triumph. The general felt exceptionally brave today. Thirty years of playing at long distance war had built up an overpowering urge in him to see the real thing.

Hauptmann Mittelstadt, on the other hand, was frightened. And old Sergeant Pechmann didn't look as fond of Rechnung Island as he had been the day before. They were about as far from home as men could get. Mittelstadt felt as if he were among aliens, not friends or allies. These beasts were leading him into battle for the sheer amusement of it. Kawamoto acted like a pasha stalking the tiger. The German's face disguised his fear when he smiled at the general. Better to humor the maniac. Mittelstadt cursed himself for coming on this outing. War and glory demanded goals. It was foolish to jeopardize your life for no objective whatsoever. What glory could there be in death on a purposeless mission? Here he was, the most important man in the South Pacific, embroiled in a two-squad firefight. He could imagine one of the vicious Americans cutting the insignia off his uniform as he lay dead in the putrid sod. They would laugh, speculate on his presence here and walk away from his bleaching bones. "This should be amusing," Mittelstadt commented to the general crouching beside him. Kawamoto nodded.

Pechmann glared at the general. Kawamoto was in the fight for himself. For his own diversion. That was dangerous. Pechmann had seen his share of war. He knew the marines were fighting for each other.

"Yes," said Kawamoto. He stood. It was unbecoming for a general to crouch. He looked at the terrain. Not exactly the location he would have chosen for a pitched battle. "The presence of a superior military mind assures your victory," he told the soldiers around him. They were in complete agreement. Taniguchi was a military genius. "Tell your men to fire at will,' Kawamoto brilliantly ordered the *hancho.*

Mittelstadt did not stand. His mind ran again to the Americans. What sort of men were they out there? He remembered the rough boys who lived down the street when he was a child. They grew up and went to work on the waterfront, when he went off to the university at Rostock. What animals they were. How much worse must these Americans be? Out there, with guns.

* * *

A WHIPLIKE CRACK split the air over Hawk's head. The bullet continued on through the trees. No one heard it. The single shot was followed by a volley. The angry slugs buzzed and slapped at the air. The next volley didn't stop. It lapsed into a continuous roar. The shots thumped into the soft earth or whined off the tumid trees, taking layers of shattered bark with them. The Japanese could not be seen.

"Twenty-five or thirty of 'em," Hawk muttered to Canlon. He raised his voice. "Get them flanks farther out. Hold the grenades till you see something." The men on the end of the northern line complied by crawling deeper into the jungle, returning desultory shots. They could not restrain themselves, however, from slinging grenades at the disembodied noise.

Hawk calculated that he was outnumbered two to one. That was all right. Two to one didn't mean a whole lot in an action of this size. He didn't have to win, anyway, he just had to get away in one piece.

Kawamoto ordered the traditional frontal assault. Even a student of strategy such as the general was saddled with the Japanese shortcomings in tactics. Elaborate tactics were unmanly. If a frontal assault failed, another and more vigorous one followed. A truly crafty commander might try a flanking maneuver, and less often, a double flanking. Hawk had seen all of these maneuvers before. He knew pretty much what to expect, and what was going on out in the blind jungle. It didn't make it any easier. They were still shooting at him.

The Japanese didn't have enough men to try a mass attack. They crawled through the now thorny shrubbery at a steady pace, intermittently firing and moving. They were shackled with another shortcoming: lack of automatic firepower. They didn't have a well-distributed submachine gun. Hawk thought he heard an old Berman or Solothurn, but it was rare to find an enemy soldier with a machine pistol. This was probably due to some administrative decision that there was no substitute for accurate rifle fire. Administrative decisions are usually made by old codgers whose need for firepower is leveled against tin cans and plant-eating game. In the jungle, the submachine gun was king. Several of the enemy were pushing and dragging 6.5 and 7.7 mm machine guns through the entangling lianas. They were heavy and bulky and required a certain amount of body weight to swing about. The carrying handle and flashguards tended to entangle themselves in the creepers. Infantrymen with bolt action Arisakas inevitably had to take the lead. While it may have been true that there was no substitute for accurate rifle fire, rifle fire is seldom accurate when another man is shooting back at you. The marines were shooting back with automatic and semiautomatic weapons, setting up a racket that would shake the soul of a marble statue. Automatic fire need not be accurate.

Hawk's perimeter laid down a vicious outpouring of fire that scythed a foot above the ground. The advancing enemy who weren't flat or behind cover were dead. Cavell had a grease gun, another man had a BAR. Hawk joined in with his Thompson. The others had semiautomatic M1's. Warbling cries from the invisible enemy let the Americans know the extent of their superior technology. Joe Canlon cradled a twelve gauge shotgun. He hadn't fired yet.

While the Japanese bullets were numerous, they were not literally everywhere, as were the Americans'. A rumbling steamroller of lead chewed leafy stalks and the smaller trees to the ground. The Japanese were finally close enough to be seen. As their attack faltered under the leaden hailstorm, Hawk saw glimpses of puttees, many splashed with red, slipping into the forest. "Hold your fire!" he shouted. He couldn't tell from his position at the source of the deafening barrage whether the Japanese were returning fire. The one-armed Lyles noticed a water blister on his finger where he had been pulling the trigger of his Ml.

Hawk swung his head and heavy helmet around to check the other sides of his triangle. If the attackers were smart enough to withdraw, a typically un-Japanese move, they were smart enough to flank him. He was surprised that they stopped before reaching grenade range. It was difficult to tell exactly where that might be in the confused underbrush. But they were close to it.

"Up and at 'em. Get the bastards. Let's go!" Hawk stood. Now was the best time to finish them. To hell with thoughts of a trap. Hawk was often less than prudently cautious under fire. He tried to take care of the caution department before the fight, while there was time. Afterwards, there was time only for fast action. Usually, the bolder force won the field. Of course, when this way of thinking failed, it failed miserably. It was the only way Hawk knew. That was his way.

He didn't change his clip. He carried the old snail drum in his Thompson because it held fifty rounds. He calculated that it still held more than a straight clip. He carried the bigger drum out of caution—he didn't play with death. But when it came right down to it, he didn't stop to think long enough to make a reasonable estimate of how many slugs were left, he just got up and ran.

A skirmish line of crouching, firing marines arced in the wake of the fleeing Japanese. Impossible as it seemed, the American fire increased in intensity, with men pulling madly against their triggers. Spent casings blew from the breeches of their weapons, glinting gold against the backdrop of multishaded green. Joe's shotgun erupted. Smoke swirled about the leafy ferns and the other mincing plants that grew close to the ground. "Slow it!" Hawk screamed. "Goddammit, Cavell, stop!" They were moving too fast now, emotion at a fever pitch had overwhelmed them. Fear turned to anger. Hawk couldn't see the enemy. He went forward, ahead of everyone, bent at the waist, his open shirt dragging and flapping.

Hawk stopped. He went to one knee and gave the others a hand signal. It told them to remain in place. The ferocious blue eyes scanned the jungle. They were familiar with the task. They wouldn't be ambushed. They were to the rain forest what an infrared snooper scope was to the night. They filtered out everything but the gray, green, khaki, and flesh colors of the Japanese hiding in the forest maze. His eyes twitched. He saw only the coconut and malaguna, the coleus and the pendanus.

He gave another hand signal: converge on this position. Cavell took it to mean converge on Hawk. Hawk moved on, crouching, slowly moving the gas compensator of his muzzle from one side to the other. Drops of perspiration fell from his nose and beard. His lips were parted, and he breathed through his mouth. His boots felt big and awkward as he lifted one past the other.

Coming to you, Jap, he said to himself. Coming to you, baby. Show your ass, Jap. Just breathe, sweetheart, I'll do the rest. He heard Cavell behind him to the right. He didn't have to look. He knew who it was. Good old

Cavell. Now they could divide the speeding twenty-five caliber slugs between them. Hawk had been willing to absorb them all. But he would share them if Cavell was stupid enough to come up here.

Taniguchi spoke calmly to his corporals. Kawamoto had just completed one of his loudest and most irrational tirades. Had it not been the honorable general's tirade, one might have called it a panicky release of cowardly tension. Since it *was* the honorable general's tirade, one had to call it an inspiring exhortation to victory. The exhortation was rather thin on inspiration, since that part of it that could be understood dealt primarily with Kawamoto's blaming everyone in the eastern hemisphere for getting a general into this situation. He blamed everyone but himself. The corporals crouched on either side of Taniguchi and Kawamoto stood over them. The general's hands were on his hips, in a position that demanded victory.

Taniguchi was now in his element. There was no emotion in his face or in his voice. His stocky body was poised, but not tense, as he explained what had to be done. His men loved him. They bowed respectfully to him when he finished and scurried into the tropical verdure. Taniguchi stood and waited for Kawamoto to approve of his plan. Kawamoto instead lapsed into another loud and unintelligible tirade. The general was better at blaming than he was at planning.

"Please forgive my suggestion, honorable General," Taniguchi calmly urged. "The enemy is very close, and we should keep our voices down."

The *hancho* knew his urging might go unheeded. He had an overlapping plan of contingency, however, for it was his hope to draw the enemy to this spot. What better way than with the ravings of a lunatic?

"You are endangering the life of a general in the Imperial Army of the emperor!" Kawamoto screamed. "You disgrace! You incompetent! You coward! Your head is yours for the moment only!" Taniguchi bowed subserviently, one ear cocked to make sure that more serious matters were being taken care of. Kawamoto was merely a nuisance to the action. Taniguchi was used to nuisances. The *hancho* would have liked nothing better than for a .30 caliber slug to penetrate the general's bisonlike forehead, although it would be degrading for such a thing to happen on his patrol.

Taniguchi had been chosen for this mission because it was felt that Kawamoto would be perfectly safe under his care. When his superiors read of the death of the general, they would not take into account Kawamoto's personality. They would consider only his rank. And Taniguchi did not want to give the Americans a dead officer of the emperor. For no matter how much he might hate Kawamoto, he hated the Americans ten times as much. He had earned his right to hate them. Always better equipped, always with more men, always brutal, never relenting, never losing. No, he would bring Kawamoto back alive. He would bring the European, cowering behind a yara tree, back too. It was a matter of pride in his craft. Taniguchi was invincible in small unit actions.

* * *

HAWK LOOKED DOWN. His boot rested in a syrupy splash of blood and body leakage. A man had taken a hard hit here. A broken ribbon of red meandered over the leaves for a few feet, then there was dark wet earth, and then nothing but trampled cane grass. The Japanese had carried off all of the dead and wounded. That one was probably dead by now. It had been an orderly retreat. They were a well-disciplined bunch. No moaning could be heard from any quarter. The vibrating hum of the insects and an incessant ducking-snapping of a locust followed the end of the firing. The Japanese were stoic sufferers. These were, at any rate. Then he heard a loud Japanese voice.

The tone of the voice was authoritative. It wasn't the voice of a wounded man. It was angry. Hawk's brooding eyebrows drew close together. The owner of the voice was either a jackass, or he was leading Hawk into a trap. He didn't count on a Japanese being a jackass. He signaled an advance. He stopped the men near the spilled blood and set up his perimeter again. They moved as silently as they could. Canlon mentally questioned moving their position for such a short gain. Joe didn't like anything about this. He pumped his shotgun.

Hawk continued in the direction of the voice. Leaves rustled to his left. What the hell was that? He held back the trigger of his tommy gun and wagged the muzzle across the moving leaves. The slithering muzzle flash blazed into the thicket. A sound of something solid being hit followed. As he approached his dead victim, still unseen in the concealing weeds, Taniguchi struck the weakest side of the ill-prepared marine triangle.

Several concussion grenades started the action. American voices screamed in pain and terror. Hawk immediately understood that he'd been suckered. He knew men were already hurt. He wheeled around without checking his kill and returned to his men. He had been only seventeen feet from General Kawamoto when he stopped and turned around. The dead man in the thicket was Taniguchi's lieutenant. Had the *hancho* delayed the attack another thirty seconds, Kawamoto would have learned a great deal more about his favorite subject—killing—than he cared to. Sergeant Hawk was a very able and willing teacher.

As Hawk ran swiftly back toward the unnerving cacophony of fire, a figure dashed by him. He saw a face and an elaborate uniform. He didn't try to fire at the man, he recognized him as a Caucasian. In the confusion, he gave the sight only a fleeting thought. Was that a Salvation Army uniform? The Red Cross had been down on the beach, might the Salvation Army not also be here? That was all he thought of the apparition for the moment.

Ferns shimmered around the belching muzzles of the Japanese machine guns. Their range was unerring, the American firepower was neutralized. When Hawk burst upon the scene, he knew he had a serious situation. One corpse lay stretched and limp on the short side of the triangle. It was bathed in red, the neck torn open, and the helmet splintered. The soft brown earth was maroon with blood. His men had no appreciable cover, just what they had scraped in front of themselves in the last few seconds before the attack. They could only hope that their return fire would keep the enemy at bay. A strong force was attacking on one of the short sides of the triangle, and a diversionary force was attacking on the other. The long side went unchallenged. The opposing troops were mere feet apart. Hawk could see darting heads and legs being drawn up under the advancing Japanese. They were coming forward with an unchecked aggressiveness. Canlon was in the process of strengthening the two sides under attack, trying desperately to move men from the long side.

A burst of fire caught one man as he rose slightly to turn around. A smear of red lashed out from his face. He was lifted from the ground and fell heavily backward on one leg. A corncob grenade landed in the middle of the hollow triangle.

Lyles, the wounded scout, dropped his rifle and rolled over on the grenade. It didn't explode. By all rights, his stomach should have been blown out. After about twenty seconds, he rolled off of it and tossed it back into the jungle. Another grenade came in from the right and fell wide. The Japanese grenades had to fall much closer to their targets than did the American's, because of their poor range.

The enemy machine guns raked the triangle. The American fire virtually ceased under the fury. Enemy riflemen edged closer, firing all the while. Several marines were screaming now at various points along the perimeter. The corpsman was dead. A man on one of the points of the triangle had lost a foot to a grenade, and his cries were the loudest. Hawk caught a glance at the straining tendons in his neck and the contorted muscles of his face as he gave into a fit of shrieking.

The sergeant crawled across the center of the perimeter. Bullets fell like raindrops. He reached Canlon. Joe managed to sob, "They got us, Hawk." Joe had no appreciation of the overall situation. He heard only a weighty mass of noise and saw nothing but the ground and glimpses of trees.

"I'll be goddamned," Hawk snarled. "Them no good sons of bitches." Anger quelled any fear Hawk might have had. The tightening of the chewing fire meant failure to him. Tactics that didn't work. Machinery that didn't operate. He was infuriated. He snatched a frag grenade from his web belt, and straightened its cotter pin on the foresight of his Thompson. He pulled the ring and the pin slid grudgingly through the two holes that held down the spoon. Holding his hand around the body of the pineapple, he gripped the safety lever down. Hawk threw an elbow out and pulled himself toward the unchallenged Nambu machine guns.

His eyes were nearly closed as he pulled himself forward, an inch at a time. His mouth was jammed shut, drooping defiantly at the corners. He thought of nothing. The sight and sound of the lightning spewing from the conical flashguards prevented his brain from functioning. The glut of sensory impressions blocked the nerve rails upon which rational thought ran. He was operating on messages from his spinal cord. Move. Forward. The incredible, involuntary tensing of his muscles became so great that even that function was about to cease. Cold Sergeant Hawk was nearly frozen. He looked into the two mouths of the spitting guns. The huddled gunners couldn't be seen behind the vaporous discharge of the shuddering breechblocks. The darting flutter of fiery silver blinded him. The dragon mouths were desperately attempting to aim lower, to stitch him. The gunners lifted up on their stocks, hoping to lick him with their glowing steel tongues. The sergeant opened his hand, and the safety lever flew off.

Hawk's arm lashed stiffly up from the earth. The

grenade turned end over end. It was a poor throw. He went mad with rage.

Taniguchi's corporals had made one mistake. The machine guns were placed hastily and too close together. They should have been on alternating sides of the triangle with interlocking fields of fire. Taniguchi had told them that. That proved to be too difficult in their estimation. Now they would pay for not listening to the *hancho*. Hawk's grenade went behind the 6.5 mm gun. The crew had plenty of time to duck. They managed to reach adequate cover, and the grenade killed not a single man. The blast and the scissoring shrapnel did however break up the steadiness of the Japanese fire.

As the grenade went off, Hawk jumped to his feet. Pure hate lifted him and pushed him forward. You had to have it to do a thing like that. Simple anger, or skill, or bravery, or the grossest pride wouldn't make you do it. You had to hate them, you had to want them dead more than you wanted to live. You couldn't learn such a thing, you had to live it. You had to hate—every minute of every day of your life.

The two machine gun crews were absent from their positions, but the other attackers raised their weapons and tried to track him. He charged the Nambus, his boots hitting like hooves. He heard the shots slipping by him. They slapped the air, struck the ground and some ricocheted off of one another. The bullets hitting the earth turned over the leaves like they were pages in a book. Ignoring the enraged barks of Japanese voices, he raced through their crisscrossing lines of fire without a scratch, kicked over the heavy machine gun and fired into a prone crewman's back. Other crewmen lay cringing nearby. He scoured the earth with passionate .45 fire, tearing up the legs, torsos, and heads he found concealed there. The obscene excess of noise was matched only by the excess of hate gushing through Hawk's bloodstream. He spun around and booted the 6.5 mm gun over like a toy.

An enemy rifleman came crouching out of the jungle behind the former machine gun position. He adjusted his Arisaka and jerked a shot off at the American. The shot hummed past Hawk's eyes, sending out shock waves that bathed his face in electric vibrations. Sparks blazed like feathery stars from the Thompson, knocking down the rifleman. Two more of the enemy charged out of the brush, running right into the same burst that killed the first man. They fell over one another. It all worked like some grotesque script; they couldn't hit him, and he couldn't miss.

Taniguchi watched Hawk. The *hancho* had excellent cover behind a thick tree, only a stone's throw away. He could have leveled his Bergman and stitched the marine. Probably. Taniguchi clenched his teeth. So young, so full of fire, so invulnerable was the marine. He wasn't as young as the other Americans lying dead in the bullet-raked perimeter, but he was still young enough to think that he couldn't be killed, still full of that youthful emotion and totally devoid of caution. Today would be the marine's day. He was on a roll. War was all odds, mathematics. The young American could no nothing wrong today. Tomorrow the odds would change, and he would die falling over a trip wire like a clumsy infant. To fire at him today invited death. Don't fight a man on a roll. Don't make a pass with death. Taniguchi would remember his face. The face of death, with its cold and ghastly orbs that served as eyes, its wide mouth viciously tucked in blind rage. Taniguchi slung his submachine gun. He waved his arm, signaling a withdrawal. He had inflicted the greater casualties by far, with his superior skill in jungle warfare. Why let a lone and lucky man even the score? Better to fight skillfully again tomorrow.

The action ended suddenly. Hawk didn't pursue them. He didn't have the men for that. He sat among the bloody dead and let Cavell and Canlon direct the end of the firefight. He was still sitting there when they carried one of his wounded men by him.

The man carried a flower someone had given him. "Get outa step, you're joggin' his head," Hawk said. The stretcherbearers paused and started over. Joe Canlon walked to Hawk and stood over him. "You okay?" Joe asked.

"Yeah. I'm okay."

Joe nodded and walked away.

5

KAWAMOTO WOKE UP IN A FOUL MOOD THE NEXT DAY. HE had learned his lesson with regard to the more dangerous forms of entertainment. He could say he had been in a firefight. There was no need or desire to do that again. On the trip back to his quarters he had called Taniguchi every name he could imagine, had publicly humiliated him, and later completed the paperwork on a radical demotion for the *hancho.* In spite of all that, when the general saw his own little *swali bungalo* after surviving the battle, he felt less animosity. *Hanchos* of twenty-year tenure were difficult to bust, even for a general. He admitted that he had been a little harsh with Taniguchi. He might tell him so. He was a little awed by the *hancho.*

But not too much. He yawned and stretched both arms until they prodded his mosquito net loose. Like all madmen, Kawamoto could not lie idle. He had to be doing something, and it had to be ninety percent self-indulgent and at least fifty percent valueless. His brain churned feverishly as he sat up. Today he would shoot prisoners. He didn't feel physical. Martial arts were out this morning. The firefight had shown him that guns were where the power lay. He yawned again. He would practice shooting men today. Or maybe children. That was a greater character-builder.

* * *

"DID you thank the captain for them rockets yesterday?" Joe Canlon asked sarcastically. He had been avoiding Hawk. He went to get his beer rations, and upon coming back saw him sitting against a barracks wall. He sat beside him and rolled his three olive drab cans between them. Hawk scratched his back like a horse on the corrugated iron of the wall. Joe had two beers finished in almost as many swallows.

"Yeah."

"Want a beer?"

"Nah."

"Good, I need all I can get. You can have one of mine if you want. Two is just as useless as three for me."

"Nah. Thanks." Hawk pulled a beer can up from the other side of his hip and took a drink. He stared out at the green peaks of the waves. The ocean was restful, lapping contentedly at the brown beach like a kitten cleaning herself.

Joe had been kind of cool toward Hawk since the firefight. He half blamed him for the outrageous casualties. He was ready to make up now. Joe couldn't hold a grudge. He didn't think Hawk even knew he was mad at him.

"What's the matter with you? Thinkin'? Gettin'

philosophical?" Joe asked. "A man can think and drink a free beer, you know."

Hawk looked over at him with an unsympathetic blank expression. He turned back toward the sea. "What do you want from me?" Hawk growled. "I told you I don't want your beer. You need some money or something?"

"God! What a bastard! You try to be nice to a guy and he acts like a horse's ass. Here, take it, you need an extra beer."

"I gotta beer in my hand. Why don't you get the hell away from me or something?" They sat there without speaking for several minutes, alternately slurping and belching. Hawk realized Joe wasn't going away. Something was on his mind.

"So what the hell *do* you want?" the sergeant asked in a slightly more civilized tone.

"Nothin'! I said nothin'! I was givin' you a beer! Damn guy." Joe took his opener in hand and put two triangular holes in the top. He took a greedy swallow. "There, now you ain't gotta worry about it. I never open a beer I don't finish."

Hawk pulled a bottle of rubbing alcohol from behind his back. "Three beers make everybody mad," the sergeant muttered. He reached behind his back again and produced a dirty, nibbled biscuit. He set it on top of his beer can and poured a healthy dose of alcohol through it, letting it filter down into the can.

"That's a good way to kill yourself," Joe commented.

"Best way I can think of."

Cavell strolled up and sat on the sand in front of them. Two other men from his squad, Henson and Stilley, soon joined him. They were among the few uninjured men of the late patrol. They too rolled their beers in front of themselves.

"What are you two guys doing?" Cavell mumbled disinterestedly. Hawk and Canlon glared at one another. "Actin' like a couple shitasses," Hawk said.

"You was. I wasn't," Canlon corrected him. Joe became the master of ceremonies since he had the opener. "Hawk's tryin' to go blind—drinkin' straight alcohol," Joe informed them.

Hawk tested his beer. "Says the asshole that drank a whole platoon's Aqua Velva in one night," the sergeant snarled as he poured another little shot into his beer. "Besides that, it ain't straight alcohol, it's a...a mixed drink is what it is, like them Yankees drink."

"Don't they have mixed drinks in Mississippi?" Henson asked as he down half of his first beer. A garble of voices followed. Hawk listened to them silently.

"They got *no* drinks in Mississippi."

"They got no *nothin'* in Mississippi."

"I know a guy what went blind from drinking."

"It'd be awful to go blind."

"Yeah, we'd have to give all this up."

"You gonna drink all three of them beers?"

"You goddamn right. Get your hands off them beers."

Hawk stood with his beer. Things were getting rowdy. He didn't like crowds, especially rowdy ones. Beer made nice guys mean. Hawk was always mean. He didn't like drunks. He didn't like anything silly. He wanted to be alone for a while. No one asked him where he was going when he stood up and walked away. Joe shrugged when the others looked to him for an explanation. "He's been kinda quiet," Canlon said.

"Has he mentioned yesterday?" Stilley asked.

"No," Joe's voice cracked. They all took a quiet sip.

Stilley shook his head and gave a short laugh that had a sob in it somewhere. "I ain't never seen nothing like that," he said.

"Yeah. I guess he saved our ass," said Joe.

Cavell looked up at Hawk's retreating figure, slouching across the beach in the direction of the field hospital. "Yeah, he's all right," Cavell sighed.

"That's southern hospitality!" Canlon shouted after Hawk. "Walk out on your buddies!" Hawk didn't turn around. Joe was feeling pretty good on three beers. He wondered if Hawk was going to the hospital because of blindness. He laughed for no apparent reason.

"He don't have to drink with me," Henson said as he batted the flies away from his knotty nose. "Just so he goes out in them woods with me." They all chuckled weakly, and held stupefied, silent smiles on their faces until they finished their beers.

Joe looked over at the cliff and then in the direction of the hospital tent. Hawk had gone in. Canlon looked back down at the sand. His smile was gone. "Wish we'd get outa here," he said.

Lyles was on a cot in the hospital tent. He'd had a slug pulled out of his arm the night before. It was close to the bone and the doctor had to fish around a little to get it. He told Hawk he was ready to go back and do it all again. When Belva Cook asked him when he thought he could return to the company, he said the sooner the better. Hawk hoped Lyles wasn't putting on a show for his benefit. His cheery attitude had already caused the cancellation of an order that would have gotten him at least three weeks on Manus Island, and maybe even a trip to New Zealand afterward. Manus wasn't exactly Paris in the springtime, anyway. Hawk left the badly wrinkled young face of Lyles still smiling. The sergeant knew he would see him again, soon.

"You'll notice that there aren't any more of the Seabees here," Belva said as the two of them walked down the aisle between the cots of ailing men. Hawk nodded. He hadn't said much. His brooding eyes took in the bright reds and dried browns shining through the white bandages. His nose absorbed the antiseptic odor. He regretted that the wounded ended up in places like this. It was unmanly or something. A chill came over him. He was about to take a drink of his beer when a doctor entered the tent. Hawk held his beer behind his back as the surgeon passed them.

"How are you, sir?" he asked the surgeon courteously. The officer didn't answer. He passed quickly on his frock-fluttering way, too busy for something as inconsequential as Sergeant Hawk. Hawk smiled. Yankee.

"They moved them out last night. When...your boys came in," Belva continued. "They're gone for good," she drawled in her Texas accent.

"Gone for good," Hawk repeated sullenly.

"They figured out what was wrong with them. The sap from a certain tree in the jungle was causing that skin deterioration. When they bulldozed or dynamited one of the trees, little drops of its black sap would get on their skin and burn right through it. They're taking them up to Alaska, where there ain't no trees."

"Yeah?" Hawk responded interestedly. She took it to be mock-interestedly. But he was interested. Strange ailments. Quick evacuations. The secret weapon?

Maybe. Probably not. Trees that rotted your hide off seemed more logical in this hellhole. There had been no more disappearances, not like C Company. He remembered the man in the Salvation Army uniform. He remained distant and quiet. What was that jerk up to?

"I think I'd like it up there. This heat is terrible," said Belva. "It's not as cold in Alaska as you might think. The ocean gives it a temperate climate—near the coast, of course."

"I reckon so." Hawk looked directly at her for the first time. She smiled. He smiled back and sipped his beer. Belva didn't want to fight it anymore. She liked him quite a bit. He was so brave and beautiful and tortured by something. He was probably shy. His quietness, she surmised, was probably due to shyness. In spite of all the war she'd seen, she didn't realize he was only fighting his way back to the edge of sanity. He was turning to walk away.

"Can I have a drink of that?" She heard herself say. She stressed her accent. Southern men liked southern women.

"Well...it's kind of a mixed drink, you see. It might make you sick."

"Oh." She tossed her dark hair off her forehead. "You don't have to drink that. I can get you some beer."

"Ah, this is good enough for me. Well, guess I better be gettin' on back," he said, again turning.

Her heart jumped into her throat, and she said, "Would you like to go swimming tonight? I can get away. I know a place."

Hawk looked at her. He was still quite numb to reality from the day before. Her sensual body didn't register strongly on him. He was, however, somehow touched by the pretty face and the vulnerable expression. He wasn't completely dead. He knew he couldn't possibly say no. He wasn't sure if that was because he didn't want to hurt her feelings, or if it was because if he turned her down he could never talk to her again. He didn't want either one of those things. But he didn't want to go anywhere. He would have liked to put the conversation in a vacuum and maybe come back to it in a couple of weeks. "You're off limits," he said simply.

"Ivania Broeder is supposed to be off limits to Captain Jordan, too. It doesn't bother them."

Hawk tightened his lips. Her comment irritated him in several different unidentifiable ways. "I ain't much of a swimmer. I guess I could watch."

She laughed. "I'll see you here at dark then?"

"Okay."

She watched him walk away. He didn't turn around again. She leaned against the tent post. She felt guilty. Nothing good would come of it. She had promised herself that she wouldn't get mixed up with a serviceman. She told her parents that. She had spent a year put off with men, suspicious of their every word and glance. Then she met Ivania Broeder. She hated her. So vain and aloof. Ivania was even more suspicious of men. She talked about them like they were some sort of viral disease. She enjoyed being untouchable. Belva saw a part of herself she didn't like in Ivania. She was naturally a friendly person, and after all these men *were* fighting a war. Most of them were really nice. Homesick children. Scared children. She hadn't fallen in love with any of them. Until now. Now she met this strange creature who seemed to belong to this terrifying time and place. But nothing good could come of it. She would love him, and he would have to love her or she would end up hating him. She felt a sadness in her chest.

That wasn't Hawk's last brush with nurses for the day. As he crossed the tire- and tread-marked sand of the beach, Ivania Broeder passed him. He was shocked when she stepped out of her path and stopped in front of him. His eyes studied her. He said nothing.

"Sergeant James Hawk, I believe? I heard about your patrol yesterday," she said. It was a friendly approach, and her smile was beautiful, and yet there was something of the queen granting an audience in her words.

"Yes, ma'am. A rough one."

"I heard what you did."

"Got a bunch of boys killed."

"No, I mean about killing all those Japanese." She was still smiling. The smile hadn't changed in size or shape since first appearing.

"Only way out, I imagine."

"I spoke with Clinton about it. He says you can't be decorated because of the top secret nature of our presence here. I think that's awful."

Hawk didn't know she was trying to irritate him. She picked the wrong way. He killed to live, not for decorations. He didn't know what she was getting at. He liked her. It would have been hard for her to irritate him.

"Yes, ma'am, probably so."

"You should protest."

Protest—regret—refund—these words weren't part of Hawk's vocabulary. He put up with shit just the way it was. "Yes, ma'am," he said.

"Well, congratulations, anyway. I must be going."

"Yeah. See you around, Lieutenant."

And off she went, mildly amused by her audience with a trained killer. Hawk bit off a plug of tobacco. I couldn't think of anything to say, he thought. And then he forgot her. Had she spoken to him day before yesterday, he would have remembered every word out of her mouth. Today, he was out of focus. He was about ten feet behind his eyeballs. His brain was revolving over and over, thinking of other things. He thought not only of the men who died yesterday but of the men here now who would also soon die. He could see them and talk to them today, and tomorrow they would be gone—just like the kids on that patrol. There was something important about that. He couldn't quite grasp it. He took a slug of beer over the wad of tobacco. He finished the can. He felt better. He started thinking more slowly, and then, not at all.

Ivania Broeder looked back over her shoulder at him. He was still standing where she had stopped him. What a brute. How well he suited this disgusting place, filled with disgusting men. Here they didn't indulge themselves with ruining the lives of women. They thrived on destroying one another. That was fine. If only she could be elsewhere. She ducked into the hospital tent.

Belva Cook was watching her. And Sergeant Hawk.

That afternoon, Jordan requested Hawk's presence at the CP. The captain cleared the office of curious ears and made Hawk comfortable in a camp chair. The office sat behind his desk, trying to look nonchalant. Hawk received permission to smoke, lit a cigar and stared at Jordan. "I don't have to tell you what a remarkable thing that was that you did out there," Jordan began. He paused. Hawk said nothing. His intense gaze bored into the captain's eyes. "I didn't bring you here to talk about it. It wasn't all glory, you know. You lost a lot of men."

"Yessir. I know."

"And the whole thing was your idea, you'll recall. Do you want to admit that it wasn't such a good idea?"

Hawk looked down thoughtfully and shifted in his chair. "No, sir. I couldn't say that."

"I didn't think you would."

"May I explain why, sir?"

"Go ahead."

"Them Japs was headed up our way. I expect they was gonna set up them two Nambus and thin out the construction men. I lost some boys. They was damn good men. But they was fighting men. That was their job. They died in a fight, not on a bulldozer gettin' sniped like a buncha rabbits. The government's put some of us into rifle platoons and some of us doin' other things. We was doin' what we do. What we do has a way of ending up like the detail yesterday. Sir."

"I see. No regrets. Go get 'em, marines. That's all there was to it?"

Hawk rocked his head back slightly. He had a terrible temper. It was so bad he could never lose it. He knew that and he could control it. "No, sir. That ain't exactly how it was. Them recon reports you was talking about told me I didn't have to worry about no Japs till I got ten miles out. We hit 'em a little over ten minutes out. I regret anybody got hurt. Damn right. But we can't sit around regrettin' everything that happens." Hawk spoke the last sentence slowly. He *had* been sitting around regretting the patrol. "If we do that, we're all gonna be eatin' fishheads and garbage rind soup in a POW camp, because the goddamn Japs don't regret nothin'."

Jordan didn't like the rebuff. It was obvious from the expression on his little boy's face. "Okay, Hawk. I respect your version of the action and your opinion. When people in my company do things, I take the heat. You're not the Lone Ranger. You know, you don't have the time in grade for all of those stripes you're carrying around," Jordan said ominously. Hawk didn't want a demotion. There were a lot of kids in the Marine Corps. He didn't want to be outranked by any more of them than he already was. The sergeant remained expressionless.

"We need men like you to win this war," Jordan continued, having already played his ace. "No one can deny it. It's unfortunate, but it's true. The Japanese do pretty much what they want to us, and it'll take strong measures to whip them. I need you, but I don't have to like you. Like you say, that's not my job. I'll work with you. We need your experience. You're willing. Maybe you're even right. Understand, you've earned no special privileges."

"Yessir." Hawk studied the officer's smooth face. This was leading up to something. It had been rehearsed, for some reason. He was setting Hawk up for another rotten detail. Get on with it, shitass, Hawk thought.

Jordan sat back in his swivel chair. He felt relieved that he had been able to force a little respect out of Hawk. He took it further. "Personalities conflict. You probably don't like me, either," the captain said.

"I didn't like not gettin' them rockets yesterday. I can

tell you that. Otherwise, I got nothin' against you. Sir." Hawk sighed. "Unless you got something to do with us being here on Stocken Bay."

"The rockets were out of the question. I didn't want anyone to know you were out there. I put it down as a contact mission, instead of a security mission—which is what it was. They wouldn't care for that. We're not here to be secure. For your information, I requested the rockets, just as you asked. I had nothing to do with their refusal, just as I have nothing to do with our being here." Jordan was nervous now. He shouldn't have defended himself. He had lost all that he gained. "Like...I said," he began with an annoying stutter, "I didn't want to discuss all of that. My point is: I'm the captain, and you're the sergeant. I'm the decision maker. I relied on your experience. You think you did a good job. I don't think the overall outcome was good. We don't need heroics, we need teamwork."

Hawk drew silently on his cigar. On a whim, he decided to give Jordan what he wanted. "Maybe you're right, sir. Maybe I did force a decision that was too big for me." Shocked, Jordan looked up with a triumphant smile. Hawk smiled back. What a kid.

"Thank you for that, Sergeant. Now for the business at hand. I'm sure you're aware that the Japanese have been using gas."

"No, sir. I...didn't know that."

"Everybody knows it. Don't kid me. They just don't know what kind. The Japs have used gas before. It's nothing new. They used it in China. Hell, I think it was in the papers. This is the first time they've used it on us, though. Talk about a stroke of...luck. It's a new kind of nerve gas, called Tabun. The Germans developed it.

Deadly as hell. You don't have time to say your prayers, that's for sure. The Germans are letting the Japs try it out. They say the Japs aren't as afraid of reprisals as the Germans are. That's why we're here."

Hawk remembered the man in the odd uniform. Had he really seen that? Was any of this real? He decided it was too questionable to mention. "Yessir. Nerve gas. Hmph. I don't think so."

"Yes, and...what? What do you mean you don't think so?"

"Two platoons disappeared. That's what they're sayin'. Nerve gas don't make you disappear."

"Listen, Hawk, we weren't there with C Company. I've been briefed by Colonel Hulmore...and...and Major Caldwell, himself, from intelligence, on this. Are you saying that they're feeding me false information?"

"*No*, sir." Hawk managed not to smile.

Jordan exhaled harshly and leaned forward on his desk. "Okay, Hawk, what was it?"

"It was nerve gas, sir."

"That's right," Jordan laughed unexpectedly.

"We're beginning to understand one another, I think. I respect your ideas, but it *was* nerve gas. It kills quickly and horribly, and the Japanese simply dragged the bodies off before we could get out there."

"Yessir. Bodies are heavy for Japs, sir."

"Meaning what?"

"If you'll check the operations report, sir," Hawk said casually, "you'll see that there weren't any enemy units even close to that sector. At last report, C Company had spotted something like a half dozen infiltrators or less out in front of their position. Nothing big. I don't know much about gas. I been to some talks on it.

It's got to blow in on the wind or be shot in by artillery. Now we know there damn sure wasn't no artillery that night. You know what else? There wasn't hardly any wind." Hawk cleared his throat. "Something else about gas. They got the kind that sort of evaporates pretty soon, and they got the kind that hangs around..."

"Persistent and nonpersistent."

"Yeah. This nerve gas is serious stuff. It's probably that persistent kind. After it got quiet and C didn't answer the phone, E Company moved into that hole in about fifteen or twenty minutes. Six Japs couldn't haul off seventy or eighty bodies that quick, not even with a goddamn truck, and a truck couldn't get in there. And we both know, sir, E Company's still on the line—right where C used to be. Ain't none of 'em died. How's that for persistent?"

"Hawk, I don't know how they did it. I don't have the details at my disposal, and neither do you. How do you know so damned much?"

"Just what I hear. There's men that were over there, you know, sir."

"Maybe you hear wrong. Do we need a rumor control officer for one hundred twenty men?"

"No, sir. But we need some facts."

"I'm telling you the facts!" Jordan stood up in angry frustration. "You come in here and...and I call you in here to tell you something...and..."

"Yessir. You're probably right, sir. It couldn't be nothin' else. I was thinkin' out loud."

Jordan sat down. He stared at Hawk. He quickly realized that wouldn't work. "I *am* right. Colonel Hulmore is right. Now, I'm going to tell you where you fit into this, if you will permit me. Perhaps you can settle a lot of your own questions, as well as everyone else's."

"Yessir."

"Colonel Hulmore says we can't let this situation go on. We've lost our initiative in the Pacific Theater. The Japs are sitting tight, and we're letting them. They need time, we don't. *We* is the United States Marine Corps. We are the PTO. Nimitz and MacArthur have developed a wait-and-see policy. Rechnung is the testing ground on the gas warfare issue. The Corps doesn't like to wait and see anything. As you can see, we've done everything humanly possible to get them to make a move."

Hawk said nothing. Jordan thought he saw an incipient sneer appearing around the sergeant's nose.

"They want me to find the gas, Hawk." Jordan looked down quickly. "The whole war is standing still. Even in Europe. The Russians are scared shitless. They're not set up for gas defense. The Germans are moving on all fronts. They're playing innocent."

Ignoring the current events lecture, Hawk said: "How are you going to find it, sir?"

"When they use it."

"When they use it, sir?"

"When they strike, you will react immediately. You will capture the gas containers, the men using them—or both."

"Damn...when they strike?"

"We're bivouacking the Seabees down there under the cliff. The Japs are preparing a strike right now. They will do so soon. Then, you take over. It's important, Hawk. I've tried to make you see that. It's got to be done; it's got to be done quietly if possible. We don't want the whole world under a nerve gas cloud. You can do it. That's the only reason we picked you. We know you can do it."

"No gas masks?"

"Not yet. We don't even think they'll help."

"This is crazy."

"We're getting masks. This is the first time they haven't been issued in two years. It's like the Japs planned this whole thing out carefully."

"I don't like it. It don't seem right. I gotta watch some men get killed and then chase the Japs after it's over?"

"It's the only way. If we hit them in full strength, they'll either gas the shit out of us, or dispose of the gas they have. We have to react on a small scale and react fast. We have several optional reactions, depending upon what the goals are to be and how close you are to the Japs."

Hawk squinted out the window. He could have said a lot of things. Instead, he said: "When?"

"We finally intercepted the order on that. They'll be ready to use it sometime after a Monday, two weeks from today. By then we'll have the masks and the exact date, probably. The local commander has been given a lot of discretion, it seems."

Hawk flicked his cigar out the window with his middle finger. "I don't like it."

* * *

BELVA COOK LED Hawk through a grove of frangipani trees. On their far side was a tiny inlet, covered from the open sea by drooping palms. A narrow strip of wet beach skirted the bay. She put a blanket on it and sat down. She wore a robe, with presumably a bathing suit under it. Hawk had no intentions of going swimming—or of doing anything else. He was concerned with the situation on Rechnung Island. If what he had been told was true, he was also concerned with the rest of the world. He was officially in the center of this mess.

He had to get the weapon. Whatever it was. And he was by no means sure of that. He would lose some more men. Probably a lot, and in all probability the losses would include himself. If he failed, someone else would have to do the same thing all over. Hawk was a humble man, but he was practical. He knew full well that if he couldn't get that weapon—be it gas or rocket ships—no one could. Not given the same set of circumstances. He had that much confidence in his ability. If he failed, a lot of other men would fail after him.

He didn't know it yet, but a lot of other people felt the same way about his ability. It was no random accident that Dog Company landed on Stocken Bay. It certainly wasn't because of Jordan's record. He had none. Dog Company was here because Hawk was in it. A general asked Colonel Hulmore to find a man who could get the weapon. The individual had to fit certain specifications. A week later, they came up with Hawk's name.

"They say that there is a man out there," Colonel Hulmore reported in reference to the front line on Rechnung, "Sergeant James Hawk is his name. But...I don't know. He could just be suicidal. I worry about his intelligence. He certainly has the experience. He was in the Raiders. He'll do, sir." That was what the colonel had said.

When Hulmore received word of the patrol into the

valley, he was shaken. He didn't want to lose Hawk—yet. That would mean another selection process. Jordan didn't know about any of this. He found out the night of the day of the patrol, in a rather harsh way. He received a severe reprimand for letting the star of the show try to kill himself. Privately, Jordan was enraged. His company was a theatrical prop for one man. He believed in teamwork. Every member of a team can be replaced.

The general was a little wiser and a lot older. One man could make a difference. Especially if the man was a tough, bullheaded bastard. His only other option was to bring in special help: Allied commandoes, Army Rangers, OSS agents, or some other specially trained-attack team. The general wanted a marine. He would have liked Raiders, but they were in a fluid state of nonavailability bordering on the nonexistent. The next best thing was an ex-Raider. The general didn't have much confidence in special training. He wanted someone who could do the job. Someone who had done a lot worse things. It was too important to turn over to some kids who were fast at running obstacle courses and running down mountains.

A seabreeze filtered through the screening palms. It tumbled over the narrow beach. Hawk's eyes fell upon the overcast sky. It was a murky gray-black pond. The clouds were smeared balls of cotton, floating on the pond's surface. The moon sat in a round pocket on this dirty blanket of cotton. The edges of the pocket were burnt orange with the moonlight.

"Pretty exotic for a boy from Mississippi, isn't it?" Belva asked. She was thinking of Bing Crosby movies.

"Mississippi'd look pretty good right now."

"Are you worried about something?"

"Yeah, sort of."

"The secret weapon?"

"Yeah. Do you know about it?"

"Everybody knows. That's why we're here. Gas, isn't it?"

Hawk shook his head. Everybody did know. "I don't know. How long will you be here?"

"As long as you are, I guess."

"You ain't heard about a pullout any time soon, have you?" Hawk lay back on an elbow.

"No. Do you think the Japs will use the weapon?"

"Hell, yes, they'll use it."

They were both quiet for a while, watching the lapping waves of the bay. Then Belva said, "No one is leaving. They're even trying to keep the wounded here. All of the evacuees go straight to Alaska. They've brought in five more doctors."

"Yeah. It's a nice place. Doctors? Why?"

"I can't imagine. They're all eye, ear, nose, and throat men. Three aren't even practicing physicians. They're researchers. Kind of a waste for a combat area. Don't you think?"

"Maybe," Hawk answered. She sure ain't no Sherlock Holmes, he thought. He liked her. Belva waited patiently for him to explain to her what the researchers were doing here. When he didn't, she figured he knew she was playing dumb. She decided to change the subject.

"Want to go for a swim? I wonder how deep the water is?"

"Must be deep. I don't think so. I ain't much of a swimmer."

"I'm just going to wade. Come on." She stood. He

didn't. She removed her robe. Hawk glanced up. What he saw temporarily blasted any other thoughts from his mind. "Do you like my swimsuit?"

"Not as much as I like what's under it."

"Come on." He got up with the alacrity of the average eighty-year-old. She stood in the water and pulled him by the hand to its edge. "It's cool tonight, isn't it?"

"Kind of."

"I saw you talking to her today," she said, standing close in front of him. She had a detached smile on her face. The water washed across her ankles.

"You...uh...who?"

"You know who. She likes you. You like her, too, don't you?" He assumed she meant Ivania Broeder. She had confused him by putting their relationship into the context of a torrid affair. He hardly knew Ivania.

"I...uh...Ivania Broeder?"

"Yes. That's who." She smiled. "That wasn't so hard, was it?"

"Yeah, I guess I like her. She's a nice-looking woman."

"Is that all that matters? Would she look as nice in a bathing suit?"

"Well, no. She's kinda...thinner and all. No, that's not all that matters. I don't even know the woman, anyway. What are you talkin' about?"

"I know she's better-looking than I am, but I'm built better. And she's a smart aleck."

"Probably so. But, you see, I don't know nothin' about her...or you either. I mean, why're you bringing it up?"

"You know why I brought it up." She put both hands on his chest and kissed him. "I want to be your friend."

"You got it, kid." He put his arms around her in a tight embrace. He tasted her thick soft lips for half a minute before letting her go. She looked up at him with half closed eyes and brushed her hand through his sandy hair.

"You know, you're a nice-looking man."

He gave a short laugh and walked back to the blanket. "Is that all that matters?"

6

KAWAMOTO'S MOOD GREW WORSE. HE HAD TRIED TO apologize to Taniguchi in a safe and indirect way. Taniguchi refused the apology in an equally safe and indirect way. That insignificant peasant, Kawamoto thought. He strapped on his sidearm. To make matters worse, Mittelstadt wouldn't go with him to the prisoners' compound. The German was polite, but that didn't make any difference. Kawamoto liked an audience when he shot prisoners.

The general stalked angrily along the gravel track that led to the compound. Two HQ aides and two common soldiers accompanied him, at a respectable distance. They entered the fly-infested confines of the compound. The guards closed the rickety barbed wire gate behind the party. "Ten," Kawamoto growled to the major in charge of the POWs. Ten guards went into the nipa-roofed huts of the prisoners. The starved creatures were brought out slowly. They groped with their lizard arms and frequently stumbled. Each was accompanied by a surly guard. They were lined up with their backs to Kawamoto.

This was to be in retribution for Kawamoto's humiliation. These were American marines. The vengeance of Kawamoto was severe. Somehow it wasn't enough. These scarred, stooped, hundred-pound creatures were only shadows of the men Kawamoto had faced in the jungle. They weren't worth killing. They were much more fun alive. He planned on walking down the line and shooting each one rapidly. He unsnapped his pistol and stepped up to the man on the end of the line. He held the eight-millimeter Taisho three inches from the man's head. The prisoner never flinched. He gave no indication of knowing the gun was there. He had no time to cry out. The blast sprayed a funnel-shaped cloud of gelatinous material from his head. The guards laughed encouragingly as the corpse fell into and knocked the next prisoner down.

Kawamoto wasn't encouraged. He didn't come here to please three-balled guards. They weren't evil enough to understand that he had done the man a favor. He returned his pistol to its holster. He didn't like doing favors. He kicked the dead man. The dead man had taken advantage of him. He turned away angrily and looked at the guards behind him. They stood at attention and looked at a safe place over the general's head. Kawamoto's anger eased into a depression. He should have brought the sword. He screamed at the marines to return to their quarters. Most of them didn't move. One on the far end of the line shuffled anxiously. Kawamoto smiled and told the major to have his guards escort them to their pen. The general strutted back to the wire.

The gate was open when he reached it. He laughed. It wasn't his usual boisterous howl. It was a series of grunts. Grunt, grunt, grunt. Then he stopped laughing and the depression returned. He needed a change. He would go back to Verhangen Prison. Before he went, however, he had one important task to perform. He would do it a little earlier than anyone expected. This particular task was certain to cheer him up.

* * *

JORDAN SAW that the human factor would be a problem. The Seabees didn't like their purpose in the Hulmore plan. They were grumbling. They no longer wanted to be camped down in the jungle. This all had to be smoothed out before two weeks were up. Informed of the situation, Hulmore took immediate action. He brought in twenty Seabee replacements. They were men who had no idea of what was going on at Stocken Bay. They were kept isolated from the others and were finally stationed near the now inactive jungle construction site. Eleven tents were erected for them. They were men fresh from the United States who had never seen action. They had no officers. All were low-ranking seamen. They were issued weapons and two marine guards. Hulmore figured that when the other Seabees saw that no harm was coming to the new men, they would go back down in the jungle without complaint. He didn't want a lot of nasty talk getting back to Nimitz. He had two weeks to convince them.

Things didn't work out. The twenty-two men were gone the next morning. No trace of them could be found. There was no need for wild rumors this time.

The facts were self-evident. The men had disappeared. Two marines, sent to relieve the others on watch, reported the chilling incident. Jordan moved the entire company into the jungle. He sent Hawk on a recon patrol. It was an outing termed to be something less than what they had discussed two days before. Confused about this mission's goal, Hawk returned with nothing to report. Other patrols brought back questionable evidence of a light and scattered Japanese presence in the forest on the night before. Nothing unusual. The regular peeping toms. By midday, Jordan had the entire company pulled back into their positions on the cliffs. The tragedy projected for two weeks from now had happened.

Little conversation followed the event. The company became morose, going into a tense holding pattern that awaited the next mysterious event. They had nothing against fighting. They were committed to that. This was a little different. The next mysterious event proved to be a surprise more ridiculous than deadly.

Jordan assembled the company. He covered his nervousness well. "We have nothing new on what happened last night," he told the men. The Seabees were allowed to lounge about the edges of the marine formation. "But I have some good news. The Commandant is especially pleased with the performance of your hazardous duty here. You can be proud of your role in the provocation of the use of a Japanese secret weapon. It is felt that a special honor is owed you. It is one that will enhance our esprit de corps and encourage us to continue in our unfinished duties here.

"The men of Company D, and our attached naval

unit, will be allowed to wear distinctive shoulder patches on our combat fatigues. This patch will set us apart from all other military units, and necessarily set us above them..."

"What is this?" Canlon muttered to Hawk.

"And, today, we are being given the privilege of designing this patch ourselves. We'll have colored pencils and paper here on these tables and each of you will submit an entry. Your officers will select one entry from these submissions and in a week or so, you will be wearing your patch."

"What the hell is this?" Canlon mumbled again.

"I think it's a joke," said Hawk.

"It is," Henson informed them. "They're gonna bring out the USO. They're shittin' us. I've seen 'em do this before." Hawk thought that was a good explanation. The USO would be more bait. He liked it. A few dead chorus girls and draft dodging comedians didn't bother him.

When Hawk was steered to a wobbly table, sat down and handed a box of crayons, he realized that this was no joke. A marine major, never before seen at Stocken

Bay was directing the operation. It had to be legitimate. That's the sort of thing majors did. "Just use your imagination," the major smiled and slapped Hawk on the back. Hawk looked at the men at the tables on either side of him. They were coloring away. He looked back over his shoulder at Canlon, still standing in line. Joe laughed at the expression on his face. "Get busy, Sergeant," the major directed him with a serious tap on the blank paper.

"Aye, aye, sir," Hawk rumbled. This started several

others in the line giggling. Hawk looked back at them without a smile. The plucky little major turned again to Hawk. He had a shrewish scowl on his face. "When I come back, your patch better be in the box and another marine sitting here," said the cranky major.

"Aye, aye, sir." He couldn't resist another deadpan look over his shoulder. The men in line decided that this was better than a USO show. Hawk drew a circle and wrote a familiar two-word obscenity across it. It was childish and far from original. There were fifty other submissions exactly like it. But it was all he could think of under such creative pressure. He got up and dropped the paper in the plywood box. Canlon sat down after him.

"How do you draw an asshole?" Canlon shouted.

About an hour later the winner was announced. Everyone thought they had the joke figured out when they heard the winner's name: Oscar Chevron. A chevron wasn't a patch, but it was close. Chevron had probably just become the father of quadruplets or something. When Oscar went up to shake hands with the major, someone shouted, "How many kids you got, Chevron?" The joke had, however, no punch line. Chevron wasn't married, it wasn't his birthday, and he was in for the duration. The major picked up his crayons and left in a huff. He was either in a hurry to get away from Stocken Bay, or he was mad about the fifty obscenities. It was left to Jordan to announce the second, third, and fourth place winners. Second place was a pretty good drawing of Veronica Lake. It would have been too hard to embroider. Canlon took fourth. The red object he had drawn was mistaken by the officers for a comet or a starburst. They liked it.

After the men were dismissed amidst a great deal of confusion, Canlon cornered Chevron and got him to redraw his submission. Enough stolen crayons were around to enable the winner to duplicate his feat. Hawk joined the crowd of men gathering near Chevron. They were still trying to figure out what it was all about. They laughed as the drawing took shape. Then, after a point the men fell silent. A gruesome three-quarter view of the death's-head starkly appeared on the paper. The teeth were grinning and oversized. It wore a cloth-covered helmet, with tricolored flames coming out of the helmet. The words "Death Before Dishonor — Company D—Jap Bait" were written around it in colorful lettering. Hawk didn't find it original. The Raiders had used something like it. But this one was a little too good. The skull didn't inspire esprit de corps. The men drifted sullenly away. Everyone had to admit it was a winner. It was Company D, all right. It was more original than Hawk's submission, more artistic than Canlon's, and maybe even easier to embroider than Veronica Lake. Most of the men felt that a cornball bird or an insipid Olympic torch would have done just as well.

Soon Hawk and Canlon were the only men standing with Chevron. "Hey, that's sharp," Canlon commented stupidly. "Don't you think so, Hawk? That oughta look good on my shoulder," Joe said with the sincere enthusiasm of an eight-year-old. He held the paper against his arm. "Don't you think, Hawk?"

The sergeant looked at the grinning skull. "I gotta see the captain," he said and walked away.

"How long did he say it'd be before we get 'em?" he heard Joe ask Chevron. Now that the patch episode was over, Hawk was able to fit it into the overall situation. It was no joke. The Marine Corps is not a bunch of fun guys.

Hawk passed the captain's guard and knocked on the open door. "Request permission to enter the captain's..."

"Get in here, Sergeant. What the hell do you want?" Jordan asked.

"What's this patch shit about, sir?"

Jordan tried to look angry. But Hawk was angry and that made him nervous. The crazy bastard might get violent. The captain stood so he wouldn't be so vulnerable. "Sit down, Hawk," Jordan ordered. Hawk sat. Jordan paced in front of him. "Did you just use profanity?"

"No, sir." Hawk's belligerent Mississippi delta accent filled the room.

"Is *shit* profanity?"

"Sorry, sir. I didn't notice."

"The patch is good for morale."

"The rule is no insignia on fatigues, sir."

"There's a new rule for us, that's why it's good for morale."

"A patch ain't good for a *goddamn* thing. Now is it, sir?"

Hawk was standing. Jordan swallowed. "Speak freely, Sergeant," the captain squeaked.

"I gotta know what's goin' on, Captain. If I'm the one goin' after this weapon, I oughta know what it is, you see? I was supposed to react the next time they used it. Instead, you send me on a regular halfass patrol." Jordan looked away from Hawk's level gaze. "If I'm a decoy, that's all right. Just tell me what's going on."

"I told you. It's nerve gas. I just pass orders along here."

"No, sir. It ain't nerve gas. The patches are to make us easy to identify. The men the Japs got have flat disappeared. No bodies. Somebody thinks they're still alive —right?"

"Who do you think you are, Sergeant? Do you think you can cross-examine your commanding officer?"

Hawk took a step forward. His voice was low, and his smile was like Chevron's skull. "You're goddamn right I can. I dig the holes and I stuff them boys into 'em. Nerve gas might be new, but I know one thing about it. It leaves you real dead."

Jordan's facade cracked. He couldn't play the superior any longer. He felt as if his father were yelling at him. It hadn't been too long ago that he had been. Jordan sat down. "I don't know, Hawk. They weren't ready for you to react. They came in here this morning after hearing about what happened and said they wanted serial numbers tattooed on every man's arm— and they're going to pull out the Seabees and all other noncombat personnel. They're pissed off that I let you go into the jungle again. Hulmore tells me that I have no authority over Sergeant James Hawk. That's what he says to me. Then the whole bunch comes back in about two hours. They say the legal officer told them they couldn't tattoo the men. The Seabees and everybody else are staying. The next thing that they send is a major with a boatload of crayons. I don't think anybody knows what's going on. The Japs weren't supposed to hit us for two weeks. Maybe they aren't telling you everything. The less you know the better—if you're captured."

Hawk stared at the spotless planking beneath his dirty boots. His mouth was pulled to one side. He sighed and came to attention. "You're right, sir. Sorry I barged in here like this."

"It's all right. I'm sick of this, too, Hawk." Hawk saluted and walked to the door. "And Hawk," Jordan said, "it *is* nerve gas. Trust me."

"Yessir. Maybe so."

Hawk walked across the beach to one of the enlisted men's barracks. He went inside and threw the owner's gear off one of the bunks. Shouldn't have been there anyway. Lay shit everywhere around here. He needed a decent place to sleep tonight. He pulled off his shirt and sat against the two-by-four headboard, with his hands locked behind his neck. He stretched his legs out on the bed and crossed his booted feet. A jagged piece of glass was propped on some empty crates across the aisle from him. It was someone's shaving mirror. You needed those with nurses and majors about. He looked into the mirror at the vicious animal staring coldly back at him. He snorted and smiled. Chevron's skull smiled back at him. Across his arm was tattooed the service number 6247347. The fact that he had that tattoo was in his service record file. His smile quietly went away. He stared without blinking at the tattoo. Then he closed his eyes.

* * *

A LIEUTENANT from Hulmore's staff asked for and received permission to enter Jordan's office. Jordan knew what it was about. "Orders from Battalion Headquarters, sir," the lieutenant snapped a salute. He handed Jordan the written order. "I'm instructed that there will be no reply, sir. You may make a comment off the record, and I will relay it to the colonel." Jordan looked at the half sheet of paper.

For your eyes only
TO: CAPT. CLINTON S. JORDAN,
D COMPANY CMDR

Sensitivity of status quo becoming unduly burdensome to war effort. Option C. Activate Hawk. Destroy upon reading Colonel J. B. Hulmore

So they were tired of waiting. They wanted Hawk to react in spite of the enemy's trail being a cold one. Jordan felt some sympathy for Hawk for the first time. Did they think he could work miracles?

"No comment," Jordan muttered. "Thank you, Lieutenant." The lieutenant's boots clicked as he returned confidently back to his inkwell in battalion headquarters. Jordan shook his head. Hawk would have the safest job of all. He would get lost in the boondocks while the rest of the company got gassed. Jordan wanted to prove himself. He wanted to direct field operations. But there were none. There was only this. He had to find a way to do something positive. He couldn't let Hawk do it all. Something would develop. "Get Hawk!" he shouted to his corporal.

* * *

KAWAMOTO LED Mittelstadt down a cell-lined aisle of Verhangen Prison. The German found it difficult to suppress a sneer as he surveyed the long-abandoned facilities. Rats, bats, birds, and other small vermin played among the sticky spider webs. An occasional skeleton lolled in the close grottoes of the cells. Efflorescence left multicolored bricks jutting from the walls and ceiling. All the inhabitants of Verhangen wore helmets as protection against the crumbling masonry. An unidentifiable black ooze dripped from the walls and an odd mixture of odors emanated from the dark recesses of the poorly lit dungeon. The dry and dusty smell of caked seabird droppings somehow coexisted with the claustrophobic stink of wet stone and fungus.

"You need not worry. Your quarters will be quite comfortable," Kawamoto looked over his shoulder as he assured the German.

"Ach," Mittelstadt raised a hand and shook his head as if the thought of unpleasant quarters had never crossed his mind. Dirt terrified the German. He began to sweat in his heavy uniform.

"I came this way to show you my pets. This area is poorly kept. Here, watch your head," Kawamoto continued. He ducked through a brick-toothed hole in one of the walls. The instant Mittelstadt stepped through the hole, a reverberating roar shook the room and startled the hell out of him. He looked up and saw a gaping mouth filled with long teeth and a massive tongue. A tiger was leaping at him. He jumped back before noticing that the animal was behind bars. The big cat stuck its paws through the bars and lashed at him furiously. *"Mein Gott!"* Mittelstadt gasped.

"The tiger despises everyone but me. He is a man-killer. He is perfectly calm when we are alone together. He gets restless when he sees anyone else," the general explained. "You see, I worked with a very fine trainer in Singapore."

"Fascinating," Mittelstadt said. He watched the rippling stripes glide against the parallel running bars. He hadn't realized the immensity of such creatures. The tiger watched him back, with an angry yet patient expression. Mittelstadt looked shyly away from the orange, target-circled eyes of the beast. The repulsive presence of the animal caused him to back involuntarily out of the room. He nearly stumbled in doing so.

"I will show you what he can do to a man," Kawamoto grunted.

"Yes, of course...but, some other time, perhaps. I would like to get established in my quarters first—if you would be so kind."

"Certainly," Kawamoto couldn't hide a disappointed drop of his lower lip. The tiger roared again when the general left. Though he expected it this time, Mittelstadt couldn't prevent himself from giving another startled jump. "We will put off seeing my other pets, until you are more in the mood," Kawamoto said. "I have some excellent attack dogs. Dobermans. I'm sure you are familiar with the breed."

"Quite."

"This way." They walked across a hallway where two aisles intersected. The roof above them had long ago collapsed. Mittelstadt looked up and squinted. He saw the pure blue sky and breathed deeply. There was nothing like clean air. Pure air.

* * *

HAWK LEANED into the shadows of the barracks bulkhead. He lit his cigar and dropped the match. He could see Cavell assembling the men under the gray wall of the cliff. The dusk sky was pink through the green of the trees high atop the ridge. A slow wind blew across the pale orange beach. Option C. Hawk snorted.

Option C meant that they were desperate. He didn't have to bring the weapon back, nor did he have to destroy it—just find it. They didn't know what it was, he realized that now. They wanted any kind of information. He could hear the cerebral men at the top of the chain of command: just send a squad of those dumb bastards out there, hell, what have we got to lose? They didn't say it in those words, they used bigger, and more vague terminology, but that was what they meant. They weren't shitting anybody but each other. He inhaled a heavy dose of smoke and sighed it out. That was okay. He could do it. He wasn't worried. The promise of physical action drove any concern from his mind. Physical action was his specialty.

"Sergeant Hawk?" He recognized the haughty, precise voice of Ivania Broeder before he turned to face her.

"How you doin', Lieutenant?" he returned solemnly. Belva Cook crossed his mind. Where had she been all day?

"You are going on a mission?" She had a superior smile on her face. Hawk didn't see it. He only glanced over his shoulder at her and looked back toward the cliff. "Yes, ma'am."

"A serious mission?"

"So they say."

"You don't think so?"

"I just wait and see."

"I don't think so, either."

"Yeah?" He put his back to the wall and turned his head to face her. The fading sunlight caught the outer strands of her golden hair. It also caught the furrows of corrugated iron on the wall. The glare made him squint.

"Yes. I think I would like to leave this place, whatever the mission. Nothing could be worse than this."

"Oh, you might change your mind."

"We are here for one purpose, to be gassed by the Japanese. I've become uncomfortable with that thought. The captain has done everything but commit murder to get me out of here. He can't do it."

Hawk nodded. "Bad situation. Jordan's a good kid."

"A scared kid."

"Probably. If he's got any sense."

She swung around in front of him. "I'm desperate to get out of here." Her eyes were flashing, her lips were parted.

He knew she was genuinely afraid. He shrugged. "We all are," he said.

"I mean I really am. It's making me sick," she said. "Tell me where you are going?"

Hawk pulled his lips in and looked intently at his boots. "Oh...can't rightly say. All over, most likely."

"No idea?"

"Nah...here and there...you know."

"Take me."

Hawk smiled. He looked around. He expected to see Jordan standing behind the corner of the building with a pair of handcuffs. "Hell, you know I can't do that." He drawled the words and continued to smile.

"Don't act like a bumpkin with me, Hawk. The Japs are going to kill us here. You at least have a chance."

"Not much of one." He stopped smiling. "I don't know what you heard, but we ain't goin' to San Diego on this mission."

"We're written off here. We're a target, a setup. I was only sent here because a bitch of an officer hated ray guts. All women hate me. I love my country and all that cheap crap, but they are going to kill us—don't you *understand?*"

Hawk cleared his throat. The word *kill* no longer had much of an impact on him. It was just another verb that described an everyday activity. "Yeah. I understand. You're just scared."

"You're goddamned right I am. I was on a hospital ship at Tarawa and another one at Saipan. You think you're a hero because you ducked a couple of bullets? I've seen more dead and mutilated men in one day than you'll see in your whole life. Don't pat me on the back and tell me I'm scared. You don't know what you're talking about. I've wallowed in this war."

Hawk put a thick hand around her little throat. Her startled eyes opened wide and she tried to pull away. She couldn't move. His expression didn't change. He let her go. "That's what a quiet night on the line feels like. Sometimes it goes away at daylight. Ever feel that on a hospital ship?"

She swallowed and put her hand to her throat. "No...but I feel it here. Listen, I've learned not to argue with men. They're always right. They always know more; they've always done more. They always hold all the cards. Okay, you've got the cards. We're both martyrs and you're a bigger one. All right? Look. I'm no southern belle in a hooped skirt, I've been around the world and now I'm stuck with a bunch of kids playing soldier and I want out before they get us all killed. So, will you do it?"

"You'd be AWOL."

"Oh God, spare me. I'll get a leave. Just say you'll do it. I don't care where you're going. I have to get off this beach."

"You gettin' a leave and gettin' permission to come with me is two different things. You don't get leaves to go on combat missions—especially this combat mission."

"Let me worry about that. I'll just show up in the jungle or something. You can say you found me and had to bring me along. You'll be in the clear. You won't lose your green campaign ribbon over it, if that's what you're scared of."

Hawk rubbed the back of his head. "Ah, hell, I can't. There'll be some shootin' and all that shit..."

"I can help with the wounded. There's no chance here. We're just waiting for the Japs to do God knows what to us. Please?"

Hawk looked down at her beautiful face. He was touched. He did like her more than Belva Cook. And she wasn't as nice as Belva Cook. "No," he said, "you see, we'll be going after this weapon. We have a good chance of getting gassed by the Japs ourselves. But if we catch them, maybe the beach will be safe. Now, if I didn't honestly believe that—I'd consider it."

"All right," she said. "I won't beg you. Maybe you're right. I hope so. I'd still rather take my chances with you. You think about it."

"Okay."

"I—" she looked down, feigning shyness. "I need a man, not a scared kid."

Hawk was too enamored with her to laugh in her face. "Yes, ma'am. He can pull a lot more strings than I can. You don't need to be goin' where we're goin'."

She smiled, still in a superior way, said, "Good night," and left.

"Night, Lieutenant."

He watched her walk toward the nurses' quarters. He bet she'd look good in a dress. She was built for fancy dresses.

"Wasn't that sweet?" Belva Cook asked.

"Hey," he said. "Where have you been?"

"Listening to you and that woman that you don't even know."

"I don't. She just came up to me all of a sudden and..."

"I know. I heard. If you hadn't called her Lieutenant, I wouldn't believe you. She's really scared, isn't she?"

"Said she was."

Belva took his hand. "James, do you think we're in as bad a spot as she says?"

"Nah." His cigar went out and he relit it. "You wanta come with me?"

"You'd take me?"

"Sure."

"Like hell. I sure as hell don't want to go. You want *me* to get shot, but not her, right?"

"Forget it."

"Well, thanks for asking, but I don't like dirt and loud noises. If you had any sense, you wouldn't go. Why is your name always at the top of the shit list?"

"Lucky."

"Of course, we could have a lot of fun, if I went."

"Nothing but."

"You're such a bastard."

"Why?"

"Don't go."

"Why?"

"Why? Are you stupid? You're not going to find anything but Japs."

"They'll be a lot of disappointed people if I don't."

"Who's going to be disappointed when you get killed?"

"You."

"You're damned right." She put her arms around him. "When will you be back?"

"Pretty quick."

"Really?"

He looked into her eyes and smiled confidently. "I guarantee it," he said.

* * *

THE PATROL WOUND through the jungle. Carter Spencer was at the point, his rhinoceros eyes shifting nervously. Cavell had selected the men for the outing. Hawk and Jordan rubber-stamped his choices without substitutions. Cavell picked them for attitude more than anything else. He wanted fifteen men charging the next surprise machine gun attack, instead of one. The men had no special training or proficiency with weapons. Only three or four qualified as expert marksmen. Henson, Stilley, and Canlon were in the group. They volunteered and Cavell took them. He didn't like their attitude, they were too normal, but they were old friends. Chevron was along. He had to live up to his patch. He would have a good attitude. Good attitude meant meanness, the desire to commit evil at the cost of your own life. It's hard to find, actually, contrary to what you hear in most pulpits. When you need it, it's just not there.

Carter Spencer was a truly vicious individual of few redeeming qualities. He was usually put on point in the fervent hope that he would get killed. He was loud and he was ugly, and he was a bully and a braggart. It's not easy to be a bully in the Marine Corps, without rank. He managed. His greatest source of entertainment was pissing on sleeping men, and then brawling in the aftermath. He had killed a Japanese woman and her baby. They gave him a severe tongue-lashing and permanent combat duty. He liked it.

Spence had never had anything approaching a friend, until Stocken Bay. A boy named Rackaby took up with him. Rackaby liked to think of himself as a streetwise hoodlum. He was pretty close to his goal, having been raised in an eastern slum. He didn't have the physique or the recklessness to be a Spence. Rackaby didn't fight without a knife in his hand. He hung around Spence and laughed at his pranks.

Hawk wasn't too fond of either of them. Just because a man likes to fight, doesn't mean he likes to fight Japanese. That was a different sort of perversion. Quiet disciplined men were often better at that. Blowhards invariably turned out to be chickenshits in a life-or-death situation. It is one thing to hit a man thirty pounds lighter than yourself, and quite another to stare into a gun muzzle.

The forest was cool this morning. Sort of like

Mississippi in late October. It wouldn't last. He bit off some tobacco. His sharp eyes searched for evidence of a stealthy passing. Hawk was in his element. If his brain waves could have been tested, they probably would show that he was as happy as ever he could be. Chewing tobacco, good weather, a full clip, and a helmet on his head. Of course, by normal standards he was quite mad. War was his only purpose. He knew it. He wasn't proud of that, but he had pride in his craft. It wasn't a good craft, but it was his. He might as well enjoy it until he lost a leg. Or something. He spat and stopped the patrol.

An earlier patrol had turned up some questionable signs of the enemy's coming this way. What there was of a trail ended here. He had to pick up a new trail now. He brought Spence back from the point and had the men fan out in a circle. Hocker, a college graduate who took to wearing his glasses more and more often, shot an azimuth as best he could. Hawk had been leading the men straight into the rear of the Japanese lines. That seemed the logical place for the Japanese to retire. Hawk expected to bump into the lines and report back that he could go no farther. He wasn't taking the patrol's purpose seriously, although he knew something could always happen. He and Canlon sat at the center of the circle of searching men.

"You ain't thinking of going through the Jap lines, are you?" Joe asked. He lit a cigarette and waited for Hawk to tell him to put it out.

"Shit no. I ain't that stupid. This is a waste of time. There ain't nothin' out here. Nothin' we're gonna find."

"I still think it's a rocket ship. It ain't gas."

"Yeah. I been thinking about that. What's the easiest way to make a bunch of men disappear?"

"A rocket ship."

"Yeah—well, what's the second best way? I'll tell you. Call 'em up on the goddamn phone and tell 'em to get their ass out." Hawk spat.

Joe thought about that. "You mean order 'em out?" Hawk nodded. "Yeah, I see what you mean. The Japs tapped into a phone line and ordered 'em forward?"

Hawk shook his head. "Easier than that. Somebody on our side pulled them back and shipped them out."

"Who'd do a thing like that?"

"Hulmore." Hawk spat.

"He'd do something like that, all right. But why?"

Hawk looked up. Someone was returning from the forest. "Why don't mean much in this old world, does it, Joe?"

Cavell walked up and reported sighting some broken foliage, toward the west. The enemy lines were due north. Hawk waded out into the dewy leaves. Cavell stood over the suspicious area. Hawk went to one knee. It was all so vague, even to an experienced tracker. Maybe it was something, and maybe it was just wishful thinking. If the Japanese had made this trail, they were pretty fair woodsmen. That was unusual. Though they adapted well to the jungle, they were urban by nature and didn't worry about things like trails.

It was dangerous to follow a trail like this one. An overactive imagination could see signs everywhere. A creative person could spend the rest of his life following it. "Why would they go that way?" Hawk asked Cavell. Cavell shrugged. Hawk spat. "All right, Cavell, take Spence and follow it if you can. We'll hold up here."

Hawk continued to look at the bent stalks as Canlon brought the men back. Joe finished the task and stood over Hawk. He looked at the collapsed tubers and shriveled leaves. "Kinda weak, ain't it?"

Hawk shook his head. "It bothers me. It looks true. Cain't figure it. A diversion would be more plain, so's you couldn't miss it."

Cavell came back. Sweat languished in the holes in his face. "If it's a fake, it's a good one. You can hardly see it. It's going west. All the way to the beach over there, maybe. Spence is still on it."

"Good," said Hawk. He took another reading from Hocker and studied the map of Rechnung. The newly found trail was going in a direction parallel to the enemy lines. It would not intersect them before reaching the western shore. "Wild goose chase," Canlon mumbled.

"Nah. We're onto something," Hawk said and spat across the leaves. Birds flapped in the distance. "Great," Joe said, "maybe we'll get killed."

"Maybe. Watch that rear yourself. Put out some flankers. Keep the same interval and keep it quiet." Hawk pushed back his helmet and looked around. Something was watching him. A drop of sweat shot down his nose. "Come on. This place gives me the willies."

Halfway between that point and the coast they made another discovery. The trail they followed became obvious. An even more obvious trail of trampled brush crossed it and led to the south. "That goes back to our lines, don't it?" Hawk asked Hocker.

"Yes, Sergeant." The two paths became one large one, heading west.

"A lot of men came that way," said Hawk. "Just a few—hardly any—came this way." He looked around again. Eyes were on the back of his head. He had the feeling so strongly, he considered ducking. "They, uh, met here and went on to the coast." He glanced at the leaves behind him.

"Yes," Hocker agreed, "unless the trail veers north toward the Japanese. We can follow this trail on our way back." He pointed to the path leading south. Hawk looked around, this time, conspicuously.

"Yeah. Go see how far Spence is from the ocean, Joe," Hawk ordered.

The column stopped when Spence came back and reported he had followed the path to the sea. Joe was with him. Hawk sent Cavell to reconnoiter the beach. Several of the men held low conversations. Joe was his usual loud self. He had made friends with a man named Tolliver. The only thing the two of them had in common was a tendency to laugh a lot. Joe brayed like a jackass when he laughed. Tolliver, a hillbilly sort, laughed like a cartoon character. Hawk called a meeting of Cavell, Hocker, and Spence. He left Joe out because of Tolliver. Hawk didn't have much of a sense of humor, or much use for anyone who did. The four men crouched in a semicircle. Hawk sighed. The unseen eyes were still out there, somewhere.

"Shut up, Joe!" Hawk opened the meeting with a shout that was louder than Joe's laughing. Joe didn't stop, but it made Tolliver nervous. Taniguchi heard all of this. He peered through the ferns. He watched Hawk. His Bergman submachine gun was tucked beneath him.

"I don't know," Spence was saying, "it looks like the

trail stops here." Cavell nodded in agreement. He didn't say anything.

Hocker unfolded the map of Rechnung. "We're on a peninsula," Hocker said, pointing to their position, "and over here is Verhangen. This is the closest point to Verhangen on Rechnung. The Japs might have gone directly over there."

"You can see that other island from the beach," said Spence.

"Okay. Let's have a look at it," said Hawk, waving Joe to him. They walked beyond the other men, through the sand-carpeted forest edge and onto the beach. Enemy footprints crossed and recrossed one another in the sand, until disappearing in the smooth, darker sand made wet by the high tide. Hawk looked out over the ocean to the rocky island in the distance.

"See that flat hill over there?" the sergeant asked Joe.

"Barely."

"There's an old German prison on it. Don't you know them Jap bastards got that son of a bitch dug in good?"

"Yeah, I remember 'em sayin' we'd have a hell of a time takin' Verhangen. Rechnung was supposed to be the easy one. They oughta be shellin' that damn thing twenty-four hours a day," said Joe.

"That's a fact. About Rechnung. We was scheduled to take this sucker in two weeks' time. You know if you wanted to keep a secret weapon a secret, Verhangen would be the place to store it—where it's safe. I bet they bring the gas in from Verhangen."

"That'd be a good idea, I guess," said Joe. "Then if we ever did take Rechnung, they could saturate the whole suckass thing and kill us all. We'd be all built up for a jump on Verhangen and they'd make a clean sweep." Joe lit a cigarette. He had a worried look. "You know though, Hawk, there ain't no way *we* could get over to that damn place and find the weapon."

"Aw, shit no. In the whole South Pacific, they gotta have some kinda plan to deal with that kind of thing. People...trained for it, I mean."

"Right," said Joe, "that ain't our goddamn job."

"But," Hawk spat, "I'd like to know if they went over there. That *is* my job." Hawk spat out his tobacco. It left his mouth tasting like rotten pecans. "Search this here beach and then we'll follow that other trail back home," he said, unsnapping his canteen.

The men combed the beach. Hawk watched them, lost in thought. When he looked back toward Verhangen, he saw something white in the water. He lit a cigar. The leathery trails tightened beneath his eyes. All you have to do is be in the right place, and something will turn up. That was Hawk's luck. He knew it wasn't *good* luck. He waded out into the surf. A piece of paper lurched along on the tops of the waves. He dipped the barrel of his Thompson under it. When he pulled it up, it nearly tore. He took it back to the beach, took off his helmet, and spread the paper across its dome.

The word "Tabun" was stenciled in dark letters at the top of the soggy paper. Beneath it were faded Japanese characters. Hawk took a deep breath and looked over at Verhangen Prison.

"What's that?" Canlon asked.

"Probably nothing. It's a sticker off something. Probably off a Jap ration can or something," said Hawk. Jordan had told him what *Tabun* was.

"Hey," said Joe, "them's American letters. T-a-b-u-n...that's Jap all right. Japs use American letters sometimes, you know."

"Yeah." Hawk bent close over the helmet. "Look, the words are fadin' out." As the hot sun dried the paper, the letters began to flake and whiten. "Ain't that some shit! Hocker! See if you can copy some of this shit down." Hocker did what he could. The paper dried and most of the writing was indecipherable. Hawk considered putting it back into the water, to see if that would bring the letters out again. He decided to let intelligence worry about it.

They took the wide trail back to the beach. No one found any further evidence of Japanese. The trail itself was rather remarkable. It looked as if it had been made by a herd of elephants.

Hawk turned his label and Hocker's notes over to the captain. He heard nothing about any of it for a couple of days. Life went on as it had before. Belva Cook tried to spend as much time with him as she could. Ivania Broeder ignored him. The men grew more surly. Joe Canlon wanted his Company D patch. They hadn't come in yet. And Hawk started wondering. He knew what Tabun was. He came to believe that the situation on Stocken Bay was just what it appeared to be: a target for Japanese nerve gas. It was either that, or someone wanted it to look like that.

Colonel Hulmore handed Jordan a small envelope. "I want you to leave that envelope in a conspicuous place," said the colonel. "It purports to be an antidote for Tabun, a neutralizing gas. It also purports to contain plans for a U.S. retaliatory gas. When the Japanese destroy Stocken Bay, I want them to find that envelope. The material it contains is total nonsense, but it will make them think twice about using Tabun again. It will also take them several months to figure out that the formulae recited in the documents are false."

"Yes, sir," Jordan replied in a near whisper. I'm only twenty-three, he told himself. "Have you found anything out on how they deliver the gas without wind or artillery, sir?"

"No." Hulmore sat back, put his feet on Jordan's desk and belched. "Damnedest thing. I don't see how they could do it without damaging the users." The colonel belched again. "Well," he said, "you might as well get Hawk in here."

"Yes, sir." A few minutes later, Hawk slouched in from the sunlight and saluted. He didn't realize the man with Jordan was a colonel until he saw the eagle on his collar. There were no introductions. Hawk knew the bastard.

"You've done a splendid job, young man," Hulmore roared.

"Thank you, sir." Hawk had a mocking smile on his face. A windbag.

"I'm afraid the job isn't done yet, though." The colonel pointed to a chair. "Sit down, Sergeant." Hawk did. That left Jordan standing off to the side like a washroom attendant. Jordan looked naked without his desk. Hawk sat across the desk, eyeball to eyeball with the bald colonel. Hulmore smiled. The narrow top of his nose ballooned out to form an awning over two enormous nostrils. A thick crop of nose hairs hung from the nose. "What you've found, my boy, is a label from a canister of a deadly chemical agent. Did you know that?"

"I had a suspicion, sir." He didn't say that he also suspected it might be a fake.

"It's a miraculous find. Nothing less. The Japs must have dropped the empty canister in the ocean to lighten their load on the trip back to Verhangen. The label washed off. It's a one in a million find—the kind that saves countless numbers of lives and alters the course of modern warfare."

"Yessir. I just looked up and there it was."

"Yes..." The colonel was irritated at having his speech interrupted. Old people get that way, and old military people are twice as bad. Old colonels are the worst because they don't have too much longer to make general. "Do you know what Tabun is, Sergeant?" The colonel leaned forward accusingly. Hawk leaned back from the repugnant face.

"No, sir. Not really."

"It's a highly lethal new nerve gas developed by the Nazis. They've never used it. There is no way that you or anyone in your patrol could have known that, is there?"

Hawk looked at Jordan. The captain looked ill at ease. "No, sir." He supposed Jordan shouldn't have told him about Tabun. He would cover for him.

"Good. You see, the label you brought us was too decomposed to be of any use. We have only your written notes to go by. All we could tell was that it was a label. There were traces of glue on it." Hulmore stopped and stared intently at Hawk.

"Yessir." Hawk stuck with his story.

"The label said something else. 'Vault 17' was

written in Japanese characters—according to your notes. That is where the Tabun canisters are stored, we're sure of it. Vault 17, Verhangen Prison, on Verhangen Island." Hawk said nothing. He suspected that. "The Japs get this gas from Europe. They have none of it themselves. The Germans probably wouldn't trust them with the formula for it. We think their entire supply is in Verhangen Prison. We can get it all. To be more specific—we can destroy it all. We don't need it. It is—let me stress this now—very important that we *do* destroy it before the fool Nips recklessly escalate the war. Do you understand the ramifications I'm referring to?" Hawk shifted uneasily. "Listen, Sergeant, did you know that one third of the American dead in the First World War were killed by gas?"

"No, sir."

"That's right. And that was plain old mustard gas, for the most part. I was there. I can tell you it wasn't very pretty. You don't know what mustard gas can do to a man, do you, young fellow?"

"No, sir." Hawk's patience was running thin.

The colonel looked triumphantly over at Jordan. Jordan was younger than Hawk. He knew even less about it. "Well, this isn't mustard gas, Hawk, it's nerve gas. It shuts down the nervous system in seconds. You don't see it, you don't smell it, you're just dead. Understand?"

"I understand, sir. I don't think that's what it is, though."

Hulmore sat thunderstruck. The sound of seabirds drifted through the window. Jordan gagged and found his voice. "Sergeant Hawk! Don't interrupt the colonel!" The colonel held up his hand. His expression changed from that of a teacher to that of a peer. His voice changed, too, from that of a shitball to that of a regular guy. "What do you mean, Hawk?"

"Well, sir, that second trail we found, that was the one they brought the prisoners down. I'm pretty sure of it. They took them sailors prisoner."

"Did you find any evidence of that?"

"No, sir. Just the trail. A big wide trail, sir."

"Japs can make a trail, Sergeant. If you're implying that it's not nerve gas and that the men are alive, forget it. I respect your opinion. I like a thinker. You just happen to be wrong. Can you accept that?"

"Yessir."

"Good boy. Now, let me go on because I'm in a rush for time. As I said, we can destroy their whole supply of gas, right there in Verhangen. We don't need the gas, we've got our own. We need a team to go in there and a man to lead it. You've been assigned the job," the colonel smiled. "You, and the same men who went on that patrol that found the label."

Hawk frowned. "Uh...well..."

"We know right where it is. Vault 17. We'll have the map and aerial photos tomorrow. We can put you in a location where you're virtually assured of success." The colonel continued to smile, as if he were telling Hawk that he had just won the Irish Sweepstakes.

"Uh...well...I don't doubt it could be done maybe, sir, but that's one hell of a heavily fortified Jap island. There ain't no way we could get out, sir."

"Probably not, probably not. Not all of you, anyway. Yes, that's for certain. Verhangen is a stronghold of the first magnitude. But really, Hawk, do what you can. That's all we ask. Modern warfare is depending on you.

Think of what this means to civilization— not to mention your own country." Hulmore wasn't bashful about flag-waving. He knew Hawk had been in the Raiders. The Raiders went through a severe indoctrination in patriotism.

"Well...yessir. I mean...you see, we're just poor old fightin' men. This seems like something for spies, or commandos or something."

"With black turtlenecks and little girl hats?" the colonel laughed. "That might work in Europe, Hawk. They can work with the people that know the language of the locale. They have well-developed resistance groups. Here it's just the Japs and us. We know and shoot each other on sight. No, fighting men are just what the general wants."

Hawk lost confidence when he heard of the general. That meant Hulmore was just the mouthpiece for this order. The colonel didn't have the sense or imagination to change his mind about it. "Yessir, but you need brigades, regiments of fighting men to push that place down."

"It has to be done a little more subtly than that, Sergeant. Now," he exclaimed loudly in settlement of the matter, "let's talk turkey." Hawk knew who the turkeys would be. "I see by your file that you have two years of formal education. You read and write well. Is that two years of secondary education? Or what?"

Hawk wanted to continue arguing the difficulty of the mission, but he had to answer. "Uh...yessir. Well, not really, sir. I mean, I didn't actually finish the second grade."

"You didn't finish second grade?"

"No, sir. I was gettin' kinda old for school by then,"

Hawk explained. Hulmore looked at Jordan. "You're self-educated, then, I presume?" the colonel asked. "What I'm getting at is this, Hawk; you will have to do a certain amount of organizing. You'll have to have the patrol broken down into security teams, assault teams, demo teams, you'll have to read maps. You'll have to memorize some Japanese characters, so you will be able to read and understand them. Are you capable of all of that?"

"I reckon so. Yessir. I can look at something one time and remember it. But...gettin' back to the point..."

"I'll take care of the points, Sergeant. You'll take the orders. You made it through bootcamp, so I'm sure you understand that much." Hulmore handed him a piece of paper. "Here's a list of words you may need to know. I realize that this may be beyond some of your men, but I want as many as possible to learn this material. Jordan, get that mimeographed, would you? And here's the roster. Pick your teams out of it."

Hawk looked at the list of names. It wasn't just a list to him. They were people, most of whom he knew. Henson. Stilley. Canlon. Just dumb riflemen. Hocker; maybe. Cavell, the only one that fit. Spence, an idiot. Rackaby, a kid in his teens, way back in his teens. Lyles. Lyles must have jumped out of bed just in time. Miller, the transfer from C Company. They wanted him dead. Rojas, a demo man from somewhere else. The men would be watching out for their own, not Rojas. Chevron; shit. Tolliver, the stupidest son of a bitch in the Marine Corps. Eddie Frobisher. You finally bought it, Eddie. Howard, a veteran like Eddie. Fred Mittelstadt. He didn't know him. Must have TB or something.

"Yessir," Hawk mumbled. "Sir, these men...I know

these men. You're expectin' an awful lot out of these kinds of fellas."

"You better believe it, Hawk. That is all. Report here tomorrow night at 1800 hours." The colonel saluted first. Hawk should have jumped.

"Uh...yessir...may I say something, sir?"

"Not at this time. The briefing will be then. That is all, Hawk."

Thus ended the pleading of the case of the condemned men. Hawk saluted and walked briskly to the door. He opened it and went out—without saluting again. "Son of a bitch," he said. He walked down the steps and across the beach. "Didn't even let me say shit," he said aloud. "Didn't give my boys a chance to volunteer or nothin'." He slipped a cigar out of his pocket. The word suicide was running through his mind.

* * *

"SUICIDE's when you kill yourself. This is murder," said Joe Canlon. Surprisingly, most of the others took it well. That made Hawk feel better. If they didn't mind, he didn't care. "Can't we get out of it?" Joe asked. He stood over Hawk as the sergeant sharpened his jungle knife. "Don't we get to have a say in any of this?" "Nope. Got your numbers memorized?" "Shit no! I can't read Chinese! Listen, Hawk..."

"Learn seventeen anyway. You'll need that one. Maybe."

"I ain't learnin' shit. I may not be the smartest guy in the world, but I know you can't force a man to do something like this. You got to have volunteers for this kind of deal, it's in the books. I know that much for a fact. I can tell you that much."

Hawk ran his knife along the whetstone. "I ain't heard nobody else griping."

"Hell, no. A bunch of goddamn lunatics is what they are. I ain't crazy. That whole plan is bullshit. We're gonna all get our ass killed."

Hawk frowned. He cleared his throat. "You want me to get you out of it?" Joe shuffled and looked to the right a left. There was no one else around. "Can you?"

"Said I could," Hawk grunted.

"Will you?"

"Shit, yeah. If you want. Say the word."

"You know it's crazy, don't you? I've known you a long time. Don't you, Hawk?"

"Suicide."

"Why are you doin' it?"

"I'm alterin' the course of modern warfare."

"Shi-i-t." Joe shuffled some more. "Shi-i-t."

"You won't get your patch."

"Shi-i-t," Joe looked up. "Why not?" he asked seriously. "I'm still in the company." Joe glared at Hawk's grim smile. "I earned it, Hawk."

"Okay, you'll get it. You dumb shitbag." He ran his thumb along the sharpened white edge of steel. "Ready for Jap bellies. Go to bed, Joe. You're gettin' on my nerves." Hawk looked up. "You're my buddy, Joe. I'd like you along. But I don't want you gettin' killed. I'm doin' it for Swede Jansen and Gist and Billy Ray Harkrider. Them was fine men. Men you could count on. They're countin' on me. So...go to bed, Joe."

Joe walked away. He turned around and came back.

"If...if everybody else is goin'," he said. "I'll go. I

don't mind goin'. I'm goin'. I just don't want nobody thinkin' I'm stupid or nothin'."

"Nobody'd think that, Joe."

Thirty-four Seabees and a squad of marines turned up missing that night. Jordan didn't order a pursuit. It was no mystery. It was accepted now that someone would dissolve every night. Air recon couldn't pick up the Japanese in the darkness. The nurses stormed Jordan's office. He could give them no solace. No one could leave Stocken Bay. He assured them that new, immediate, and drastic steps were being taken to alleviate the situation. Countermeasures were being made operative, the American forces were no longer sitting ducks. This attack would be one of the last the Japanese would be allowed to mount.

Hawk knew Hulmore wouldn't evacuate anyone at this point. It might tip his hand to the Japanese. Things had to look normal. The nurses moved into their barracks and barricaded it. They were issued weapons. The Seabees moved into the sparse lines with the marines. Everyone prepared to defend their lives.

Ivania Broeder had a better idea. She walked into Hawk's barracks and brought him outside. "You see what's going to happen here, don't you?" she asked him. "I know you're leaving again."

"Yes, ma'am. I gotta admit it, this time. It's a rough think to take."

"You bet your ass it is, mister. Can you let them do this to us? They are going to come down here and kill *every*—damned—one of us."

"I...shit...I don't know. If you knew where I was goin'..."

"I know exactly where you are going. You're going to

a briefing at 1800. Right? There, you will learn that you are going to an objective rallying point north of Verhangen. It is a small uninhabited island. From it, you will be able to walk across a reef to Verhangen Prison.

Once inside you will climb a chimney to a subterranean chamber and destroy a Japanese cache of German nerve gas with cyclonite. Does any of that sound familiar?"

"Yeah, but not all of it. Where'd you find all that out?"

"What difference does it make? Let's get to it. Will you take me? You can leave me on the ORP island. At least if I'm captured, I'll be alive. Nobody is leaving Stocken Bay alive, except you."

"Look, lady—I'll grant you, you shouldn't be here. It's a bad break. But it ain't none of my doin'. If I went around doin' what was right, I'd be taking ten nurses over to Verhangen and sending my pay check to the orphans in Poland. I just can't. I'm already stuck with enough eight balls to make them Jap-assed bastards happy."

"The other nurses don't want to come. They have confidence in the gods of war. We know better, though, don't we? You can bring that tramp you've got the hots for with us. You don't want to see sweet little Belva get her hide fried off, do you?"

Hawk sighed and looked out to the sea. "Goddamn," he muttered. He was a rebel and a rule breaker. He may have even been a criminal by nature. It was hard to tell. The war had given him so much moral freedom, it was difficult to commit a crime. The awesome authority of the U.S. government or the Marine Corps meant very little to him. He operated under his own code of ethics. Those usually fitted neatly within the Corps ethics. This time they didn't. "Awright," he growled, "if Belva will go, I'll take the both of you. I guess you know the Japs are gonna catch you for sure?"

"I'll talk to her," said Ivania.

Hawk shook his head. "I'll talk to her first. I want the first shot, before you go paintin' a rosy picture."

The sergeant told Belva what Ivania wanted to do. He grudgingly admitted that it might be a good idea. "God, I'm scared," Belva said. They stood in the shadow of the hospital tent. "Should I do it?"

"I guess...hell..."

"It sounds dangerous."

"Dangerous as hell. But so is this. The best you can hope for is to get caught by the Japs. Sometimes they treat women okay. You could get hurt if they catch us before we get to the ORP. I think we'll make that, though. I don't know...I got some tough old boys goin' with us. We'll get by."

She turned away. "Oh...I don't know. I don't know, James. You're talking over my head. I'm not a marine, you know. Maybe they plan to evacuate us."

"That's what I thought. I don't think so anymore. Look how many times the Japs have hit us. You're still here. Next time your number might come up. Next time your number might come up. Next time might be in five minutes."

Belva shook her head. "I don't know. How can they do this to us?"

"I don't know. Hulmore, I guess."

She shook her head again. "I'll talk to you tonight. I'll talk to Ivania and see what she has to say. Maybe I will go." She looked down and moved away to go into the tent.

"Hey," he caught her arm. "Is that a maybe goodbye?"

She spun around and embraced him. "God, this is awful," she said. "Will you take care of me?"

"As much as I can. I'm into something up to my ass, too. I can't help none if you're here and I'm on Verhangen—that's for sure."

"I have to go." She was crying. He didn't stop her again.

7

THE RUBBER RAFTS SLID OFF THE SAND OF RECHNUNG with a grating slurp. The moon rose in the east over the tree-tops. The ocean was paved with calm and silver dimpled waves. Joe Canlon had already counted two extra people. He rambled on about it until Hawk told him to shut up. No one else had any comments about the additions. They figured the sergeant knew what he was doing.

An easy wind blew over the surface of the black water in a constant caress. It was cool, but Hawk was sweating as he paddled the little boat. His newly issued gas mask thumped against the bloated side of the raft. Verhangen Prison was visible against the gray night sky. Huge moonlit clouds floated over it in threatening silence. The sea was flat. The crossing should be simple. It was a placid stretch of sea. The Japanese had crossed it many times with their strange and deadly weapon. Perhaps they would be crossing it tonight.

Both the Americans and Japanese patrolled these waters. They were too vast for thorough vigilance.

Hawk expected to cross without difficulty. Belva Cook huddled against him. "I'm glad I came," she whispered. He didn't answer. She would change her mind when he left her on the little island. He glanced over at the boat next to him. Cavell was in its prow, striking the water with sure strokes. "I feel safe with you," Belva said.

Hawk waved to Hocker. He was in the boat behind Cavell. Hocker took the lead. Spence and Rackaby were with him. They were used to leading. Hocker's job was to find the rocky little islet that would be their objective rallying point.

They paddled for an hour. At times they moved in astonishing silence. At other times, it seemed to Hawk as if the swishing paddles were vying to see which could be the loudest. Hocker skirted the northern shore of Verhangen. He then struck a southerly course. Another hour went by. Everyone suspected that he had missed the target, but no one said anything until another half hour passed by. Hawk finally waved Hocker over.

"We've gone plumb around the goddamn thing, Hocker. You missed it," Hawk whispered angrily.

"Yes, Sergeant. We'll have to go back."

"All right. We're too far out, kid. We gotta get in closer. It ain't this far offshore, you know." Hocker nodded in agreement and went back into the lead. He paddled directly for Verhangen. He didn't *want* to get closer. There would be searchlights and patrol boats along the coast. But Hawk was right. He knew he had to go closer. Hocker blew his cheeks out. Hell, he was eventually going into Verhangen itself, he might as well get used to the idea.

Joe Canlon followed the convoy like a reluctant

caboose. He cursed himself for not taking the opportunity Hawk had given him. He got himself into this just because his friends were doing it. He could easily get out of here and make some new friends that did nicer things. Joe was often amazed at men who found it a privilege to serve, and here he was among the worst of them. He kept himself going by telling himself that he could back out at any point. He had been using the same psychological trick since Parris Island, and it was wearing thin. The water under the thin bottom of the boat was cold and Joe was shivering.

"Can Hocker find it?" Belva asked Hawk. "We're awfully close to the main island."

"He'll find it. It just looks close."

"I'll be glad when we get there. Will we be safe there?"

"Pretty safe."

The paddles drank thirstily, impatiently at the disinterested sea. Ivania Broeder saw the heads of Hawk and Belva close together. She studied Hawk's profile. Over their heads loomed Verhangen Prison. The moon was behind it now, casting white-rimmed shadows that looked like a solar eclipse. They must be on Verhangen's westernmost shore. She turned away and looked at the other boats behind them. Tolliver smiled at her. Water light dappled his face. She turned back and looked at her shoes, drawn up beneath her.

"There's that son of a bitch!" Hawk called in a muffled shout. "Hocker..." he pointed toward a dark little bump rising out of the ocean. It was obscured by the darker shadow of the large island. Hawk hit the water with a renewed enthusiasm and was the first ashore. "Out," he ordered the passengers. Once they had stumbled out of the raft, he dragged it across the razor-sharp coral and into the brush. Stunted palms leaned across most of the beach, making it much darker than the exposed sea had been. The coral punctured two of the boats before the men realized what was happening. The white coral gave off a subdued glow beneath their feet.

"We done lost two boats," Canlon observed. "How we gonna get back?"

"There won't be as many of us on the way back. If there's any," Henson told him. Tolliver giggled. Joe didn't say anything else that night. He no longer appreciated Tolliver's sense of humor.

The plants grew close to the ground. They crouched together beneath them, talking in low tones. Hocker unfolded a map and an aerial photo and spread them out on the pile of explosives. Several hands reached out to prevent the photo from curling up. Hawk switched on an amber-shielded flashlight. The map had a detailed vertical-cut drawing of the prison on one quarter of the page. The date, 1904, was written under it. "Look at that date," Stilley said. "That map's forty years old."

"That's a lot older than you'll ever be," said Henson.

"We're not going in tonight, are we?" Stilley asked.

Hawk looked at the map and rubbed his mouth. "What do you want to do, wait till next week, Stilley? Cavell, check out that reef. What time is it, anyway?" It was late. Too late. Cavell reported that the moon was high over the ocean and shining down on the reef that connected the ORP island to Verhangen. The reef lay under a burst of daylight. That was that. It was all postponed until tomorrow night. It had taken them too longer to get over here. The Japanese would have an entire day to find them.

The *hancho* Tamatsu Taniguchi slid his field glasses back into their case. What fools these Americans were! Did they think the Japanese were blind? It was the young sergeant from the jungle firefight. So rash. He couldn't see him, but he knew it was Hawk. Sometimes he thought his own people were fanatical, until he saw the American marines in action. War did this to men. All men. Unlike most combatants, Taniguchi knew that all men were the same. The *hancho* was always rational, always wise. He didn't tell the private standing beside him what he had seen. He had told no one that he saw Hawk find the Tabun label. Instead, he went back to Verhangen and waited for Hawk. And here he was. Taniguchi had expected something a little more ingenious, like a submarine drop. Rubber rafts and flashlights—indeed!

Taniguchi climbed wordlessly out of the old watchtower. He walked down a decaying corridor of the prison, to the quarters of his old friend, Major Sasumo Keizo. Keizo opened his door and smiled when he saw the *hancho* standing in the hall. Keizo was in his nightshirt.

"Come in, Tamatsu!" Keizo and Taniguchi had enlisted together, several centuries ago. They were boys together. Their children played together and waited together for their fathers back in Japan. Soon they would both be grandfathers. Their wives were close friends. Keizo had taken a commission when it was offered to him and had risen slowly through the grades. Taniguchi had often refused a commission. He was a man of action. Keizo pulled a bottle of rice wine from the shelf of his nightstand.

They sat on the floor at Keizo's three-legged table. Taniguchi swallowed a drink in a single gulp. That would be his last drink. Taniguchi was a temperate man. Keizo listened intently as the *hancho* told the story of Hawk: the firefight, the Tabun label, and the fact that the American was squatting below them at this very minute. He was sure it was Hawk. So rash.

"You should have reported this, old friend," said Keizo.

"I am reporting it, dear Sasumo, to you, an officer in the Imperial Army. A security officer. My obligation is met."

"And mine begins? What would you have me do? Stay silent as you have done?" Keizo was still smiling. He loved Taniguchi.

"It is out of my hands," said Taniguchi. Taniguchi smiled.

"You know why they are here, then?"

"Yes. To kill the German and destroy his weapon. Perhaps to kill Kawamoto."

"Ah, you are too optimistic. I too would be silent were that the case. Tell me, old friend, what do you think of this...weapon?"

"It is abominable, of course. It will destroy us when the Americans react in kind..."

"Precisely," said Keizo. "You want them to destroy it, don't you?"

"We are at war, dear Major." Taniguchi liked to needle his friend by using his title. "I want this American *hancho* killed. He deserves death, never doubt that.

And I want to win this war—for that is the only good that can come of a war."

"Yes, but do you want to win it this way?" Keizo asked.

"If I thought that we could win with it, I might give it some consideration. As I said, I believe it can only harm us. Kawamoto is mad. He must have a great deal to do with this operation. He has had ties with the Germans for years. I wouldn't be surprised if he was acting under his own authority. He cherishes weapons as a child cherishes its toys."

"I would *never* use such a thing," Keizo said. "It is without any semblance of honor. If you say nothing of these Americans, I will say nothing. Let them have the weapon."

Taniguchi nodded seriously. "My brother, I knew that you would feel this way. You have always been too kind. You, who loved the flowers and the butterflies. Why you became a solider, I shall never know. But... Major...it will not be that easy. The Americans will need our help to get into Verhangen Prison. It would be impossible for even skilled attackers to get the weapon. These men are blunderers. They are doomed to failure. I could have killed them before they ever left Rechnung."

"But you knew what they were after?" Keizo asked.

"Perhaps. Let them have the weapon. Leave certain areas unguarded. Let them have the German if they want him. And certainly let them have Kawamoto—if they are interested. I'm sure they feel he is far more useful to them as our commander. It doesn't matter. Kawamoto's days are few. Colonel Sakae is already talking of assuming command."

Keizo sipped his drink pensively. "I will do as you say." He smiled and looked into Taniguchi's weathered face. Keizo knew that he himself would bear most of the responsibility for this. He was the officer in charge of Verhangen's security. "Only two old friends could talk as we do, Tamatsu. We talk of treason. We talk of disgrace to ourselves and our families. We talk of a loss of honor and of the loss of our heads. We talk of comforting a hated and brutal enemy."

Taniguchi laughed bitterly, the way veteran soldiers do. "We are too old to talk of these things, Sasumo. Let these children talk of their honor. The worst must first be explained since the concept is beyond them. You and I have honor within us. Wise heads such as ours are safe from the vengeance of a fool like Kawamoto. He fears real men. As for our enemies, they will find no comfort." Taniguchi took a deep breath. "They will get into Verhangen Prison. But they won't get out."

* * *

HAWK AND BELVA SAT TOGETHER, looking over the reef at the enemy fortification. "I want to go home," she said.

"What do you mean?" he asked.

"You know what I mean. I don't want to surrender to the Japs. That gives me chills. What about Bataan? Do you think you can get out of there once you get in?"

Hawk shrugged. "It don't look like it. Not this time. I..."

"Please come back."

"I'll be tryin'. Remember, if I come back, it'll probably be under fire. If you want to live through this, your best bet is surrender."

"I can't do it. I'll just have to take my chances."

Daylight came with an unnerving blaze of brightness. The Americans huddled closer to the ground. The vegetation seemed scarcely adequate by the light of the day. The dawn brought another revelation. Verhangen Prison. The reef that arced into Verhangen was a few hundred yards long. The high walled prison was another couple of hundred yards off the beach, perched on a flat hill. Between the hill and the beach were aprons of barbed wire and watchtowers mounted with searchlights. More searchlights peered from the prison wall. Every searchlight was fringed with machine guns. Enemy lines, strong enough to repel a full-fledged marine invasion, were also between the prison and the beach. There would be wire patrols, beach patrols, men on the walls, men in the lines, men in the watchtowers, and men in the water.

Hawk laughed when he saw it. He lay on his stomach, peering from the ferns. "Look at that shit!" said Cavell, lying next to him. Cavell had made a statement the night before to the effect that marines could do anything. "That's impossible. It just can't be done," he said by light of day.

"That's right." Hawk agreed. He laughed again and shook his head. "We're pullin' out tonight. They might think they got a sucker, but I ain't sucker enough to walk my men into that."

"They're gonna be pissed off when you come back," said Cavell.

"You ain't just a-shittin'." Joe Canlon crawled over. He had been listening. "We ain't got enough boats to go back," he said.

"You worry too much, Joe," Hawk said.

"Can you do it? Can you back out?" Joe asked.

Hawk spat. "I'm the leader of the operation, the man in the field. I have to make judgment calls. I call this one a problem. It's worse than anybody expected. We can't even get onto the island. We'd get shot to pieces on the goddamn reef. If it had a hundred to one chance, I'd do it. It just can't be done."

"Hulmore would read it more like fifty-fifty," said Cavell. Joe glanced over at Cavell. He didn't like him.

He could tell that Cavell half wanted to go through with it, knowing it couldn't be done. Joe liked civilized people.

Everyone breathed a little easier. They were still terrified of detection by a barbarous enemy. But now they felt safe from commitment to a futile effort by their own barbarous leader. All they had to do was hang on until nightfall. Plans were made to double up on the rafts.

* * *

THE CORRIDORS HAD to be evacuated so that Kawamoto could bring his tiger up to his chambers. His chambers were on a labyrinthine floor in Tower 2, the same chambers occupied by Verhangen's former warden. Kawamoto alone was able to escort the beast. He did so by means of a hand resting gently on the monster's thick neck. He took the tiger into his bedroom, shut the door, and returned to a mat in his sitting room. He called for Hauptmann Mittelstadt. The German appeared a half hour later and Kawamoto poured him a drink. Mittelstadt was uncomfortable. He had always thought Kawamoto strange, but today he was afraid of him. He had considered seeing Sergeant Pechmann in his place. He feared offending the general. Being alone with Kawamoto in the isolated stone of the tower room made the shaved hair on Mittelstadt's neck tingle. He didn't know the tiger was in the back room.

"Manliness courses through my veins, much thicker than blood," bellowed the slightly drunken general. Mittelstadt watched him cautiously from beneath his brows, being polite, but always watching him. He knew that the general could leap up without provocation and throw a deadly kick at him before he could move a muscle. The German sipped his drink slowly so that there would be no danger of intoxication. "I am the sort of man who makes other men look like women," Kawamoto screamed. "A man such as I comes along once in ten generations!"

Mittelstadt didn't quite know what to say. So, he said, "Yes. Yes, of course, my General."

"Have you ever felt the wildness and the power of the untamed beast?" Kawamoto shouted.

Mittelstadt started to answer that he felt it right now. He had inadvertently forgotten his pistol. He had expected something more along the lines of a parlor discussion. "Exactly...to what are you referring?" the German asked. He tried to sound diplomatic, but it wasn't in him.

"Man and nature, nature in man, the power...the tiger...the tiger," Kawamoto babbled, stood and walked to the bedroom. He threw open the door. The beast was sprawled comfortably on the general's bed, all aglow in horrifying black and orange stripes. He scarcely looked at the two men. He was drowsy. Perhaps he didn't see Mittelstadt. Mittelstadt knew the animal would kill anyone but Kawamoto. “Feel the exhilaration, honorable Mittelstadt? That is nature. You and nature. Face to face. Feel the power?”

“Yes. Would you mind closing the door?” the German said evenly. He backed slowly toward the exit. “You are letting your fear destroy the pleasure,” Kawamoto complained, “Enjoy it. Enjoy the awesome strength of nature, look on it, and revel in it. And—don’t move or you may catch his eye.” Mittelstadt froze. Grunt, grunt, grunt, Kawamoto laughed. And then he shut the bedroom door. “You felt it?”

“Yes, yes, of course.”

“I...feel this within me always. I am power. I have used your weapon again. Several times, in fact.”

“You...but...that was forbidden, General.”

“War is limitlessness. Nothing is forbidden. Just as nothing is forbidden to nature, or to a man, who is truly a man...”

“I...see...” A knock at the door ended the peculiar exchange. Corporal Omato announced that the general’s dinner was ready. Mittelstadt, wide-eyed and breathless, opened the door and let the corporal in. As Omato rolled the tray in, Mittelstadt danced by him and out into the hall. “We can discuss these things at greater length later, General,” Mittelstadt called back, “If you will permit me, I must catch up on some paperwork that has been accumulating.”

“By all means. I have something else here now to show you. I suppose I can show you another time. Good day.” Omato and Mittelstadt left. Kawamoto sat alone at his table. He lifted the lid from his plate. Upon it lay the cooked heart of the American marine. He swallowed large amounts of rice and wine with his meal. When he finished, he rammed his fist into the heavy tabletop. It splintered. Grunt, grunt, grunt, Kawamoto laughed. He stood and walked to the wall. He rammed his fist into the wall, three times. The stone did not surrender as the table had. Kawamoto only smiled and held up his bloody fist. "Was there ever such a man as I?" he screamed to the empty room.

8

The marines noticed that evening was coming on too quickly. A fine mist blocked the tropical sun, and the air became cool long before dusk. The mist turned into a fog that swirled about the leafy boughs. The sky was whitewashed away. Verhangen Prison could no longer be seen. No one regretted that. Grayish-white dough pressed through the sieve of leaves. Hawk was the first one to realize what this meant. "The Good Lord Himself done turned a hand against me," he whispered. He knew his number was up. He had always expected that it would come suddenly, without warning. Not this way. He had to force his own ending intentionally in a well-planned assault. The others, in the way of underlings, were secure in the knowledge that they were going back to Stocken Bay. Hawk knew that plans could be changed, and that he had a job to do. Now he could do it. Dogs bayed in the foggy distance. They were probably somewhere down by the wire.

Hawk lit a cigar and watched the men preparing to leave. "Change in plans, men," he said in a loud voice.

"I reckon we gotta do it." The men looked at him, too stunned to complain. It was a surprise in name only. Disappointment upon terrifying disappointment had been their lot since leaving the United States. Someone said, "Shit," but that was about it. "We gotta chance on making it to the island anyway. It ain't gonna make it no easier to get in or out, though. We have to do it, boys."

Cavell walked by. He had been loading a raft. He nodded his head as if he were in complete agreement. The others unloaded the rafts. Some began lining up on the beach, as if they were paratroopers ready to jump. They listened to the distant dogs.

"You ever notice something about dogs?" Tolliver asked Canlon. "They don't bother women. I noticed that back home. A man can't walk down the street without a pack of dogs following him, but they don't bother women." Tolliver laughed his cartoon character laugh.

Canlon threw down his cigarette. "So what?" He snapped.

Tolliver laughed again and said, "Come on, Joe, what you wanta go back for? They'll just kill us over at Stocken anyways." Joe didn't answer this time.

Carter Spence stood beside them. He hitched his Ml higher across his apish shoulders. "What's Hawk gonna do with them two whores?" he asked Canlon. "What's the story on them?"

"Who cares? I'm worried about my own goddamn story," said Joe.

Hawk shuffled to the rear and drew Belva aside. "Think you'll be all right?" he asked.

"It wouldn't matter, one way or the other, would it?" she replied.

"I guess not," he said. He looked away quickly and sighed. It was a shallow sigh, the sigh of a frightened man. But Belva knew James Hawk wasn't frightened—for himself. "Well, hell, I guess we better get goin'," he said with a sort of forced impatience. He didn't kiss her or say anything else. He didn't look over at Ivania Broeder. He had seen her earlier, standing in the white mist, her collar high around her face. She watched him all the time now, he noticed. He still liked her. He didn't want the two women to surrender to the Japanese. But he had faced hard choices before. They were no longer hard for him. They were just another step in making it from daylight to dusk. He walked away from both of them, thinking clearly and with determination about the impossible task that lay before him. He knew that he had done everything possible for them, and that perhaps he had saved their lives. He couldn't think about it anymore. He waded through the men. "Let's go," he said.

With a casualness that would have given Hulmore heart failure, Hawk took the point. He didn't see where he was any more valuable than anyone else. If he got killed, Cavell was to take over. There was a strict pecking order. Every man had a number. Tolliver was last. Every man had to go on and never turn back. Get the weapon. No matter what. Joe Canlon was number four in the chain of command. He was behind Spence. He started thinking about that for the first time. He hated Spence. The new guy, Fred Mittelstadt, was pissed off because Joe was ahead of him. Mittelstadt outranked Joe, but Canlon was Hawk's buddy. Mittelstadt had been a member of C Company, and he was on this mission for revenge. He was dedicated. He had been decorated several times, and was the most decorated man in C Company, before it was liquidated. He was a farmer from Texas.

The tide was low. They had little difficulty negotiating the sharp reef. A man could see only about five or six feet in front of himself. They kept a close interval. Hawk left no one, other than the two women, at the ORP. Hulmore's elaborate plans, involving security teams, assault teams, contingencies, and rear guards, lay wadded up in a ball under Hawk's bunk on Stocken Bay. Hawk's plan was get in, blow it, and get out. He would use whatever and whomever he had to do that. He wasn't bound by any rigid instructions. Those never worked. They were just something to give broad-bottomed men like Hulmore something to do.

Hawk carried his Thompson, one hand on the trigger, one of the forestock. The safety was off. An icy wave occasionally lashed up to the height of his knees. His eyes narrowed, as if they were staring into sunlight, instead of gray-white nothingness. He predicted that it would be over soon. They would stumble into an enemy patrol, shit would fly, and that would be it. Slaughtered like true suckers. He spat into the loud and eternal ocean. He walked slower than was even his custom.

The sea sprawled on every side of him, out beyond the limited perimeter of his vision like outer space. Within an alarmingly short period of time, he felt his boots walking on firm, smooth ground. He had reached the sands of Verhangen. Surprised that he had made it this far, he prepared to take the next step. A drainage ditch ran from the prison to the sea, crossing the entire beach. He had to find it and get the men inside it. He ordered a halt and went on ahead in the blind fog. The dogs barked in the distance. They seemed no closer than they had been when the patrol was on the ORP. He could not see the grim features of Verhangen Prison above him. He did think that he could see the shadow of a watchtower. Its searchlight was unlit. The night grew dark, as well as foggier. He walked in a half crouch, expecting to stumble into an enemy soldier at every step. He slung his Thompson and slid his knife from its scabbard. His foot plunged down an incline and he caught himself, one foot in a hole, and one foot out. He had found the ditch. It wasn't running toward the prison as it should be, unless he was turned around. What the hell, he thought, it's a ditch. He retraced his steps, found the others and led them to it.

The three-and-a-half- to four-feet deep trench offered a degree of comforting concealment. Hawk moved along it, bent low and at an especially cautious pace. He was convinced that he would have to kill a number of men to get into the prison, and each one had to be dispatched neatly and more quietly than the one before. He was concerned that the ditch was running in the wrong direction until it finally took a sharp turn toward the right and the prison walls.

The men moved quietly, carrying only necessary equipment and gas masks. Their radio had been left on the ORP island. Hocker depressed the transmission bar without sending a voice signal before they left. That was the last of the communications unless they made it back to the ORP.

They crossed under the first coils of barbed wire. The wire was merely strung from one bank of the ditch to the other. It was over their heads and posed no barrier whatsoever. From the aerial photos they knew there were several lines of wire preceding the enemy entrenchments. The second line of wire proved to be more protective than the first. The Japanese had taken an extra spool and strew it in the ditch bottom, beneath the coils that spanned the banks. It created a jumble of sharp strands, running in every conceivable direction like some mad spider's web. Hawk wanted to get through this with a minimum of effort. He tried to push the lower strands aside, starting from one bank and pushing toward the other. He discovered that the lower strands were cross-wired and attached to the upper strands. Pushing wouldn't work. He called for the cutters and weaved his way into the morass of steel snakes. A free-swinging strand lashed his face, one of its barbs stabbing him along the jaw line. It didn't slow him. The second man, Spence, also with cutters, followed him. By the time the last man crawled through the wire, it was totally demolished. This would be advantageous, were a quick exit necessary.

The sergeant halted the men again and went on alone. He knew they were close to the enemy beach entrenchments. Within fifty feet he heard Japanese voices. It gave him a chilling sensation. Usually when he heard the familiar Japanese accents, he was on his own ground and prepared to defend it. This time he was on their ground with stealth as his only defense. Being on the defensive and being stealthy were against his nature. He moved steadily down the ditch, a swallow frozen in his throat. He heard more voices and laughter, coming from either side of the ditch. He passed under the forbidding noise, until he came to a mass of broken concrete chunks that effectively dammed the trench, and his progress. He removed his helmet and crawled up the sharp stone to look around. Behind the dam were enemy trenches and revetments, intersecting the course of the ditch. Twenty feet from his head was a Nambu emplacement. It had no crew. A sense of unreality washed over Hawk as he looked at the machine gun. What are we doing? He gave a quick hand signal.

He saw no enemy soldiers in the immediate vicinity, and he would rapidly take advantage of that. Speed was everything. When Spence tapped his boot from below, he snaked over the concrete and into the Japanese lines. He looked both ways, seeing nothing but a few tin cans and pieces of paper, and dashed across the trench to where the drainage ditch picked up again. He sat against the sloping side of the ditch, breathing heavily and watching the others surge over the top of the concrete dam. Detection at this juncture seemed a certainty. Between ten and twenty thousand troops were on Verhangen. That made the ratio of men per square yard pretty high. But all of them made it over without a sign of difficulty and without a sign of an enemy trooper. Hawk felt dizzied by their unchecked advance.

He didn't stop to congratulate himself. He moved rapidly forward. He felt the presence of the prison before he saw it. The old wet stones appeared out of the fog. The tops of the walls were lost in the white cloud-bank. The ditch ran under the wall, with only a barred grill blocking the entranceway. The bars were set into a concrete casing, too close together to be crawled between. Fortunately, the earth had washed away from the casing, and it was a simple matter to slide in the greenish mud beneath the concrete and thus get under the prison.

Without a cursory inspection, Hawk threw his legs through the hole. He was the head of a long column and had no time to hesitate. The green slime was slick. He shot into the blackness. Spence waddled through the opening and slid even more rapidly down. He collided with Hawk's back. "Cain't see nothin'," the sergeant told Spence. They let themselves down the irresistible incline, their boots pounding against each other's shoulders. Another man was behind Spence, and they could already feel his weight on their backs. At length the ground leveled off, and Hawk rolled out of the way of the steady stream of men sliding down the drop. "Gimme the light," Hawk muttered into the confused mob. He soon felt the rubberized plastic of the flashlight's cylindrical body in his hand. The amber-hooded bulb cast little illumination. It revealed a muddy, gray-green-yellow earth below them and a damp wall of stone to the right. They were in a tunnel of some sort. Hawk cut the light. It didn't help him much, but it would help enemy observers. He looked up. He could see wisps of fog blowing through the grill above. Evidently everyone had made it inside.

"Where's Hocker?" Hawk's hoarse whisper came from out of the darkness.

"Here, Sergeant." The reply was from some distance away.

"Come with me, we'll lead the way. We'll just follow the wall. Keep your map out." Hawk put a hand on the clammy wall. He felt the plush gentleness of a fungus growth on the stone. He picked one boot up over the other on the irregular ground. The quietness of the men was surprising. At times when they were all stopped, there was the total absence of any sound. It was nerve-wracking, and almost painful to the ear. The men began anxious shuffling to relieve the silence. "Stop that noise," Hawk ordered.

About that time, his hand met an empty space in the stone wall. He felt a small square opening. "Swing that map over here," he told Hocker and turned on the light. The amber glow revealed a gruesome little vent or drainage shaft. "Reckon that's a way up?" he asked Hocker. According to the old drawing, a cylindrical well opened into the sewer beneath the prison. Presumably, they were in the sewer; it was supposed to connect with the ditch outside. A ladder was attached to the side of the well, and the well itself extended through the entire height of the prison, right through a tower, designated Tower 2, and above to the roof, where it became a chimney or smokestack. This opening bore no resemblance to the well with the ladder.

"No," said Hocker.

"It's a way to somewhere," said Hawk.

"Let's stick with the map," Hocker boldly advised.

"Cavell!" Hawk called. Cavell came within the glow of the light, a shadow lying in each of the holes in his face. "I'm goin' up this here thing. You go on ahead and see if you can find that goddamn ladder."

"Right, Hawk. Do I get a light?" Cavell asked.

"Yeah. Get him a light. Hey, y'all asleep? Where's them lights?" A shuffling followed. "There you go. Don't use it too much." Cavell nodded and took the flashlight. "Rest of you stay here." Hawk put a hand on either side of the square opening. It was slick with a greasy substance. He pulled himself into it. It was moist and close-smelling inside. "Shit. Gimme a boost," he mumbled. Someone's back came beneath his boots. He pressed against the sides of the shaft and lifted himself. He slipped on the wet rock, caught himself, and pushed higher. By pushing with his back on one wall and his hands and feet on the opposite wall, he was able to force his body upward. It wasn't easy work. After a few minutes of this scuffing pace, a message flashed across the inside wall of his forehead. *Get me out of here.* He stopped and breathed heavily. It was closer in the shaft now, trapping close. He labored to breathe. *Claustrophobia.* He became a little dizzy.

He pulled higher, his pace slowed. His foot slipped and he barely prevented himself from plummeting down the shaft. He paused to rest again. That quiet was in here. Only worse. An earsplitting quiet. He flipped the light on. It lit a few feet of sepia stone above. A drop of water hit the bridge of his nose and splashed into his eye. He turned off the light. Hell of a place for a rifleman. He scuffled up another few feet. The shaft was getting smaller, becoming tapered. It was hard to maintain a grip. He knew the men couldn't get up this. He would go only a little farther and stop. His helmet bumped into something. He held up the light. Wooden planking lay across the shaft above his helmet. Off went the light. He listened. Nothing. He pushed on the sodden wood. It rose. Light blazed into the black shaft. He let the planking down quickly. That bastard led to somewhere with lights. He awaited a reaction from above. No sound. He would have to raise the trap door, if indeed that is what it was, to the height of a foot or more in order to see anything. And anything could see him much easier than he could see it.

He bit off a fresh plug of tobacco and fought it around his mouth for a minute. He'd be taking a big chance by looking out that trap door. It would be the least of the chances he'd be taking over the next few hours. Might as well get used to it. He knew he wouldn't leave Verhangen without a Japanese eye falling on him. He tried to spit between his knees. He could tell by the hot wetness that he had missed and hit his pants leg. He took off his helmet and set it on his boots. He pushed the heavy planking up. Light slapped across his eyes once again.

He pushed the wood higher and pressed his head against it. The shaft had a sheltered alcove as its source. Beyond the alcove, he could see men in various states of undress moving about. A long room ran toward the alcove and a hallway ran in front of it. Bunks were in the room. The alcove was in a deep shadow, though any amount of light looked bright to Hawk. The barracks room looked inviting compared to the slimy pit he had crawled through. It was tempting to jump out in spite of the several dozen enemy troops.

But he was led not into temptation. He lowered the door and spat into the darkness. He pulled at his nose and thought for a moment. The alcove was probably a cell, and he was probably in a toilet. It had been planked over to prevent someone from falling in. He could, possibly, climb into the alcove for a better look around. It didn't offer a great enough degree of seclusion. It could be an avenue into the prison, but only after lights out. The ladder had to be a better way. He needed to get as many men up to where the weapon was kept as possible so that they could provide security during the demolition. This just wasn't efficient. First there was the climb, and then there would be fifteen men tiptoeing through the Japanese bedroom.

Hawk put on his helmet and lowered himself down. He descended rapidly, without regard for the noise or the wear and tear on his field jacket. The others helped him out of the shaft.

"What'd you see?" Canlon whispered.

"Bunch of 'em."

"Who?"

"Goddamn elves, what do you think, shit for brains?"

"Cavell found the ladder. Don't look bad, I guess," said Joe.

"No shit? Where 'bouts?"

"Up there. Come on, they're waitin' on you. Hocker said he told you not to go up that damn little thing," Joe chided him.

"Yeah? Well, when Hocker starts callin' the shots around here, he can climb in the goddamn holes," said Hawk. Joe led him along the wall to where the rest of the patrol had gathered.

"Found a ladder here," said Cavell. "It's the chimney on the map. It's got some bad steps on it. I don't know how much screwin' around it'll take."

"Let me see that bastard." Hawk looked up and squinted. He could see an iron ladder encased in thick and porous brown corrosion. It went up endlessly. "This must be it. It was in the picture."

"Yeah, but where are we going?" Hocker asked.

"Well, I got that figured, too. They said the ammunition vaults and the gas are probably on one of the two underground floors. I just seen the lowest floor and it looks like they're using it for a barracks. We have to go up one more level. It's got to be there. If it ain't, we'll never find it anyway. We'll have to split up and hunt it and all get bumped off by our lonesome."

"We're in the sewer, and this goes all the way to the roof," said Hocker. "Can you find the right floor?"

"I imagine. I just climbed a shitter, I think. High tide must wash in here and clean the shit out." Hawk shined the flashlight on the wall, looking for a high water mark. He saw nothing at first and raised the light as high as he could reach. About nine feet from ground level was the fringe of grass and dust that marked the highest point of the rising water. "Damn. We can't stay here if the water gets that damn high."

"That must have been a storm," said Hocker. "It couldn't get that high or it would flood the Japs outside."

"Well. We'll see." Hawk said and mounted the rickety ladder. The rungs complained with creaking echoes as his heavy boots pounded skyward. He could see no lessening of the darkness above him. He climbed beyond the point where he judged the lower floor barracks to be. It only took seconds, instead of minutes as did his first ascent. He left the flashlight on, climbing with it in his right hand. He saw no means of communication leaving the well.

Hawk was an aggressive man, used to operating in hostile environments. His aggressiveness was of the true variety, not the blowhard type taught at vacuum cleaner sales seminars, or even the type taught in average military training. Such a man develops a certain temperament, a restrained madness. Virtually everything with which he comes into contact tries to destroy him. He faces every situation with an eye toward mastery. It becomes habit. His thought processes are directed toward forcing things into submission to him. There is little room for kindness. There is little room for second guessing in such a mind. After a while, the hostile environment *does* submit, and the hostile man becomes accustomed to success. It is expected. But at some critical point, he knows that this environment has the power to rise up against him and destroy him. New levels of mastery will be reached, or he will be destroyed. The levels of mastery are finite, like man—but the environment is infinite. He had reached a critical point. He could not go on forever undetected, and yet detection meant a plunge into the infinite.

He was brought face to face with this fact. A heavy iron door gleamed beneath his amber light like the shell of a dirty reptile. He ran the faint glow over the hinges. A crusty sprinkling of brown rust covered them. They would creak when opened—if they would open at all. A lever latch jutted from the door. He lifted it slowly. It wasn't locked. Initially stuck, the lever came up easily. If he hadn't known better, he would have thought it had been recently lubricated. A steel plate about a foot wide formed a threshold in front of the door. He climbed from the ladder and on to it. A slight push opened the door a half inch. A pale half-light came from beyond the groaning door. Putting his hand around the door's thickness, he opened it wider. It was quiet within. Muffled echoes came from a great distance. A long hallway proceeded from the door. Shadowy rooms lined the hall and corridors intersected it at uniform intervals. It looked somewhat abandoned. Abandoned—but not quits. The floor was neatly swept.

Single light bulbs shined from each corridor intersection.

His hand on the door felt gritty. He looked at his palm. It was black with graphite. Hawk's eyes shifted back and forth across the hallway. He spat down into the ladder's well. He opened the door wider, sticking his head into the mournful light and taking a quick glance behind the iron-jacketed hatch. The critical point had been reached. The rat had to come out of its hole if it wanted to feed. One boot plodded into the corridor. His whole body followed.

He spat onto the clean floor. It hit with a loud snap. His mocking eyes challenged the unknown quietness that confronted him. He slipped his knife from its scabbard and padded along the wall. He discovered the rooms were in a fair state of repair and were used for storage rather than as cells. The absence of any windows told him that he was still underground. The absence of soldiers meant that this was probably the magazine he was looking for. But there should still be guards and probably work details bringing ammunition in and out.

None of this was immediately apparent. Only empty halls were to be seen and only distant sounds could be heard. He turned down the first corridor that he came to. The same type of roughly hewn little rooms opened onto it. Crates of ammo filled most of the little spaces. He noted the board placards over the doors to these rooms. He couldn't read the Japanese information painted on them. He moved from room to room, checking the corridor before each advance. Cells began to appear on the opposite side of the hall as well as his side.

Most of the cells were vacant. Some contained supplies. He went farther and farther from the safety of the well. He dashed into one of the cells. He felt feverish in spite of the coolness in the damp room. The cell was filled with rifle grease, judging by the looks of the cans spilled from one open crate. Then he looked across the hall and saw it—the first indication that he was on the right track.

The board over the cell across from him had "Vault 3" written on it in Japanese characters. He stared at it in wonder for a moment. Would it be that easy? He dashed to the next storeroom. It was locked. He stood in the shadow of its doorway. Across from it was a cell marked "Vault 4." Vault 4 was open. He ran across the hall and into it. It was pitch dark inside. He flashed the light. Seventy millimeter howitzer rounds sat comfortably against the back wall. He had seen the gun that ate those bastards often enough. He looked out the door. He was nearing the end of the corridor. One cell was left. He dashed to the locked door, stood back and read "Vault 2." The numbers ran four, three, two.

"Well, shit," he whispered. Either the cells weren't numbered in sequence, or his Japanese lessons weren't paying off. A little line over a big line was supposed to be a two. "Crazy Jap bastards," he cursed the inefficiency of the enemy. He peered into the next corridor. It was vacant. It looked like the one he had just finished inspecting: little rooms waiting patiently in crumbling brick walls. He took a right and ran into the first room he saw. His sense of direction told him he was heading south. He resolved to never pass an intersecting corridor for fear of getting lost. He would go west at the first corridor and south at the next one to get back to the ladder. He didn't want to take a chance on marking the walls. The layout was confusing, not being a simple block pattern. It rather resembled the poorly planned streets in a small town. Rooms had probably been partitioned and added haphazardly at different points in Verhangen's history.

Vault 10, marked with a crosslike character, was across the hall from him. He could see Vault 11, farther south. The corridor stretched on for a considerable distance. This has to be it, he thought. It's got to be here, even if it ain't numbered right. It'll have to be on this row, somewheres. He heard a loud outburst of laughter.

The laughter wasn't close, but it was on this floor. He couldn't possibly hear the goings on at other levels. Piss on it, I'm too close now. He abandoned caution like an inexperienced burglar. He ran down the corridor without stopping. Vault 7, the 7 looked like a r; Vault 5, the 5 looked like a chair; Vault 6, the 6 looked like a stick man. On he ran, reading the irritating numbers—Vault 12, Vault 8, Vault 14, Vault 15—and there it was. It was right in the middle of the corridor, in the most vulnerable location—Vault 17. The door was shut.

He pulled on it. "Son of a bitchin' door's locked," he breathed. He twisted the T-shaped handle. It opened. "God Almighty," he gasped, and ducked inside and shut the door behind him. He cuddled against the stone, taking deep breaths and peering out a crack in the door. It was *still* quiet outside. He stared into the darkness of the vault. It can't be this easy, he thought. If I had the cyclonite, I could blow the son of a bitch and be down that ladder before a cat could lick his ass.

He remembered where he was. He remembered what was in the room with him. The weapon—the monster. He rubbed the sweat out of his eyebrows and took off his helmet. What was this thing that sat in the dark with him? He could feel a strange presence, the presence of something so evil, it could no longer be considered an inanimate object. His thumb angrily slid forward on the flashlight's button. The amber glow pitifully lit the morgue like room. The vault contained several metal bottles of the type gas is kept in. Hawk was familiar with them as being the types of bottles that hold acetylene gas and oxygen used in welding. He realized, however, that these bottles served no constructive purpose. This wasn't Santa's workshop. It was the den of Satan—and James Hawk.

The nasty little heads on the bottles glared at him like a formation of alien soldiers. So they were right. It was gas. Tabun. Nerve gas. He walked closer to the forbidding canisters. The closest one had a label on it, with another label glued loosely and flapping over it. The label attached directly to the bottle was one like the one he found in the waters off Rechnung. It said "Tabun," and in Japanese, "Vault 17, Verhangen Prison." Flapped over it was a label written in English letters, but in a foreign language. It said, *"Vergeltungswaffe Orient."* Hawk recognized *waffe* as German. Three canisters had this double labeling. One of the three was connected with a hose to another of the bottles that carried only the Tabun label. Several bottles had only the Tabun label and a few had labels marked "Sarin." He took his soggy pencil from his pocket and laboriously etched all of the unusual words on the back of his map.

His gut reaction was that *Vergeltungswaffe Orient* was worse than Tabun. Otherwise, it wouldn't have the deceptive double labeling. Whatever it was, it was bad medicine. Apparently, it had Tabun mixed into it. He glanced over and saw a tall bottle with no labeling at all. He tilted his head and came closer to it. Its hull was thicker than the other bottles, and it was perforated, giving the indication that it had an inner hull as well. Fins were welded to its bottom half. "Rocket," Hawk whispered. That was how they delivered it. It would take only a few men to launch it, and without a warhead it would be silent in comparison to artillery.

Along the top of the room, he spied a number of vent openings. They were boarded shut and thick layers of plaster had been applied to the boards. The vents probably led all over the prison. Hawk smiled. Several thoughts ran through his head. He could hardly take on the responsibility for unleashing gas on the Japanese. Still, Sergeant Hawk was a truly vicious individual, who could do just about anything. After all, it was their gas. He looked at the valves on the bottles. One need not even have a wrench to open them. He had only to pull the safety cotter key and twist the bolt valve. And, as a footnote, die in the process. He looked at the army of diminutive bottle-heads facing him. "See you later, little buddies," he snarled.

He found his way back to the door opening onto the ladder without any difficulty. Cavell was on the ladder, waiting for him. Cirilo Rojas, the demolition man, was with him. "We're ready," said the efficient Cavell. "Did you find it?"

"Yeah. Quiet as church on a weekday," Hawk said as he clambered out to the threshold. He closed the heavy door. "We're supposed to bring the men up here and secure the area while you rig the shit to blow. I'm thinking we can get by without all that."

"You mean, no cover?" Rojas asked from his position a few rungs down the ladder. He and Cavell had the explosives paraphernalia strapped to their backs.

"Cover means a lot of racket. Gettin' them men in and out," said Hawk. He didn't mention that he now had a hope of getting out of this alive. "But I'll leave it up to y'all."

"Jesus. I don't know," said Rojas. "Just tell me what to do."

"If they catch us, that's the end of it," Cavell interjected. "Our job is to blow it—not get out of here. Securing the area will make sure we blow it. Getting out —that's just a bonus. It doesn't count for anything."

Hawk studied Cavell's scarred face in the dim light. He was the ultimate soldier, all right; quiet, schizophrenic. He had his single purpose. Hawk was only a brutal man in brutal circumstances. But he was afraid Cavell was right. "What do you say, Rojas?" Hawk growled. "Answer me."

Rojas shook his head. "Shit, man, I'll take the cover," said the demo man. He knew he was the tie breaker.

"Okay," Hawk nodded. He wouldn't overrule them. Maybe they were right. Maybe they just lacked imagination. Hawk believed in traveling light and moving fast. People that farted around were the people that got caught. "Bring up six men. I ain't bringin' the whole goddamn Marine Corps up here." Cavell nodded and signaled with his flashlight. The ladder began to shake and hum under the weight of several men. Canlon's face was the first to appear below Rojas. "Takin' six inside, Joe," Hawk said. "I want two by this door here." I would have to be the first stupid son of a bitch up the ladder, thought Joe Canlon.

Hawk looked inside the door again. He ran to the first intersection and looked around. He couldn't believe such luck. He waved Cavell in. Canlon, Tolliver, Lyles, Chevron, Hocker, and Rackaby followed. When he saw the six that randomly entered, Hawk realized the value of a prepared assault team. The chosen men's excellence at the art of stealth was marginal. But Hawk was a rifleman. He wasn't trained to think that this adventure could be successful. He led the way to Vault 17, taking the two turns without hesitating, never slowing or taking cover as he had done on the first trip. Detection was no longer the issue. Just do it. The six-man security team each carried M1's and M3's. They now had their M3's in their hands. They wouldn't hide if the enemy made a sudden appearance.

Hawk reached the long corridor fronting Vault 17. "Joe, stay here," he said, unconsciously giving his friend the safest position. "Tolliver, Lyles, and Chevron, go to the end of this row and cover it. Hocker and Rackaby go up the other end. Don't shoot till you got to." With both ends of the corridor covered, and the only intersecting corridor also covered, Vault 17 would not be the object of a surprise visit. Hawk and Rojas entered the vault. Cavell covered the door. Rojas lit a bright lamp and went to work.

Rojas molded shaped charges of C3 onto the bottles. Hawk watched skeptically. "How's that gonna work? How'll they all blow?"

"Electricity, man. Leap frog circuit. The current fires the fuses," said Rojas disinterestedly.

"You ain't talkin' about stringin' a goddamn wire

from here to kingdom come, are you?" Hawk went to one knee beside him.

"What do you want? You want to light a fuse?" Rojas asked.

Hawk nodded yes.

"How long?"

Hawk looked at the door. "Give us thirty minutes."

"You got it. You want to roll these things into a pile? We might get some kind of secondary explosion out of all this shit," said Rojas.

"Yeah. Yeah, okay," Hawk said, walking to the door. "Cavell, come in here and help us. Roll these bastards into a pile." The two of them began manhandling the heavy bottles toward the center of the room. The grunting and scuffling were quite noisy.

"I guess that'll work," said Rojas.

"That's what I like to hear after crawlin' through a million Japs," Hawk wheezed.

"It'll work," said Rojas. "It's gonna be one hell of a mess when it blows. There'll be gas everywhere."

"That's right," said Hawk. "You finished?"

"Yeah, want to light it?"

Hawk smiled and put his hand on Rojas's shoulder. "That's why I brought you, ain't it?" Hawk looked at Cavell and tossed his head toward the others in the corridor. Cavell slid a brick down the hall to signal them. He waved them back toward Canlon. Rojas opened the door. Behind him, an orange sparkler crawled slowly along the floor of Vault 17. Hawk shut the door and led a calm exit. They passed Canlon's checkpoint and returned to the ladder. He waved each man down the chimney. He was the last to leave. He looked once more at the empty corridor, shook his head, and closed the heavy iron door. He felt his way over the yawning well to the ladder.

* * *

CORPORAL OMATO HAD BEEN DEPRESSED. He was from a family that prided itself on its military history. He came out of a fine school and became a flunky to Kawamoto. At first, he thought it would be a splendid opportunity. Kawamoto's horrid personality was, however, taking its toll. Omato's self-image had dropped below that of a toad.

Omato knocked on the general's door. No answer. He requested permission to enter. No answer. It was unlike the general to be unresponsive. Omato was afraid. A blind American prisoner had been left with Kawamoto. Perhaps he had overpowered the general during some sort of torture. Torture was Kawamoto's favorite early evening pastime. Should Omato barge in? If Kawamoto was dead, everything would be all right. But what if he were only injured? Omato would be blamed for not insisting that he stay and guard the prisoner. The corporal hated torture, although he had been forced to become quite good at it. He was the general's number one accomplice. Kawamoto wouldn't ask an officer to do the degrading things that he asked Omato to do. The corporal swallowed. What would his family think if Kawamoto executed him for some malfeasance? It was a complete loss of honor. Harakiri would be the only solution. Harakiri would be a relief to Omato. He threw open the door.

One never knew what to expect when one opened the general's door. Nothing could have prepared Omato for what he found. Not even his years with the general. The floor was red with blood. A corpse lay spread-eagled in the center of it. Its stomach was torn open. Kawamoto was on his hands and knees, covered with blood, bending over the corpse. He was eating undigested food from the corpse's stomach with his hands. "Come in, Omato," said the monster on the floor. "Let me teach you the ways of the wild beast."

Omato blinked his eyes, suspecting some flaw in his vision. Perhaps this was only a crimson filter over his eyes, or demented hallucination. "Come," Kawamoto motioned to him, his hands purplish red. Omato shook his head and backed toward the door. "That is an order, Omato," said the general. Omato slammed the door and ran to his desk. He opened his top drawer, removed his dagger and plunged it below his navel. He rapidly proceeded to disembowel himself, praying fervently that he should be dead before the devouring creature, Kawamoto, found him at his task.

* * *

TANIGUCHI PHONED MAJOR KEIZO. The serene voice of the security officer answered the call. "The marines have left," Taniguchi informed him.

"Did they see the prisoners?"

"No. They went directly to Vault 17 and have returned to the sewer. I assume that they set a charge. I am becoming concerned over their incompetence. I cannot order an inspection to check Vault 17. Kawamoto will know that we are involved. We should have brought Colonel Sakae into this. Now we can only wait. I pray that it was not a long-delayed fuse. I would have called you sooner, but there were only the open lines available. They acted swiftly, coming in exactly where we predicted."

"They should see the prisoners," said Keizo.

"They will be with them soon enough," Taniguchi returned coldly.

"Perhaps. Perhaps not. They should know what

Kawamoto has done. Very well, old friend. I will give the order to capture them now," sighed Keizo. "We will then look mildly alert."

"Capture them? Or kill them?" Taniguchi asked. He remembered the cruel young sergeant. He wanted him dead. There was a pause at the other end of the line, and then another sigh.

"Yes," said Keizo at last, "or kill them. We must do whatever results in the least damage to our own forces."

"They made no attempt to find the German—or Kawamoto," Taniguchi said.

"Disappointing," Keizo admitted.

* * *

THE MARINES MOVED QUICKLY along the course of the sewer. Escape, freedom, and life coursed through their bloodstreams like a powerful song. They were going to make it. After all of that worry, they were going to make it. The man named Howard was the first to climb out of the grill that led to the drainage ditch outside. Eddie Frobisher was behind him. A shot exploded from without the foggy opening. Howard rolled limply down through the opening, tripping Eddie and falling into the others.

"Get back! Pull away from that hole!" Hawk

shouted. He expected grenades, and within seconds, three rolled down the slope from the grill. The men were far enough back by that time. The sewer reverberated with the loud blasts. Whining shrapnel ricocheted off the soft brick.

Joe Canlon huddled against a curve in the wall. "Typical shit," he cursed.

"They were on to us all along," said Cavell.

"The gas ain't blowed yet," Hawk said calmly.

"And it never will," Cavell replied. Another grenade rolled into the sewer and the men bowed their heads as it exploded.

"Ain't that some shit?" Hawk exclaimed, looking back toward the ladder. "I wonder if we can get back up there."

"What the hell for," Joe asked. Enemy troops began launching themselves through the grill and rolling down the slope.

"Nail 'em!" Hawk screamed in angry frustration. The grease guns opened up on full automatic, saturating the slope and the opening beneath the grill in a metallic hailstorm. Bodies toppled over one another. The wounded cried out. The marines kept firing until the wounded were silent. The Japanese ceased their attempt to enter the sewer. "Cover the rear!" Hawk shouted, waving three men to the far end of the unexplored tunnel.

A bright orange blaze appeared at the grill. A great hissing came from outside. Licking flame shot deep into the subterranean tunnel with a heart-stopping whoosh. "Flamethrower! Flamethrower!" someone squealed. Hawk watched the thick jellied stream of fire. It looked like his men were out of its reach. They fell farther back, seeking absolute safety from the terrible weapon. The sewer heated up. The men fired into the flames. It was futile. The orange shadows highlighted their frightened faces.

"Hold your fire," Hawk ordered. The smell of burning petroleum was overpowering. There was another smell, that of a burned animal. No one could find Miller in the pumpkin-colored light. Hawk looked back at the ladder. Had he done his job, or had he been duped? He had to know. He was running out of time. If he didn't go back immediately to check the canisters, he would find himself in the middle of the gaseous explosion. The flames died away and he pulled Joe aside. "I don't know whether to shit or go blind, Joe. Come on, I guess we gotta go back."

"Gimme a break, Hawk."

"Come on." Joe ran with him up the ladder to the heavy iron door that opened off the well. Without a thought as to what lay beyond, Hawk threw the door open. The halls were as quiet as before. "Stay here," he told Joe. He ran around the two turns and looked at Vault 17. All was clear. The enemy hadn't appeared. The fuse had maybe ten minutes to go. Hawk walked down the hall to the vault. His jaw muscles worked tensely under his beard.

Two men were already dead. Their end came quickly, brutally. Hawk knew that they would all go the same route. He entered the cell and climbed atop two of the Tabun bottles. The fuse hissed in his ears. Balanced precariously, he chipped at the plaster covering the boarded vent shafts. Once the plaster was off, the thick boards remained. Although the vent was no longer air tight, it was rather well blocked. He pounded and pried at the boards. They wouldn't budge. He jumped down and hoisted one of the massive canisters onto his shoulder. He rammed it through the vent. He staggered to a second vent and did the same thing. The heavy force splintered the wood. He set the bottle down with a hollow clank. He came close to swallowing his tongue when he turned around and saw a man standing behind him.

"About five minutes to go." It was Cavell.

"What the goddamn hell you doin' here?"

"We can't hold that tunnel down there. The Japs came from the other side. The men are climbin' the ladder. I don't know where they think they're going. I came to see that the job gets done." They stared at each other across the burning fuse. Hawk's eyes were those of a trapped and unthinking animal. Cavell's eyes were those of a man who has turned too far in on himself.

"What do you mean?" Hawk demanded, sweat dripping off the end of his nose.

"A lot can happen in five minutes. I'll stay in here. If they come in here, I can hold the room with my M3 and grenades."

"That's suicide," said Hawk. Cavell laughed. It was a strange, haunting laugh—repulsive, and certainly not the least bit appealing or contagious. Hawk laughed with him. In a second, neither man had the trace of a smile on his face. They once again stared into each other's eyes.

"All right," said Hawk. "You make a run for it—when it gets down to a minute or so."

"Sure." Cavell didn't smile.

Hawk nodded. He had a fleeting suspicion that maybe Cavell had snapped. But he dismissed the thought. Cavells didn't snap under pressure. They snapped after it was over. Hawk was betting the whole operation on that. "See you later, then," the sergeant said evenly.

"Later."

Hawk checked the hall. He ran the two quick turns and slipped through the iron door. Standing on the narrow threshold, he closed it. Men were climbing by him on the ladder. "Did Joe get out?" he asked Hocker. Hocker continued to climb by, his face white with fear. "Yeah, he's at the top. Cavell left Spence and Rackaby to guard the bottom. He said we couldn't hold the sewer. There's a lot of Japs down there."

"Yeah," said Hawk, "Pass the word, go as high as you can get. Go to the roof if it goes that far. I opened some vent shafts. When that gas goes up, it'll probably go all over this goddamn building."

Hocker stared out from his bloodless face. Hawk never did hear him pass the message up. Tolliver climbed by, wrestling with his interwoven Ml and M3 straps. He laughed foolishly and Hawk looked blankly at him. "Hold up, Tolliver, let me on the ladder," he said.

Joe Canlon found himself in the uncomfortable position of leading the patrol from the top of the ladder. Every time he passed another iron door he felt pangs of indecision. Should he stop or not? Each door led to a different level. He was relieved to get Hawk's order. He didn't know that none of the doors opened. He did know that he saw some kind of light above him. His heart pounded in his ears. He thrust his head through the circular opening at the summit of the smokestack and breathed the foggy night air.

Rojas, the man below him, cursed when Joe suddenly stopped. "Go on out, Canlon!" Rojas yelled.

"I can't," Joe shrieked.

"What do you mean, you shithead? Get moving, you're holding everybody up."

Rojas wanted to get into the open air before the gas exploded. Joe hung on the side of the ladder and let Rojas pass him. "I mean we can't get down," said Joe.

Rojas looked out of the opening. The smokestack jutted out of a tower roof that stood high over the main prison roof. It was far too high to jump down to even the tower roof. "We're screwed," Rojas snapped unemotionally. The fog made it impossible to tell how high they were. But it was high.

"What the hell's going on?" Fred Mittelstadt shouted from below. Joe told him. "Let me up there," Mittelstadt said. "I'll jump it. If I make it, the rest of you can do it." They let Mittelstadt by.

"You'll change your mind when you see it," said Rojas.

Mittelstadt didn't change his mind. He knew it was too far. He climbed over and hit the air without hesitating. He didn't cry out. They didn't hear him hit. They knew he was dead. It was an odd, crazy thing that he did; the same sort of thing that had gotten him decorated several times. He was no relation to Hauptmann Mittelstadt, the SS officer sleeping comfortably in a room several stories below the Americans.

Hocker wasn't so impetuous. He reasoned that the last of the iron doors would open onto the tower roof. He happened to be the man adjacent to that door. He shouted and soon had three others beating on the door and prying at it with their knives. It wouldn't open for hell.

Cavell sat in the darkness. He watched the fuse sparkle toward its cataclysmic goal. One minute left. He looked at the door, then folded his strong thin arms across his lap. There had been no interruptions, no sounds. The fuse crept up the side of a bottle and toward the detonator like a wounded spider. Thirty seconds. Half a minute and the Japanese would never gas another marine. Cavell felt a swell of satisfied righteousness about that. He also felt something else. It overshadowed his monumental pride in accomplishment. He wanted to live. He had gone to the wire and looked within himself, more than he had ever done before. It took physical circumstances to make him do this. He couldn't have done it on his own. He jumped to his feet and threw open the door. He sprinted down the hall, turned twice and dove behind the iron door by the ladder.

For a few seconds, he heard men cursing above him on the ladder. He heard Spence and Rackaby below, shooting it out with the furious Japanese. He hung onto the lever of the door. The explosion rocked the rotted soul of Verhangen Prison. Cavell's door flapped open, hard, with him clinging to it. The iron-jacketed hatch smashed him into the wall of the well. He fell, half conscious, until a leg fouled in the ladder. He heard it crack like a broomstick. With all of his indomitable spirit, he latched a hand to the ladder.

The others clung to the trembling ladder. A cloud of dust filled the narrow diameter of the well. Henson bellowed, "Gas!"

Hawk reached for the mask on his hip. "Get your

mask!" he shouted to his men. He looked up and saw Hocker without a mask. The others looked like giant insects hanging on the side of the well with their strange face gear. Hawk shook Hocker's boot. "Where's your mask?" he asked, lifting his own up in order to speak.

The dust was thick between them. "I don't know...I lost it," said Hocker.

"And you was supposed to be smart, Hocker," Hawk said, ripping off his mask and handing it to the man above him. "Merry Christmas, kid." Hocker took the mask without another word and pulled it down over his face. Hawk clenched his teeth and watched the billowing cloud that enveloped them. It smelled like dust. It tasted like dust. He rubbed his eyes. After a full two minutes, the cloud still lingered. Hawk decided that it *was* dust, and dust alone.

The sergeant looked below and saw Cavell in trouble. He climbed by the still masked men, to the bottom of the column. He pulled Cavell upright by his jacket collar. "What's the damage, Cavell?"

"Leg's broke," Cavell replied. Shots in the chimney below sounded like kegs of dynamite going off. Spence and Rackaby were having a tough time of it.

"Come on," said Hawk. "You gotta climb anyway."

Cavell grimaced. "I. .. something else is broke. I...my elbow or my shoulder or something." Hawk readjusted his grip on the injured man. He was none too gentle, and Cavell sucked air between his teeth in pain. The shots in the sewer below grew more insistent. Hawk looked down to see if he could tell what was going on.

"We need help!" Spence cried out in panic.

"Climb up the ladder," Hawk shouted.

"We can't! We can't! They'll come in on us!"

"Climb up the ladder," Hawk repeated, and shouted, "Now!" for emphasis. He slipped a grenade from his belt and tore the pin out. He heard the two marines pounding rapidly up the ladder. He took his fingers from around the safety lever and the spoon sprang forward into the abyss below. He dropped the grenade lazily, far out into the darkness at the center of the well. His other hand still held Cavell. By the time the grenade exploded, Spence was already close up under Cavell. Moans of Japanese wounded rose from the sewer.

"Spence, push Cavell up. Get his butt on your shoulders," Hawk called. "Rackaby, keep fire trained down the hole and drop a grenade if it sounds like they're comin' in the well."

"I need some bandoliers," Rackaby sobbed.

"Well, goddamn it, get 'em," Hawk said. The sergeant pulled Cavell from above by using his jacket for a handle. The bullish Spence pushed and grunted from below the injured man. Cavell managed to help with one arm and one leg. Hawk tried to think as this madness swirled around him. He knew he couldn't afford to think of only one situation at a time. That wouldn't get him out of here. Every passing minute would be another fight for survival in the bowels of the enemy anthill.

The history of Verhangen Prison was in his favor, but he knew nothing of it. The prison had to be abandoned decades ago after two horrible riots. The prisoners had been able to control the myriad of narrow corridors and could not be ejected. Eventually the entire island was surrounded by the German navy, and the convicts were starved out. Hundreds died in the most gruesome manners imaginable. Of course, the circumstances were different then; the prisoners outnumbered the military guards. This time, the prisoners were outnumbered.

Hocker lifted his mask and went back to work on the door to the roof of Tower 2. The blast in Vault 17 had thoroughly rocked the walls of the chimney. An encouraging crack appeared between the iron edge of Hocker's door and the old brick. He, and two others, forced their fingers into the crack, and by applying terror-stricken brute strength, ripped it open. They tumbled out into the open air of the Tower 2 rooftop.

Hocker and Canlon looked about themselves. Searchlights were placed at two positions on opposite sides of the tower roof. Through the ghostly night mist, they could see the hulking round shadows of the lights. "Split up," said Joe, his voice high-pitched and frightened. "Take them lights. They probably got machine guns on 'em." The two groups of men, relieved to be off the ladder and out of the dusty well, charged blindly into the swimming gray fog. The unprepared Japanese were met with a deadly surprise.

Hawk heard the roar of automatic fire as he dragged Cavell onto the roof. Japanese voices were cursing and crying out in pain. One of the big lights exploded amidst a tinkle of glass. Smoke rose over its round, dead hull. Hawk found Canlon making his way back toward the smokestack.

"Hawk, I's lookin' for you. We got the roof secured. Killed four Japs with no trouble. We got a couple of real sharp machine guns off of 'em, too."

"Good deal, Joe. We've done our job. The gas is gone. All we gotta do is get outa here."

Joe shook his head. "That ain't gonna be easy. Unless we sprout wings."

"They're still coming up the ladder," Rackaby shouted. "They keep coming."

"Take it easy," Hawk snapped. "Shoot 'em. You'll be shootin' 'em all night. You'll be shootin' 'em till we ain't got no more ammo. Don't get excited about it." Japanese voices blared from the chimney like noise from a megaphone. Hawk primed a grenade and tossed it underhanded through the door. They could hear it bouncing off the side of the well before it exploded.

Hocker came up to Hawk carrying a Japanese radio. "They'll know where we are, when they call up here and don't get an answer," he told Hawk.

"Well...tough shit. They oughta know by now where we are. See if you can get Jordan on that piece of shit. Tell him...tell him we done our job," said Hawk. His voice was distant. Hopeless.

"Yeah," said Joe, "tell him to get a plane in here. Tell him to get Hulmore to invade the island."

"You can forget that," Hawk growled. "Wasn't nothin' said about any of that. It's up to us to get our own ass out."

"What do you think of givin' up?" Joe asked.

"I don't think too goddamn much of it," Hawk returned.

"Maybe an autogiro could land here on the roof," Hocker said hopefully.

"An autogiro?" Hawk looked at him angrily. "You think them suckass pogues can get an autogiro in here? They can't even get thirty caliber slugs up to us when we're dyin' in the mud. Look, kid, I don't want to get on your nerves or anything, but this is kind of it. You're lookin' at it. All we can do is keep killin' the sons of bitches and hope for a hole to run to."

"I think they'll hit the island," Joe said to Hocker. "We got their gas for 'em. They got no excuses now." Hawk didn't tell them that command never planned invasions on the spur of the moment. Some invasions, Tarawa most notably, might look that way, but it took months. Spur of the moment was your problem.

Spence waddled up to Hawk. "We found a stairway, Hawk. I gotta couple men covering it. But, you know, them Japs can get awful damn close on those things before we can get a shot at them." Spence was holding up well. He didn't look scared. He had to put on a show for the others. He blew his nose with his thumb.

"Okay," Hawk answered simply. He felt hollow inside. The others were too scared to have that hollow, hopeless feeling. But Hawk was their heart and soul, and he felt hollow. He sat against the chimney with a thoughtful look on his face. He took out a block of chewing tobacco and bit greedily into it. Henson and Stilley were checking Cavell out. Joe Canlon came and stood over him. Hawk always had an answer. He never gave up. Never. Hawk glanced up at him. Joe was standing near him with an obviously helpless look.

Hawk spat. He shrugged and said, "Well...we can buffalo 'em for a pretty good while, Joe."

Chevron came and stood by Canlon. "It looks like you'll earn that patch," Chevron told Joe.

Joe shook his head and looked down. "Yeah. I wanted one of them patches," he grunted stupidly. Joe's boxer's voice sounded so stupid, it was difficult to take even his darker moments seriously. This time, the difficulty was overcome.

Joe threw himself down beside Hawk. He wanted to say something. He had no idea of what it was. Hawk finally said: "You was right about the rocket, Joe."

"A rocket ship? No shit?"

"No. A rocket. They shot the gas in on a homemade rocket, made out of a gas bottle. I still can't figure what they done with the bodies." One of the machine guns rattled loudly behind them. Someone was either testing it or raking the main roof of the prison below. "It's kind of funny when you stop and think about it," said Hawk.

"What?"

"A full-blowed colonel comes into Stocken Bay and says, 'Hawk, go into Verhangen and get yourself and a squad killed.'"

"What's so goddamn funny about that?" Joe grumbled.

"I did it."

* * *

Captain Jordan discovered that Ivania Broeder was gone almost immediately. He knew that she either went with Hawk or found a means to escape to a rear area. Unable to believe that she was foolish enough to go with Hawk, or that he was foolish enough to take her, he had all records of transports to Rechnung's other beach checked. This was easy to do. Of late, only high-ranking officers had been to Stocken Bay, and they came on small fast craft. No one had seen her. She could have charmed a senior officer into smuggling her out. He didn't think so. He had been with all of the officers visiting Stocken. She hadn't made any acquaintances. Hawk was another matter.

Belva Cook was gone, too. Several people had seen her hanging around with Hawk. He chose to believe that Ivania left with Belva. The only other possibility was that she had disappeared like the other victims of the enemy secret weapon. He wished that she had discussed it with him first. He didn't know if he could have, in good conscience, advised her not to leave. He regretted his failure to get her out of the danger area. He thought about it all day. Finally, just before dark, he reached into his desk and took out the envelope marked "Top Secret." It was Hulmore's decoy information. He might be able to use it.

Alone and afraid, he took a small launch to the other side of Rechnung Island. He then boldly struck out across the strait to Verhangen. He was a young man, and he was in love. That was the only way to explain what he did. He dropped a raft over the side of the launch and paddled to the uninhabited islet where Ivania and Belva waited. He had no way of knowing they were there. The fierce fog caught him before making landfall. He found his way ashore about an hour after Hawk's departure. A motor patrol boat buzzed efficiently up in his wake and blasted him with a searchlight. Excited Japanese voices called to him. Breathless with terror, he scrambled into the underbrush. The voices stopped calling and started laughing. The Japanese boat cut its engine and rocked on the oil-dark sea near the reef. Jordan had no means of escaping the islet.

Ivania and Belva, now much closer than before, huddled together in the concealing shrubbery. They heard Jordan blundering toward them. They thought he was Japanese. Belva buried her face on her forearm. Ivania sat upright with pistol drawn, her mouth and eyes as wide open as they could get. She meant to surrender, but she also meant to defend herself if no opportunity to surrender be given. Jordan stumbled at her feet.

"Clinton! What are you doing here?" she cried.

"What are *you* doing here? I came to get you. Are you crazy, Ivania?"

"You brought them with you." Belva looked up. She was in a rage and in a state only partially bordering on lucid. She reached out and struck Jordan forcefully across the face.

Ivania put an arm around her waist and pulled her back. "Be quiet, Belva. They'll hear you."

They heard the sound of many men splashing ashore. The men howled and laughed like they were on an outing in the park.

"Give yourself up!" Belva hissed at Jordan. "Go ahead, before they find us, you son of a bitch!" Belva kicked at him. "You coward!"

Jordan took the kick stoically. He swallowed with difficulty. They were going to get him anyway. He reached in his belt and pulled out the small packet of decoy information. He handed it to Ivania and said, "Maybe you can use this. Somehow." She read the words "Top Secret" stamped in red on the outside. Jordan stood and walked toward the voices. The two women listened in abject horror to what followed.

"Where are the others?" A Japanese accented voice asked.

"There are no others," Jordan answered in a trembling tenor. He felt childlike. Nothing in his life had prepared him for this. A ring of tough Imperial soldiers glowered at him from behind poised rifles. Swarthy sailors watched from nearby.

The two women heard a heavy thump. Jordan began to cry. Ivania bowed her head, dropped her pistol, and stood. Belva pulled at her. "What are you doing?"

"They know someone else is here," said Ivania. "I'm going to give myself up. I'm not going to sit here and listen to them beat him to death. They won't know you're here. Stay quiet. Hawk will be back. The Japs can't kill him. Here. Clinton gave me this. I don't know what it is. Don't let the Japs have it. I think it's important." Belva stared vacantly at her. "Take it."

"You can't leave me here alone," Belva said, taking the envelope.

Ivania looked coldly into Belva's fluttering eyes. One couldn't blame Belva for being horrified. But Ivania Broeder did. She only wanted to get away from her. She walked through the curtain of plants. A loud chorus of *Ahs* came from beyond the screening foliage.

By some estimates, what Jordan did that night could be considered foolish. As it turned out, his contemporaries accused him not so much of being a fool, as of being a coward. Cowards are considered to be overly clever fellows in some circles. He fell under the accusation because of what happened at Stocken Bay that night. The Japanese hit the beach in full force with their final reserves of the secret weapon, taking every man and woman there. The place was an eerie ghost town. They also hit isolated positions on the other side of Rechnung. It was all as high command had predicted. The enemy was on the road to a steady and sure escalation. As a result of the Hulmore Plan, they would literally run out of gas. But it was too late for Dog Company and their unfortunate companions at Stocken Bay. Jordan escaped the same fate by only a matter of minutes. Actually, the captain was neither foolish nor cowardly. He was rather brave, and very young.

* * *

"THE AMERICANS ARE on the roof of Tower 2," Taniguchi told Major Keizo. He spoke into the phone with a low voice.

"Ah," Keizo gasped hopefully, "They are going after Kawamoto?" The warden's quarters, where Kawamoto lived, were near the top of Tower 2.

"Perhaps. It may only be coincidental. Have you told the honorable general of the attack?" Taniguchi asked.

"Certainly not. I just completed a long discussion with Colonel Sakae. He has agreed that Kawamoto is no longer mentally capable of command. He says that he will assume the command if the general commits a public blunder that will justify him. It will be much easier for all of us, he tells me, if the Americans kill him."

"I have no qualms about it. The man would be an ass, were he sane enough. He deserves the most inglorious death fate allows. Perhaps we can minimize the pressure you have placed on the marines until they find him?"

Keizo sighed. Going against his general hurt him deeply. He knew it had to be done. "Very well, old friend. We cannot become too obvious about this," the major warned. "I have already ordered all of the guards away from the general's quarters in Tower 2. He only has his faithful Omato, The Ghoul, with him now. We must be careful. If we become too bold, the transition may not be orderly."

"No, Major, we will not to be too bold," said Taniguchi, whose life itself was boldness.

"Did you hear what your pets did in Vault 17?" Keizo asked.

"I heard the explosion," Taniguchi replied flatly.

"Hah, the explosion! The marines cleared two ventilation ducts. Fortunately, a bird's nest clogged one or we would all be dead. They were able to block it with towels. Two barracks of men were killed by Tabun on the floor above the vault. The men who found them were also killed. The gas seeping under the door killed even those trying to seal off the room. We cemented the rooms off. There are over a hundred bodies down there. The marines are as mad as ever Kawamoto was."

Taniguchi was stunned by this report. A hundred dead. He was directly responsible. He rubbed his forehead. It had to be done. It was Kawamoto's sin, not his. It was the sergeant. He knew it. "They will die," Taniguchi rasped. Taniguchi didn't allow his countrymen to be needlessly sacrificed. He had no patience with excess. There was no excuse for what the sergeant had done. But Taniguchi admitted to himself that he too was at fault.

* * *

Hawk couldn't understand why the stairway remained clear. The Japanese should have been charging up it long ago. He decided that it must be investigated. He went cautiously down the curving stone steps to the floor below. At first sight he saw no one. How could so much of this place be unoccupied? He found a few empty cells near the end of the steps and heard low sounds farther down the aisle of barred enclosures. Lingering moans came from deep within the center of the haunted floor of the tower. He became curious. Advancing Japanese would not be moaning. He walked carefully down the hall of tumbling bricks, his Thompson thrust in front of him, and its strap dangling right and left with each step. The noise grew louder. His face showed no emotion. The source of the noise burst upon his vision.

A large, barred room, one huge cell, occupied the middle of the floor. It was packed with American prisoners. In the dim light, Hawk saw that some wore marine battle fatigues, some wore Seabee khakis, and that most of them wore tattered rags, if they wore anything at all. At least half of the population of the foul-smelling room were lying on the floor, writhing in the throes of illness. Others sat on the stone, their heads in their hands. No one looked up as Hawk passed along the bars.

He stared silently at the men. Some looked like men he had once known, but only vaguely. Then he saw a man that he firmly recognized. He was sitting near the bars. He would know that bullet head anywhere.

"Swede! Hey, Swede!" Hawk called, looking frantically for a way to get the cell open. With all of these men to aid him, he could play hell with the Japanese designs on exterminating his patrol. Each of his men carried three firearms, including their handguns. All he needed was a few captured weapons to have a regular army. He laughed. He grabbed the bars with both hands. "Hey, Swede! It's me! Hawk."

Swede turned around with an angelic smile on his face. "Hawk? James Hawk. They gotcha, huh, buddy?"

"Nah. Shit no. I come to let you out, Swede."

The shadows fell from Swede's face as he stood. His eyes were totally white. The pupils were gone. "You've landed, Hawk? They're takin' Verhangen?"

Hawk's eyebrows nearly met in a tortured expression. Swede had been blinded. "Uh...no, Swede," Hawk explained, looking around at the other men. None of them seemed interested in their visitor. Perhaps they didn't see him in the poor light. "I...we're kinda trapped up on the roof. I need some help."

"Ah, you came to the wrong place, buddy." Swede clucked and shook his head. "These boys can't see. The Japs got a secret weapon, Hawk. We was on the line one night, and we all went blind. It makes you hoarse for a while, too, you can't talk for a couple hours. Damn near makes you deaf. They waltzed in and herded us outa our holes. I didn't know who the hell I was goin' off with—or to where. They been bringing in boys most every day. In fact, they brought some tonight. I figured you were with them, Hawk. They say they wiped out D Company tonight."

Hawk thrust his chin out. Dangerous thoughts ran through his mind. A knotted fist of anger leapt up his gullet. He suddenly was glad to be trapped in Verhangen Prison.

"You don't mean it," he whispered roughly.

"Yeah. It's all true. I think my eyes'll come back—just like my voice and my ears did. Don't you? The Japs say they won't, but they're lyin' little maggots. It's a German weapon. The German that brought it out here came in and told us about it."

"Yeah. Tabun?" Hawk remembered the man in the Salvation Army getup.

"Nah. That's nerve gas. That'll kill you. They're gonna use *it,* too, I hear. Nah, what it is, is a biological weapon, Hawk. They put a trace of Tabun in it, the German says, to constrict the pupils of your eyes. Then your eye is susceptible to the germ in the rest of the gas. It's some virus they extracted from dog shit—that's what he says—and it reacts right away on the eye and destroys the sight. They put solid particles, a kind of dust in it, for the germs to live on, I guess. It's a three-part deal. It's got Tabun, the germ, and the dust." Swede sighed. "We were just sitting there in our holes, and we hear this thud behind us. I turned around and saw this rocket with its nose stuck in the mud. It was smoking. Red dust came out of everywhere. We hit the deck because we thought it was going to blow. Then it got smokier and smokier and the lieutenant yelled that it was a smokescreen for a Jap attack. So, I peeps over my hole, and I don't see nothing, and I notice my eyes are a little fuzzy. My nose started running like they pulled the plug on my brain, and I started slobbering and sweating. Pretty soon I could hardly breathe or see at all. It felt like somebody sittin' on my chest. I couldn't talk or hear too good—I didn't know what the shit to think. Some of the other boys got stomach pains and the shits, but I never did. It wasn't but a few seconds and I felt a hand on my arm, not rough or nothing, and then I'm walking along with somebody leading me, blind as a bat. Well, I was already feeling a little better by then, so I went along. I had it figured that they were Japs by the time they stuck us in the boats, though."

"Red dust, Swede?" Hawk thought of the dust cloud in the well. He didn't remember it as being red. It might have been the germ dust, but without the eye-weakening Tabun in it.

"That's right. Like red smoke. The German told us all about it. You ought to talk to him. I think he said something like we each got less than a milligram of Tabun. Oh, they're smart, Hawk. They got it all figured. And they got plenty of the stuff, right here in Verhangen."

Hawk looked over the herd of mutilated warriors. "Yeah," he said. "I got the gas, Swede," Hawk found himself choking. "I got the gas for you and blew it to hell."

"No kiddin'? Thanks, Hawk. You're all marine. A guy can count on you. Everybody always said that. That Hawk is a tough son of a bitch."

"Thanks, Swede. I...appreciate that."

"It's the truth. Listen, you know there's one other thing you can do for me, buddy."

"Name it."

"This Jap general—Kawamoto—he comes in here, ten, twelve times a day, cacklin' and carrying on like a nutcase. He kills a lot of boys. Every day. Tortures 'em a long time, and kills 'em. A man had a heart attack yesterday, just from hearin' that he was coming in here again. I'd sure like for you to get ahold of him, Hawk. I'd sure like to see that."

Hawk breathed a shuddering sigh. His rage was

barely restrained. "I'll get him. You can goddamn sure bet on it."

Swede smiled. He continued speaking in his singsong voice; nothing like the old Swede. It was an unemotional voice, like a guru in a trance or a man disinterestedly reading lines. "Thanks, Hawk. I know you will. He lives right under us. He's got the whole floor all to himself down there. Get him, Hawk."

"He's a dead Jap," came the hate-filled response. Hawk was already in motion, stalking toward the stairs.

"Hey, Hawk, let us out!" Swede called.

Hawk nodded and remembered that Swede couldn't see. "Be right back," he said.

He ran up the stairs and found Canlon. He ordered him to push down the bars and let the blind prisoners guard the stairway. It was left to Canlon to figure how this could be done. Joe placed one of the enemy machine guns in a downward position and told Swede to shoot if he heard anything coming up. He couldn't miss. Hawk was already down the stairs and headed toward Kawamoto's floor before the prisoners were released.

As he descended the steps to the warden's quarters, the total lack of Japanese presence bothered him again. This was the one place, were it really Kawamoto's living area, that should be teeming with enemy troops. When he reached the next level, he found Corporal Omato at his post near the stairs. He was dead. He lay on the floor, his head propped against the wall. His uncoiled intestines were strewn about the floor.

Hawk glanced at the slick, colorful carnage. He had seen *harakiri* before. Something peculiar was going on in Verhangen Prison. He felt intuitively that it had something to do with the monster that commanded these unfortunate men.

* * *

CAPTAIN KAWAMOTO, the nephew of the general, had been wounded during the fighting in the chimney well. It was nothing but a minor arm wound. He was able to walk to the sick bay under his own power. On his way, he passed the response center, located near the main entrance to the prison. He discovered there that the general had no knowledge of the American attack, and that no troops had been sent to guard his floor in Tower 2. Captain Kawamoto knew that the marines had to be dangerously close to his uncle. Not even he liked the general, but his career depended rather strongly upon the old maniac. He made a quick and direct call to the general. Kawamoto himself answered. Omato usually did that task. The captain then proceeded to the hospital.

Kawamoto slammed the phone down. "Treachery!" he cried, aiming a crushing blow at the wall. "Sakae! Keizo! The madmen! Americans within touching distance of the commander of the emperor's southern outpost," he hissed. "How I will torture them."

But Kawamoto got little pleasure from planning it. He remembered that day in the forest when the marines nearly found him. The memory of it came close to shocking him into sanity. He grabbed the phone and called his most loyal battalion commander. The commander promised troops in Tower 2 within twenty minutes. Kawamoto slammed the phone again. Twenty minutes was a long time. He dashed to his bedroom door. The tiger sauntered out. He opened his door and let the beast into the hall. He walked across the hall and opened another door. A large Doberman pinscher pranced out, looked at the tiger and walked in the opposite direction. Kawamoto ran back to his room and locked the door. He pushed a heavy desk across it.

Talking to himself, quite lucidly now, he took an 8 millimeter Type II submachine gun from beneath his bed. It was a special experimental issue, yet to be distributed to the troops. The forestock was as long as the barrel and it held a long banana clip. He turned his bed over, got behind it, and aimed the Type II at the outer door.

* * *

MAJOR KEIZO PICKED up the call from Colonel Sakae. The colonel, usually an unemotional and practical man, was quite agitated. "I have managed to get a reply from my telegram to Tokyo," said Colonel Sakae. "They tell me that General Kawamoto has received no authorization for the use of any agent of either chemical or biological warfare. Let me read you the reply, as I received it. 'General Kawamoto was ordered the following: You are to allow Captain Mittelstadt to review our frontline facilities and to cooperate with him in any recommendations or demonstrations of any innovative methods of combat proven useful in the European campaigns."

Keizo slammed his fist on the desk. "I knew it. Are they relieving him?"

"They are launching a full investigation. Major. I fear that this will take at least a month."

"What swines the Americans must think we are," Keizo moaned.

"Aghhh," Sakae grunted. He didn't care what particular creature the enemy might think he resembled. He simply didn't want them to react against his innocent men with gas. "They are issuing a communiqué today, assuring Washington that the gas was not authorized," Sakae said in the flat tone of a man who has done all that he can with a regrettable situation. "If...I am forced to assume command...without clearance...may I continue to rely upon your support, Major Keizo?"

"Absolutely."

9

Hawk found this floor vastly different from the others. It was clean and new-looking. The corridors were much more narrow, and they wound endlessly about and in upon one another. He saw no rooms opening off of these hallways, and some of the corridors were only blind alleys. The floor plan had evidently been laid in this manner for defensive purposes. The warden of Verhangen had been well protected. He had felt perfectly safe here—until after the second riot. After that, he felt nothing.

Hawk pushed his chewing tobacco to the back of his mouth and folded his upper lip in upon his teeth. His pace was cautious but impatient. Blood lust caused him to grip his Thompson tightly. The corridors were poorly lit. He felt the evil of the place, simmering out of the old, newly washed bricks. Decades of sin weighed heavily on the ancient structure. He felt watched. Or was it followed? He looked over his shoulder. Nothing. No—there was a shadow, an oddly shaped shadow. He went to one knee and raised the machine pistol. The hint of a cruel smile was at the corner of his mouth. The shadow glided past an intersecting corridor—huge and powerful, and yet not ponderous, but with a rather graceful speed. Something was stalking him. Something not human.

Hawk spat onto the floor. Where's the goddamn doors in this place, he asked himself. Slowly he raised to a crouch and proceeded down the hall with his investigation. He heard breathing. A large creature was panting. Being from Mississippi, rather than Asia, he immediately thought of a horse. It wasn't a man. Not even a man like Kawamoto would sound like that. It was walking. It walked lightly. But it was big, and it breathed heavily.

Hawk swallowed and glanced quickly behind himself once again. Tobacco juice burned his gullet. What the hell was it? He spat. Come on out, shitass, and we'll figure out which one of us is the monster. He got his wish. He got it at a bad time.

With Hawk backed into a blind corridor, only a few feet in length, the great tiger strolled unfalteringly down the hall. The sergeant's eyelids fluttered. He recognized the beast as a tiger, but he had a typically American first impression. The word tiger didn't flash in his brain—it was the word circus that appeared there. A circus was the place of harmless juvenile entertainment. The tiger roared and the solid walls shook. "Jesus Almighty Christ." The first impression didn't last long.

The tiger, his sensitivity somewhat dulled by long cohabitation with humanity, found the shortness of space was not conducive to a full charge. He looked at the dirty man-thing and seemed to be thinking. He gave an angry snarl and scooted across the floor at Hawk, throwing an annoyed swipe at the barrel of the Thompson that he found jammed in his face.

Before the startled man could pull the trigger, the lightning animal reflexes had completely knocked the gun from his grasp. It rattled like a discarded toy off of two walls before spinning to the floor. The cat deigned to give it a couple of extra digs with his back feet, sending it farther down the hall. The sergeant was trapped in a corner, his only exit blocked by the juggernaut in front of him.

Hawk had felt the infinite strength of the beast. In its mere awkward batting away of the gun, the tiger had exerted the power of a dozen men. Hawk's hands stung where his grip had been torn free.

The force of a giant machine lay beneath the bright fawn-colored hide.

Hawk's numbed hand leapt for his knife handle. The sudden motion caused the tiger to scoot once again on his haunches, this time with his raging mouth open and his massive paws outstretched. There was no place to run or dodge. Where the man of average intelligence and sensibilities would have merely closed his eyes and died, Hawk ripped his arm back with furious offensive determination. Destructiveness was so much a part of him, he needed no time to think. He was as much animal as the tiger, and fighting back was so inbred, he saw only vulnerability in the invincible. In midflight of the charge, with the locomotive inertia only inches from his thin flesh, he slashed the knife blade across both of the flaming eyes. He took them both out, gouging a piece of nose bridge-bone in the bargain.

Blind or sighted, four hundred twenty pounds of

flying muscle could not be denied. The paws stabbed only tattered fatigues, but a crushing shoulder hit him full across the chest. He was catapulted into the wall behind him. His back absorbed the flat, solid impact and he rebounded to the floor. His helmet prevented his skull from being fractured, and the violent collision saved him from being shredded by the ivory-colored talons on the rotating paws.

He looked up to see the tiger attacking the wall in blind demonic frenzy. He rolled beneath the range of the free-swinging talons and staggered to his feet. He still clung tightly to his knife. Mean, raging, irrational, he drew his arm back and threw his knife-bladed fist at the side of the animal's throat. When he couldn't pull the jungle knife out, he spun to one side and backed down the corridor to watch the animal's powerful death throes.

The tiger threw itself against one wall and then the other, splashing its blood from floor to ceiling and never succeeding in escaping the corner. Hawk picked up his submachine gun. The animal collapsed. He walked over and pulled his knife from the gigantic neck as the tiger lay twitching in a curled heap. Whether it was luck, raw courage, unparalleled ignorance, or the triumph of human brutality over the animal—it was over. He looked at his shoulder. He had escaped the encounter with nothing more than a few deep bruises. He stared in wonder at the brightly striped thing, still sucking air into its drowning lungs.

He looked at his gun. The clip had been knocked out. The top of the clip was bent. He pressed it back into shape with his thick fingers. Knowing that Kawamoto still lay ahead of him, he replaced the clip with a new one. He walked out of the blind corridor, just as determined to find the general as when he entered it. The Doberman was nearly on him before he saw it.

After wrestling with the tiger, a guard dog wasn't quite as intimidating as it might have been. The dog's mouth was open to the full width of his head and a snarling hiss of sucking saliva voiced his intentions. The effect of these frightening trappings, enough to strike terror in the heart of the common sneak thief, was lost upon Sergeant Hawk. He knew that he was the larger of the two animals by a hundred pounds. A heavy boot collided with the lower jaw of the dog before he could score the first bite. Cool and alert, Hawk eyed the corridor for more dangerous attackers, and then reached down and seized the animal's throat with both of his big hands. The dog twisted powerfully, landing a snap of his fangs on Hawk's jacket forearm. The jacket ripped as if a threshing machine had caught it. Gaining new respect for the infuriated creature, he held the dog away, for its legs continued cutting at him. He slammed its head into the brick wall. Once failed to daze the mindless dog. Twice made it whine. It fought on valiantly after the third time. After that, it became gruesome. He dropped the Doberman after slamming it a few more times as insurance and dried his hands on his pants.

Hawk sensed his opportunity was at hand. Kawamoto might have already fled. But maybe he hadn't. The sergeant knew that help had to be on the way for the general, though he had no idea how much and how close it was. He meandered down the confusing aisles. He was yet to find a door.

Things were fairly calm up on the roof. The

Japanese had stopped trying to climb the chimney well. The dead were stacked several feet high at the bottom of the smokestack. Hocker had observed enemy mortar teams setting up their hardware, both on the ground and on the main roof of the prison below. The main roof formed a mezzanine between Tower 2 and Tower 1. Tower 1 was now visible in the lessening fog. Desultory bullets whined off the top of the smokestack, showering the marines with brick dust. Spence carried the Japanese machine gun from one point of opportunity to the next, dispersing, and effectively getting on the nerves of the mortar crews. The Americans were comparatively safe from the small-arms fire. Spence knew that the marines would have to move if the mortars laid down any sort of barrage. So far, they hadn't fired a single round.

* * *

Belva Cook was alone. She looked at the Top Secret documents that Ivania had given her. The Japanese had taken Jordan and Ivania without searching the island. Belva now knew that she didn't want to be captured.

That was all right for a man, but not for her. Dying on Stocken Bay looked a lot better than it did a few hours ago. She came from her hiding place and dragged a rubber raft to the beach. She pushed off and paddled into the rolling sea. It was much rougher than it had been on the trip over. By all rights, she should have been drowned or captured in the treacherous ocean. As it turned out, however, she found Jordan's light launch anchored in the strait—and then she was captured. She was taken to a small utility room on the roof of Tower 1.

Ivania Broeder was there. Jordan was supposed to be nearby.

* * *

GENERAL ROWCHETTI, USMC, looked morosely into his drink. Three members of his staff and three battalion and regimental commanders sat before him at the table in the officer's mess. One of the colonels was Hulmore. Hulmore was recounting his adventures with gas in World War I.

"It was a green cloud, twenty feet high, coming down on us through the trees," Hulmore babbled. Rowchetti had been in that battle. He didn't remember any green clouds—or Hulmore. An aide brought the general a message. "Thank you," he said and read it quietly. It read: "Voice transmission received from Verhangen Island, sent to any receiver, Rechnung: 'We done it.' "

As Rowchetti looked at the paper, an emotion filled his chest. He didn't know if it was pride or compassion. "Hawk has succeeded, gentlemen," Rowchetti reported quietly. His eyes were misty.

Hulmore roared and banged the table. "I told you I could do it," Hulmore bellowed. "Just like clockwork. I had that son of a bitch planned to where it couldn't miss."

"Yeah," the general admitted. He thought for a moment. "Well done, Hulmore. What sort of diversion did you use to get them in there?"

"Diversion? Nah, we didn't use any diversion. Wasn't any need. It would have taken a battleship to divert any Japs on a place that size," Hulmore said with a rousing laugh. The other officers laughed with him.

Rowchetti didn't laugh. "A battleship is sitting idle south of Rechnung right now. Tell me, what sort of means are being used to evacuate the strike force?" the general asked.

"Evacuation? Nah, we didn't use an evacuation plan. Hell, General, they can't get out of there," Hulmore laughed again. The other officers were watching Rowchetti. They didn't laugh as loudly this time.

The general stood. "I must be going. There are a few things I have to do tonight. Can't wait till morning. Oh, and Hulmore, I have a fine new company for you, just organized," said Rowchetti. Hulmore looked up. He was in line for a promotion to brigadier general, he didn't want to add a company to his battalion. "There will be a major in command of the company. I know it's unusual to use a major in such a lowly capacity"—Rowchetti smiled for the first time tonight—"but this poor idiot can do no better."

Colonel Hulmore grimaced and winked at his companions.

"Ah," he growled. "Who is the damn fool major?"

"You."

* * *

HAWK FELT Kawamoto was still on the floor. He had some vague suspicion that the Japanese wanted their leader dead. That was the only way to explain the absence of pressure from the thousands of enemy soldiers, both inside and outside the prison. They had made no attempt to enter Tower 2 by the simplest method, the stairs. Being a good Samaritan at heart, Hawk was willing to accommodate everyone and kill the general. He wanted to do it quickly. He knew the stairs could provide a quick avenue of approach for a flood of Japanese troops. He would be trapped here in this maze without much hope of escape.

He was soon rewarded with the welcome sight of two doors, across the winding hall from one another. They were possibly the only two doors on the floor. Standing to one side, he opened the first door about an inch. A row of snarling teeth jumped at him, biting into the wooden door. He slammed the door on the Doberman's nose. His patience had run out.

He kicked the door open and fired point blank into the dog, knocking it through the air and across the empty room. It was only a kennel. Gun smoke drifted by his face. He looked at the other closed door behind him. "Come on, Clyde Beatty, don't be bashful," he whispered. He turned to face the door and fired three rounds into its latch. He leapt to the side of the door, twisted the latch, and opened it.

An 8 millimeter barrage blazed through the opening, riddling the door to the kennel across the hall. A Japanese voice, squealing through teeth, could be heard within the room. The voice salivated and cursed, shrieking like a rooster being throttled by a hound. Hawk smiled grimly to himself.

He edged along the wall and primed a grenade. Without looking into the room, he slapped it through the door. The grenade hit Kawamoto's overturned bed and almost rolled back into the hall. The black explosion belched from the door, throwing shrapnel against the opposite wall. A piece of it slid along Hawk's neck.

His ears rang, making hearing impossible. Anger washed away his reason in a flood of adrenalin. He lunged through the door, waving the fiery gun muzzle in all directions.

The .45 slugs tore into the mattress that blocked the door to the bedroom, sending thousands of gray little feathers floating through the smoke-filled room. Holes, surrounded by spider web cracks, sprinkled the bedroom partition's sheetrock wall. Hawk relentlessly kept his finger pulled tightly against the trigger of the submachine gun, blowing ever larger holes into the sheetrock, until it began to fall away in great hunks. A flash of defiant machine pistol fire exploded through one of the larger holes in the wall. Bullets screamed bloodthirstily about the room. Hawk ignored the return fire and charged its source. Before he could cross half the room, a percussion grenade rolled across the floor. He twisted away from it and dove for the door. Falling flat on the hall floor, he felt the burst roll over him like a great flaming tumbleweed. Only a concussion grenade, and he had fallen beneath its primary force. He was on his hands and knees before the smoke cleared, crawling back into the room. He fired from his knees, barely able to hear the loud and maniacal shots. He fired until the clip ran dry, then he stood and dove through the sheetrock.

The remnants of the entire wall collapsed about him. He raised his head to find an empty room. A large, open window faced the foggy night. He crawled frantically over to it. Like some huge, frightened ape, Kawamoto was making his way along a catwalk to an iron escape stairway leading below. Hawk released his old clip and rammed in a new one. He leaned out the window and barked a roaring mockery at the easy target. "Jap! Turn around, Jap!" His voice sounded like a whisper from the inside of his ringing head. He raised the Thompson and took aim at Kawamoto's hulking back.

* * *

WHEN THE ALARM was sounded concerning the danger to Kawamoto, rumors instantly began to fly. The members of the garrison loyal to the general knew that someone had betrayed their leader; it was only a question of whom. It appeared to be a sin of omission, and that meant that security, Major Keizo, was involved. Hauptmann Mittelstadt heard of this. He discussed the situation with Sergeant Pechmann, and they decided that as long as there was the slightest chance of Kawamoto's survival, they had to stay on his good side. They wanted it known that they had nothing to do with the mutiny. To enhance this impression, they joined the rescue party racing up the Tower 2 stairway to the general's quarters. Mittelstadt and Pechmann wanted to be as far away from the fighting as possible, but reasoned that fighting wasn't as bad as being considered a traitor by the thing in charge of Verhangen Prison.

Mittelstadt and Pechmann made the mistake of sluggards everywhere by trying to look enthusiastic. Pechmann made the larger error, probably by Mittelstadt's design, of being the first to enter Kawamoto's smoking room.

Hawk dropped his sights from the fleeing general and swung his muzzle around to face the rescuers. He loosed a burst across Pechmann's pelvis. The German's torn corpse, its spinal cord severed, flung itself into the crowd at the door. Mittelstadt took a single .45 in the chest. He was just as dead. Hawk jumped through the window.

Kawamoto scrambled down the escape stairway with the choreography common to the overweight. Hawk threw the stock of his weapon to his shoulder and fired at the bouncing target. Spewing ricochets played down the wall and over Kawamoto's round little head. A tommy gun is not a precision instrument. He couldn't have missed with a rifle. He would have saved a lot of anguish if his aim had been true. There was no time for another shot, the Japanese were pouring into the bedroom. Hawk could either chase Kawamoto or try to make it back to the roof. Chasing the general meant turning his back to a firing squad and running headlong into another one. This time his reason prevailed. He turned his back to Kawamoto and sprinted up the emergency stairway toward the roof. Erratic fire followed him up the side of the building. The iron steps ended at a door on the floor above. The door led inside, to the main stairway. He stepped inside the doorway and fired down the iron escape ladder, effectively clearing it on pursuers by sheer intimidation.

"Swede?" he called.

"Yeah, Hawk?"

"I'm comin' up." Hawk ran up the steps. "There's Japs behind me, Swede, nothin' but Japs. Can you hold 'em for a while?"

"Yeah. Do I have a good fix on 'em?"

Hawk put a hand on the blind machine-gunner's

shoulder. "Perfect, Swede. If you can't handle it, I can send some boys down here."

"Take off, Hawk, you're wasting my time." Swede smiled. Several of his fellow *Vergeltungswaffe* victims stood beside him, serving as his crew. "Hawk? You got that bastard, didn't you?"

"What do you think, Swede?"

"I knew you would. That kinda makes it all worthwhile."

"Damn right. See you...later."

"Sure, old buddy. I'll see you."

Hawk ran for the roof. Disconnected thoughts filled his shocked brain. Escape? Too complicated. The general? Gone forever. No, Hawk thought, I'll get the son of a bitch. I'll put on a Jap uniform, I'll play dead, I'll do whatever it takes, but I'll get him. He allowed the challenge of Kawamoto to dominate his thoughts. He hadn't even the most rudimentary escape plan when he reached the roof.

The enemy's earlier lack of enthusiasm for pressuring the marine position vanished. They were making up for lost time. Hawk knew that Kawamoto was in control once again. That didn't bother him as much as knowing that it was his fault that this was the case.

Knee mortars were brought to bear on the roof of Tower 2. In a rare showing of restraint, they hurled only grenades. The Japanese felt the grenades would do the job as well as mortar rounds without completely demolishing the ancient structure. Were Tower 2 reduced to rubble, it might become more difficult to flush the ensconced American invaders. Sergeant

Hawk, a superbly adaptable animal, merely withdrew to the floor below the roof and let the grenades fall.

The mood of the Americans was no better for this. They sat listening to the horrendous barrage and guarded the entrances to their floor. It was piecemeal survival. They had outwitted this attempt to kill them. Maybe they wouldn't be so lucky the next time. Hawk laid his helmet back against a stone wall and closed his eyes.

10

The takeover by Colonel Sakae suffered a severe setback when Kawamoto again appeared. It was one thing to contemplate overthrowing the general when he was holed up in his room, and quite another when he was strutting about on the roof of Tower 1. Kawamoto screamed at his mortar crews on the mezzanine below. They ran about, changing positions in the most ridiculous manner in order to appease him. Belva and Ivania could see him from their three-walled room on the roof of Tower 1. It was a dirty little storage room, with a low fire burning at its door. Soldiers warmed themselves against the damp night air at the fire. They occasionally glanced inside the room at the two women. Everyone was on edge with Kawamoto back on the scene. It was like the return of a drunken, bullying father.

Kawamoto had never been in a greater rage in all of his mad years. Tower 1, across the mezzanine from Tower 2, was filled to capacity with soldiers now, all looking at the roof that protected the marines.

Kawamoto felt safe on Tower 1 because of all of the

intervening men. He resolved to correct the indignity delivered him by Sergeant Hawk. He summoned Major Keizo personally up to the tower. Keizo was too frightened to do anything but appear. He had heard nothing from Colonel Sakae. Everyone was making himself scarce. Kawamoto ordered Major Keizo to launch a banzai attack upon the floor of Tower 2. The general made it clear that he wanted Keizo in the forefront of this attack.

"Such dereliction of duty as you have shown in endangering your commander and his forces borders on such a stupidity that it might even be intentional!" Kawamoto told the sad-eyed major. "You will prove your devotion to the emperor!"

Major Keizo bowed humbly and left to organize his assault troops. He informed Taniguchi of this new turn of events. The *hancho* insisted that he accompany Keizo. Keizo was relieved to have him. Ability and experience such as Taniguchi's made the deadly task seem less so.

A handsome lieutenant entered the room where Belva and Ivania were confined. "I am Lieutenant Ohuru. I have been sent by Colonel Sakae," he said. "We are giving you the opportunity to remove yourself from the custody of General Kawamoto. We fear he has taken leave of his senses and may endanger you. Colonel Sakae is in the process of assuming command of Verhangen. You may come with me now. Please be discreet and act as if our leaving is nothing out of the ordinary." Ohuru smiled. Ivania knew that he must be an exceptionally brave man to come to the roof of Tower 1, where Kawamoto raved, for the sole purpose of saving enemy prisoners. "I will remind you that these forces you see behind me are hostile to me and to

Colonel Sakae," Ohuru added, in a low voice. Again, he smiled.

Ivania stood. Her brief observation of Kawamoto assured her that she would rather be with anyone else.

Belva stood also. She could see the portly general outside. Belva was trembling and she had a wild look in her eyes. She stepped around Ohuru and shouted out the door, "This man is kidnapping us! Help!" The soldiers around the fire looked at Ohuru. He turned to run. A flurry of fists followed, and the lieutenant was carried away under restraint.

Kawamoto appeared at the door moments later. He smiled broadly, exposing an imperfect row of greenish-brown teeth. Ivania shuddered. "He was planning a mutiny!" Belva cried to the general. Kawamoto looked to Ivania and raised his eyebrows.

Ivania looked at Belva. "Yes...yes, he was," Ivania mumbled. She was ashamed of herself for saying it, but she had to make the best of the situation. Grunt, grunt, grunt, Kawamoto laughed.

"I have information that will help you," said Belva, pulling out the packet of information Jordan had brought from Stocken Bay. Belva was the only one of the three captured who hadn't been searched. "It is important information...about antidotes to your gas, and about our own gas reserves," Belva said, holding the envelope close to Kawamoto's round face. Kawamoto raised his eyebrows and laughed again.

Ivania reached out and snatched the envelope. She didn't know it was a decoy. She thought it truly contained vital information. Of course, Belva thought the same. Ivania took a step beyond the general and dropped the envelope into the fire outside the door.

Kawamoto struck her brutally. He reached into the fire and pulled the papers out, seemingly without feeling a thing.

The general turned and walked away. He was overseeing the setting up of a loud speaker before he was so rudely interrupted. He wanted to talk to the marines in Tower 2. He owed them a special torture for trying to kill him. "Now you've really made him mad," Belva said to the fallen Ivania. Ivania rolled over and looked at her without saying anything.

Kawamoto ordered the knee mortar barrage halted. An electronic bullhorn was brought to him. He looked through the wisps of fog to the fiery roof of Tower 2. "Americans!" he shouted. He watched the smoky roof across the mezzanine. No sign of life. "American marines! Show yourself and talk terms of surrender!" Needless to say, Kawamoto had no intention of letting them live. He expected Keizo's suicide charge on them to begin at any moment. "Americans!"

Hawk heard the cries from his sanctuary on the floor below the roof. He smiled at Canlon and spat. Joe shivered.

"American marines!" The inhuman voice continued with the persistence of madness. "I have captured your women and your officer. Bring a spokesman to the roof and let him see for himself." There was laughing and scuffling out of microphone range, like some live radio broadcast.

Hawk and Canlon looked at one another, puzzled. "This is Belva Cook!" A voice said over the speaker. It didn't sound much like her, but it had to be her. "Come out, James...James Hawk!" Hawk frowned and got to his feet. He looked at no one as he climbed the grenade charred stairs to the roof. He crossed the roof's smoldering surface and leaned on the wall at its edge. He could clearly see the people gathered on the top of Tower 1. He saw Kawamoto's shaved little head, the same head his .45 slugs had so narrowly missed. And he saw Belva and Ivania. He had one more surprise. There beside them was Captain Clinton Jordan. He knew he should get an M1.

A gust of wind blew the lingering smoke around Hawk. He studied the scene. Confusion settled upon his features. He looked more old than defiant. The strange eyes looked more tragic than vicious. No surrender and kill Kawamoto—that had been his only plan up to this point. Now he didn't know.

"James Hawk!" Kawamoto screamed. Grunt, grunt, grunt, he laughed. He had a claw on Belva's arm. "Surrender and save your life and those of these two beautiful ladies—and this honorable gentleman, Captain Jordan. Why fight on? What do you hope to accomplish? There is no escape. You will be treated well as prisoners of war. You will live long and truly happy lives in devoted service to the emperor. A great future of commitment awaits you. Do not be foolish," the mad general pleaded.

They tried to force Jordan to the megaphone. He wouldn't say anything. A soldier kicked him and he was left to roll about the rooftop. "Surrender!" Kawamoto shouted to fill the dead air in his little program.

He dragged Ivania to the megaphone. "Personally—I'd rather die," she said in a cold and flat tone. Kawamoto pushed her down. She knocked Belva over.

"Now he'll kill us. You're crazy, Ivania," Belva shrieked. A soldier slapped Belva to calm her.

"I don't give a damn what the son of a bitch does," said Ivania. "We'd be out of this if you weren't such a sniveling coward."

"What is your answer, American? American James Hawk, what is the answer? You must answer now!" Kawamoto was foaming at the mouth. Those standing near him knew that he had been semi rational for a longer period of time than was his custom. They stood a safe distance away from him. He was about to explode. Sergeant Hawk didn't understand this.

Hawk leaned on the Tower 2 wall and looked down. Hundreds of Japanese troops were looking up at him from the mezzanine. Some were laughing and talking. After the general quit talking, a loud murmur came from the crowd.

"Oh, I don't know," Hawk shouted in a voice loud enough for Kawamoto to hear. The voices on the mezzanine grew louder. "I mean...what did you...uh..." The voices drowned him out.

"Silence!" Kawamoto screamed. "Silence below!" He wailed at the troops on the mezzanine. "Let me help you in your dilemma," Kawamoto shouted back at Hawk. "I see your difficulty. I understand your hesitancy." Jordan was dragged to the edge of the roof. Kawamoto pulled out a dagger. *"I will help you."* The general was either on the verge of a heart attack or a complete mental breakdown.

Jordan looked impassively at the fog- and smoke-shrouded figure of Sergeant Hawk. The captain had finally confronted his fears. There had always been that great fear just over the horizon that was the source of all his fears. That fear was yet to come. He had reached it. It was a relief to face it. It was nothing really. He had only to stand here in the night breeze and say and do nothing. He discovered something else, though. Facing the fear, meeting it, and in fact, not caring about it, had not made him any more of a man than he already was. How much of a man he was didn't matter. He wanted only to live. There was nothing left to prove or accomplish. There was only life.

Like the berserk beast that he was, Kawamoto plunged the blade again and again through Jordan's neck and into his back. He muttered something like "Very inefficient...very painful..." into the megaphone. Jordan couldn't stifle a whimper, but he managed to keep from crying out any louder. The big general lifted him by a leg and tipped his corpse over the wall, letting it fall to the mezzanine below. The crowd down there cheered.

Hawk's eyes narrowed. The men with the smiles watched him from below. He spat down onto them. His face betrayed no emotion.

"Now! Now! The women! Hawk! American Hawk! What say you now?" Kawamoto leapt up on the width of the wall with the agility of an acrobat, daring the awesome fall. He danced with unerring accuracy on the wall and howled without the aid of the megaphone: "Breeder of treachery!" The voice was now supernatural, satanic. Hawk clenched his teeth when he saw the bizarre spectacle.

"Let's talk," the sergeant shouted. But it was too late. Kawamoto had lost the slight control he once had over himself. He waved the bloody dagger in his hand. The soldiers, cringing and hesitant, pushed the struggling Belva close to him. He turned his back to Hawk and swung the dagger back and forth across her face. Her body was tossed to the men below. They cheered. Hawk winced in disbelief and rubbed a hand across his forehead.

"One more...one more..." came the cry of the devil through the megaphone. Once more, Hawk's loyalty to the Thompson submachine gun proved his undoing. He could have picked the general off with a rifle. Instead, his face white with rage and horror, he had to turn and walk away. He heard the crowd on the mezzanine cheer when the last body fell among them.

* * *

MAJOR KEIZO and Taniguchi halted their impassioned climb up Tower 2 to watch the general's rooftop drama. They watched silently as Jordan was tossed over the side. When Belva was thrown over, Keizo reached out and grabbed the barred windows. He and Taniguchi were one floor below the quarters of the warden.

"I simply cannot allow such things as this to continue," Major Keizo said in a tormented voice.

"I will shoot the pig if you ask me," Taniguchi offered quietly.

"No. Colonel Sakae must act now. Send your most loyal men to him, old friend. Tell him to act now—or that I will." Keizo looked up the stairway. "We will offer these men an honorable peace and end this disgusting display."

Taniguchi nodded thoughtfully. The Americans were the least of his worries. The marines had a way of taking care of themselves. He was worried for his friend. Keizo's heart was too big. He would have been a fine man in a world populated by men, women, and children. Here he was too vulnerable. Here there were only hard soldiers. Taniguchi could live in either world, but he recognized easily the men who could not live in either the one or the other. "If we do this thing forcefully," Taniguchi said slowly, "some units will surely support Kawamoto. You must also be careful not to offend Colonel Sakae. He is a capable and honorable man. There may be trouble, my Major."

"Let there be trouble," Keizo said, his sensitive eyes watery with tears. "I cannot tolerate this." He bowed his head as the crowd outside cheered the falling of a third corpse. It was the body of Lieutenant Ohuru, Sakae's aide, the aide who dared Kawamoto himself in an effort to rescue the American women. This was the same body that Hawk had mistaken for Ivania Broeder's.

Taniguchi's flinty eyes studied his friend. Yes, you are too soft, he thought. Dear friend, my friend, too soft and good for this life. But you are right, and I will stand by your side whatever the consequences. "Very well," Taniguchi snapped, betraying no emotion, and he ordered it done. The lowly sergeant knew that he would be the steel in Keizo's mutiny. He must see it through. It would take a man and a soldier. Though Keizo was a dear person, he couldn't handle a three-faction revolt.

"Come," Major Keizo said with a newfound authority. "We must release these Americans. They have done us a great service." Taniguchi said nothing. He followed behind his major. Keizo climbed the steps, through the warden's floor and on up to the approach that led to Swede's machine gun. Keizo could hear men above him.

"Honorable Americans," Major Keizo said to the silent stairway. "I have come to talk peace with you, a true peace. I have come without arms. Trust in me, and I shall trust in you." Taniguchi laid a restraining hand on Keizo's arm. The major shrugged it off with a smile. Keizo walked up the steps with his head held high, for he was an honorable man who had never done a shameful act.

The man he met on the steps, however, was Sergeant Hawk. Their eyes met. "Hello...*Jap*" Hawk snarled. He pulled the trigger back mercilessly on his Thompson. Keizo's body rolled to Taniguchi's feet.

Taniguchi looked down at the kind, open eyes of Keizo. He ripped his Taisho pistol from his hip and taking two steps at a time, charged up toward the landing. He saw the face of the marine behind the Thompson and ducked quickly behind the curve in the stairway. Hawk fired a burst at him.

The sergeant. The same one, Taniguchi thought. Your luck has expired, American. Your days of rage are over. He tossed his arm around the curve and squeezed off several shots.

Hawk withdrew behind Swede's machine gun. The pistol shots ricocheted harmlessly below him. Taniguchi called for a charge. He quickly stopped it when the machine gun opened up on the stairway. He called for grenades.

Kawamoto's patience with Hawk ran out before Taniguchi's. He ordered mortar fire onto the roof of Tower 2. This time the knee mortars opened up with Type .89 ammunition. Soon fourteen-pound heavy explosive sticks were raining on the rickety rooftop. Eighty-one millimeters bellowed from the earth below.

Taniguchi cursed Kawamoto and ordered a retreat. Tower 2 would be destroyed under this type of barrage.

Taniguchi had to get his men out while there was still a serviceable stairway. He picked up the limp body of his friend and led his men down amidst the falling brick dust and roar of mortars.

The Japanese had received conflicting orders.

Colonel Sakae ordered that the mortar fire be stopped. Kawamoto stood on the wall of Tower 1 yelling infuriated, but unintelligible commands. Fist fights broke out among the mortar crews on the mezzanine. Colonel Sakae appeared personally on the mezzanine and within minutes, Taniguchi was at his side. All manner of confusion followed, with no one listening to anyone else. Shots were fired and before too long, the mezzanine was cleared of the unruly mob, as everyone sought cover from everyone else. No one could tell exactly what was going on.

Hawk climbed a pile of smoking brick that had once been a stairway. He looked down at the chaos on the mezzanine. Trouble also seemed to be erupting on the roof of Tower 1. Shots came from that direction. The sergeant watched all of the frantic activity with detached interest. Then Kawamoto appeared boldly on the mezzanine. He was shouting and trying to rally his supporters. He strutted unchallenged to the middle of the roof, a thronging retinue surrounding him. He issued nonsensical orders, sending men in a dozen directions at once, and turning in large circles all the while he walked. Machine gun fire broke up this cocky act. Kawamoto and his men scrambled for cover. The general ended up in the base of Tower 2. A faint smile touched Hawk's cruel lips. He climbed back down to his men.

"What's going on out there?" Cavell asked him.

Cavell's pants leg was torn open, exposing a swollen limb. One arm hung tense and motionless at his side. His face showed the obvious pain.

"It looks like the crazy sons of bitches are shootin' at each other," Hawk said. "I guess they think those mortars wiped us out."

"They did get most of the POWs," Canlon said quietly. "We're still diggin' 'em out. Ain't found none alive yet."

"Think we can get out while all that shit's going on out there?" Cavell asked. Hawk lit a cigar. He rocked back his helmet and began pacing. "We ought to act fast," Cavell added.

"They never did seal off this tower right," Hawk said drawing thoughtfully on his cigar. "They shoulda burned us out."

"Let's don't goddamn worry about what *they* oughta do," said Joe Canlon. "Let's get outa here."

"Come here, Joe." Hawk drew Canlon aside.

"What?" Joe asked.

"You know, Joe, I can take a lot of shit, but I'm startin' to wonder just how much."

"What do you mean?"

"I gotta get that Jap general."

"Listen, Hawk. You're just mad. We'll be down in Australia in three or four days, and you'll be laughin' about this. If a man's got a chance to live through something like this, he's got to try."

"Don't give me no fairies in the meadow stories, Joe. Get the men together. We gotta do some talkin' about this real fast." Hawk continued pacing as the men assembled. He had held his rage in cool check for as long as he could. Joe was right. He was mad. He would never forget it, he couldn't walk away from it. Escape meant absolutely nothing to him. He was enough of a leader to know that this was largely his personal problem.

He outlined an escape plan. The mortars had punched holes through most of the tower floors. They could get down from one level to the next that way. He guaranteed them that they could reach the sewer. That was where the guarantees ended. It would take a lot of luck to get through the sewer. It would take a miracle to get off the island. It would take something greater than all of that to get back to Rechnung. Hawk wasn't one to call it impossible. They would have to capture an enemy patrol boat. He shrugged when he finished. "That's what it'll take."

"I can't make it," said Cavell.

"We'll carry you," said Joe Canlon.

"No. He's right," Hawk interrupted the rumbles of comradely encouragement that were coming from the ranks. "Keep moving. Move fast. Don't carry no dead weight. We ain't at New River. Forget your boy scout trainin' and just get the hell outa here any way you can. Somebody'll make it if you don't fart around."

Henson and Stilley looked at one another. Everyone knew it would come to something like this. A hopeless run for it, dropping the dead and wounded like excess baggage. No one had expected official sanction for such a retreat.

"Me, I ain't goin'. It don't look that good. I got another job to do. I'm gonna kill that Jap general that started all this shit. He's right down here under us, and he ain't gettin' away from me again." Hawk sighed. "I reckon you know what my chances are. Cavell's stayin' with me."

The men stood silently for a moment. "It won't work," Hocker said in a rational and serious voice. "We can't get out of here."

"I doubt it," Hawk had to admit it. He listened as the dead men discussed it. He heard only voices and no words.

"I'll go with Hawk," Hocker's voice came loudly out of the group. "Let's kill that son of a bitch." He was evidently speaking to a faction that wanted to try to escape. Lyles wanted to go after Kawamoto. He attacked as crazy anyone who thought they could get out of Verhangen.

Spence threw his helmet down and shouted a few obscenities. He was tough, and he was a little brave, but he was no hero. Heroes were suckers. But he didn't see a way in hell of getting out. Rackaby watched Spence and, taking his cue, joined in the cursing. No one knew exactly what their position was in the matter. There was really nothing to curse but the situation itself. Within a few minutes Spence and Rackaby had worked themselves into enough of a rage to want a more tangible target for their anger. Their wrath turned to Kawamoto. They were for killing him. They went from not knowing what the hell to do, to firm supporters of staying with Hawk. The others followed this same course, with varying degrees of intensity. Joe Canlon was the last to fall for the emotional alternative.

"Wait a minute here," Joe shouted. The crazy bastards. "You guys are throwing away our only chance. We can get outa here, I tell you. Remember how you all said we couldn't get in? Well, here the hell we are, running all over the goddamn place like we owned it. You go after that Jap and you ain't goin' nowhere but to hell in little bloody pieces."

Everyone got quiet again. Before Joe could rally more support, Eddie Frobisher, who lost his buddy Howard down in the sewer, said: "I don't want out of here. Look what the Jap did to Swede Jansen and them other men. By God if I'll let that shit go by me, Joe Canlon."

That made Joe look like a disloyal chickenshit. With any support, he could have swayed them. But he was alone. It was like trying to persuade America that Japan was just a misunderstood nation on the day after Pearl Harbor. It got quiet again. They were waiting for Hawk to intervene. He didn't. He couldn't say one word that would prolong the life of any man there. Finally, Tolliver said: "I'll go with you, Joe, if you want to try to get out."

Joe looked at his hillbilly friend. Tolliver was hanging his head. He wanted to stay. Typical hillbilly shit, Joe thought. Throw a bunch of morons in with a few hillbillies and you get the goddamn U.S. Marine Corps. Joe shook his head. "You're all a pack of saps," he said. "I'll stay, but I'll tell you one thing, if I find any ways out of this trap along the way, I'm goddamn sure takin' it. One dead Jap ain't shit to me. You men'll see that if we find a way out. I ain't worried. You'll see that." Joe turned angrily to the sergeant. "Even you'll see it, Hawk."

Hawk hung his head and waited for Joe to finish. When it appeared that he had, Hawk nodded slowly and said: "All right. Get ready."

They gave the chimney well a try as their first

maneuver. Hocker got a scathing wound from a rifle below and they had to abandon the effort. The wound made Hocker nervous. Hawk tried the stairs next. The, steps on the first two floors were little more than angled piles of rubble. Below that point, there were no stairs. A mortar round had struck the side of the building and blown the supports from all the stairs. Hawk didn't let any of this slow the pace. It was all expected. It all had to be dealt with. He led the men to a jagged hole in the floor. They were able to let themselves through it to the level below and were able to repeat the procedure.

They at last reached a floor that posed a problem. It had no stairs, and it had no mortar holes. Rojas had explosives left over. He placed a thirty-pound square charge of composition 3 in the center of the floor. After it was detonated the entire floor sagged and a split appeared along the middle area. The smoking fissure was large enough for a man to fit through. It was dangerous, however. The floor was now bowl-shaped, with a fissure in the bottom of the bowl. If the floor collapsed, a man in the fissure could be sandwiched between the two migrating halves of the floor. A man under it would be crushed. Under the circumstances, no one gave a great deal of thought to either of these things happening. The sagging stone groaned and bounced as each man fought his way through. Hawk went last. The floor held.

Up until this point, the floors they passed through had been unoccupied. The Japanese had evacuated the structure due to the mortar barrage. They were now, however, one floor above the floor that opened onto the mezzanine. A stairwell, still intact, led directly below. Voices came blaring up it, as well as the sound of occasional shots. By Hawk's calculations, Kawamoto was on the mezzanine level floor. That was where he had last seen him. The general could have fled deeper into the main body of the prison, but Hawk had an idea that this was not the case. It sounded like a vast majority of the enemy troops were in the throes of a revolt against Kawamoto. The only men loyal to him were probably those on the floor below. Kawamoto now found himself in exactly the same position Hawk was in. They were both trapped in a maze of rabid pursuers.

Hawk glanced down the stairwell. He should have stopped and formulated a plan. He didn't. He plunged down the steps at a gallop. The others followed, Joe Canlon among them. Joe looked at no one and said nothing. He kept his place in line, huddled over his M3 and scurried down the steps. A floor flooded with Japanese soldiers met Hawk's eyes. The entire floor was one huge room. Most of the men were at the windows, firing out onto the mezzanine. The interior was smoky and dark. Hawk stepped off the stairs.

He looked about the chaotic scene. The Japanese hadn't noticed him in the shadows. He didn't see Kawamoto. He was ready to go on to a lower level if the general couldn't be found. He looked at the frantic faces like a child hunting his parents in a train station. But it was Joe Canlon's dimwitted honesty that sealed everyone's fate. Had Joe kept silent, the men would have continued the descent and probably reached the ground. Joe realized his mistake several seconds after he made it.

11

"That's a general, ain't it? That's him, ain't it, Hawk?"

The other men filed off the stairs, somewhat leaderless. Spence got them into a line and on one knee. Some of them began hauling debris to the line for cover.

Hawk looked to where Joe was pointing. "Yeah," he said in a low voice and began walking toward the mass of Japanese firing out the windows. He didn't want to be betrayed by his Thompson again. Joe watched Hawk's slouching, casual frame approaching the backs of the preoccupied Japanese. Carter Spence and Rackaby stood beside Joe, watching in amazement.

"He's gone nuts. Let's go help him, Spence," Joe gasped.

Spence was big, mean, ugly, and a bully to his stinking core. He was all of those things because he wasn't brave. He wanted to be, but he just wasn't. And it pissed him off, too. After all he'd been through, he knew he was still a chickenshit. In a fit of anger, he raged, "Let's get him!"

Hawk's eyes were set, his mouth frozen, his Cutts compensator leveled at Kawamoto's pear-shaped back.

It would take a few more steps before he would trust his submachine gun to do the job. He wasn't expecting a rear attack. Joe threw himself across the back of Hawk's knees. Spence caught him before he fell and dragged him backward. Several of the Japanese noticed this odd commotion behind him. The marines behind the makeshift line of beams and stone opened fire. Kawamoto's forces began to scream and run about in circles, unable to tell where this new threat was coming from.

Hawk didn't struggle with his rescuers. The Japanese were beginning to train fire on him. His limited instinct of self-preservation took over. He crawled back to the marines' line of defense. He made no effort to see that Joe and Spence also reached the line. As the three of them crawled over the barricade, the Japanese trained a concentrated volley on the Americans. Everyone ducked beneath its fury.

A bullet went through Spence's helmet, spun it around on his head and knocked it off without injuring him.

"You gone nuts, Hawk?" Joe screamed.

"Nobody told you to come out there."

"That was crazy, Hawk. You've gone crazy!" Joe cried out. Tears fell down his dirty, rugged face. "You gotta get us outa here, Hawk!"

"I'm crazy, Joe?" Hawk glared at the pathetic sight. There was no need to berate Joe. He had acted involuntarily. It was reflex action. Hawk could have accepted the disappointment, but Spence joined in.

"Yeah, Hawk," the big man bawled. "What the hell's the matter with you?" Spence became inspired by the loudness of his own voice. He was getting even more pissed off. The bullets whining over his head made him forget that the adrenalin surging through his body had been released by terror rather than anger. He leaned closer to Hawk and screamed into his face. "You do that again and I'll snap your spine!"

Hawk's somber mouth twisted into a cruel smile.

They were lying on their bellies face to face. He reached over and grabbed Spence's collar. He gave it a meaningful wrench and spat at him, "Get *loud,* Spence! I want to hear you get loud!"

"Let me go," Spence looked down, his head quivering like a palsied animal. "Let me go, you maniac." He couldn't bear to look into Hawk's eyes. He had seen those eyes before. The eyes of the unafraid. He couldn't understand them. How could a man be unafraid?

"Please, Hawk," Joe whined. "Get us out!" Hawk let Spence go. His smile vanished. His expressionless countenance peered over the barricade toward the enemy. The Japanese had problems of their own. They were caught in a nasty crossfire. A superior number of men were firing on them from the mezzanine, and automatic-equipped Americans riddled their unguarded rear. Dozens of men loyal to Kawamoto lay dead and strewn about the floor. Dozens more clutched at wounds and cried out in pain. In spite of that, a ubiquitous fusillade chopped at the marine barricade, filling the area with splinters of wood and chips of stone.

Joe, like all of mankind, still hoped for a savior. That wasn't to be. Hawk's devotion to his responsibilities was shattered. Those above him had written him off, and he had to write his own men off. There wasn't time to be hurt about all of it. Now it was time to die. Hawk never backed down. Not even from this. Had his men known how determined he was, their terror could have no longer been contained. They had all been in desperate situations before this one. Still, it takes an extremely cold individual to write himself off completely—without the slightest hidden hope of somehow extricating himself from his predicament. It takes an even colder fellow to write everyone else off, too. Hawk did it easily. His only fear in life was of caring too much for anybody, including himself.

"All right," Hawk shouted in a strangely masterful voice over the ripping shells. The cringing men pricked up their ears and listened with diehard hopes of salvation. They stopped firing. They breathlessly awaited his orders. The only qualification for a leader that they required was a man with the guts to do it. Unfortunately, James Hawk qualified. "We're goin' into 'em! Get your grenades ready!" He glanced over the top of the barricade. The men looked at one another. This was the oracle that they had so faithfully pined for. "Grenades!"

Arms whipped back repeatedly. Spheres hurled across the room. Enemy grenadiers traded bombs with them» An erupting bedlam to rival the echo of hell's own hatch being slammed took possession of the room. The deafening convulsions blasted any remnant of reason left in a human brain there.

For all of the noise and smoke, the grenade battle

seemed to have no effect. The two rows of men continued to fire at one another. Hawk eyed the blasting muzzles of the fearless enemy. He didn't see the curtain of copper jacketed .303 bullets that the others saw. He saw Kawamoto's slick little head, bobbing behind the exposed line of kneeling riflemen. He wanted that little head. He wanted to have his way with its twisted contents. Like he had with the Doberman. "Like a dog," Hawk whispered. Hawk went to one knee. "Get that general! He's on the left! Kill him!" He screamed until his larynx threatened to burst under the vibration. He knew when he got up, the proposition of anyone following him was an iffy one. Rojas fell dead across his leg. His forehead was gone. Hawk pushed the corpse away.

The superior enemy rifle fire only increased. The pressure from the mezzanine seemed to be lessening. Kawamoto's forces were giving most of their attention to the Americans. Marine fire barked back gamely. The cavern of explosions anesthetized the men, dulling their motivation. They knew that they were on the peak of their strained emotions, but their confused minds didn't know why. Their brains did all they could to keep them physically moving. Hawk noticed that the bullets had stopped ricocheting behind him. He turned around and looked at the wall behind the barricade. It looked as if bananas were being thrown against it. Irregular blotches of white decorated the wall where bullets had harshly pocked it moments before.

"Look at that," he told Joe. "Wood bullets, they're usin' wood bullets."

Canlon looked at the mashed wood on the wall.

"Yeah..." he said. "Let's go...they're usin' wood bullets." Hawk stood amidst the flurry of rifle fire and waved the men forward. He didn't tell anyone that wood traveling at fifteen hundred miles per hour will kill you just as surely as lead. He smiled when he saw that everyone was following him. They didn't know what they were doing.

Kawamoto heard the rattling breechblock of the Thompson through all the other countless noises. He knew Hawk was after him. He remembered that loose clanking rattle well. The general ducked lower, tucking his head between his knees. He closed his eyes. If only Taniguchi were here, as he had been on that day in the forest. Taniguchi could get him out of this. Taniguchi would move through this chaos with steel nerves. These fools were dropping like flies around him. Kawamoto opened his eyes a crack. The thought of Taniguchi encouraged him. Perhaps he hallucinated that he saw him. Perhaps he thought Taniguchi was his father and he was a child again. Kawamoto saw the raw carnage spread about him and took no pleasure from it. He was as close to sanity as he had been in twenty years. The American fire was getting louder. "Ahhhh," he involuntarily whimpered. The Americans were attacking. It was impossible, but they were running across the floor, firing at him. He shivered violently, his head juggling from one shoulder to the other. "Ahhh," he squealed. "Ahhh...Taniguchi! Taniguchi!"

But Taniguchi was out on the mezzanine at that moment. He was attempting to do the same thing that the Americans were trying to do: destroy Kawamoto, rid Verhangen Prison of its perverted monster. Taniguchi was proceeding rationally, working his men closer to Kawamoto's position, taking few risks and no casualties. Taniguchi had two devils to kill, Kawamoto and Hawk. He couldn't fling himself at one and let the other go free. No, he'd get both. War was only a trade, a craft. Success didn't depend on manhood, heroics, rage, or blood. Only skill. Most men fighting wars didn't live long enough to learn that. Taniguchi knew. He waved a rifleman toward a tower window. He kept close behind. He wanted to be the man who killed Keizo's murderer.

Hawk wasn't concerned with plans, motives, or any considerations for the technicalities of strategy. A fire in his soul propelled him across the floor of the smoky room, straight into the enemy lines. They saw only a fast-moving shudder of submachine gunfire. The other marines were with him. Some of them were abreast of him. They had caught his disease. Their emotions were uncaged. Madness, whether it be brought on by fear or anger, looks the same. They were determined to kill every Japanese in the room, and then every Japanese on Verhangen Island. Nothing would stop them. Nothing but death.

Bullets aren't interested in emotional intensity. Stilley was hit between the eyes, climbing over the barricade. By all laws of physics, he should have fallen backward. Perhaps it was the reduced impact of the wooden bullets that allowed him to stagger forward, fall to his knees, then to a hand and finally onto his face. His buddy, Henson, stopped when he saw what happened. He may have gone back as much for himself as for Stilley. It might have been safer by the barricade. It really wasn't safe anywhere. A burst from a submachine gun bit into Henson's legs, climbed his back, and threw him carelessly across the barricade.

With a speed that defied rifle fire, Hawk reached the enemy lines and crashed into them. He voiced a roar that would put a young lion to shame. A kneeling soldier raised his rifle to fire as Hawk's boot kicked it aside. The little defender looked down, confused. Hawk never slowed in his running, putting a boot in the man's crotch, and when the Japanese folded backward, another stomped into his face. He literally ran over the man.

Hawk found himself face to face with the long open windows that fronted the mezzanine. Small knots of soldiers were firing and running toward him from out there. He ignored them and went to one knee, under the windowsill. He opened fire on the backs of Kawamoto's men. Several dropped before his clip ran dry.

The other marines met the line with the crashing impact of a train wreck. Equipment clattered against equipment as the men swung desperately at one another. The point-blank range made firing difficult, but for the mindlessly reckless it was accurate fire. Hawk dropped his Thompson and picked up an abandoned Arisaka from the floor. It failed to fire. He reared it back over his head and slammed it down into the back of one of two little men struggling with Spence. The surviving Japanese disengaged himself and ran for his life. Spence managed to level his M 3 and blow massive holes in the man's back.

The Japanese line had been severed by the irresistible attack, though they still had superior numbers in their favor. The Japanese fought listlessly, apparently without conviction, matching the fury of the Americans in only isolated instances. While the scattered center portion of their line mixed with the marines and fought on, the two severed flanks withdrew and joined together in a corner of the room. They set up a devastating enfilade. Their firing was indiscriminate. They made good use of their unchallenged firepower, killing more of their own in an effort to annihilate the Americans.

Hawk swung the Arisaka across the face of a bayonet-wielding soldier. He knocked the face inward, into a red concave distortion of its former self. As the body fell, Hawk noticed the enfilade. The thing he noticed most about it was that Kawamoto was there behind it, once again safely protected by a line of spouting muzzles. The sergeant mentally calculated his chances. He could run into the front end of rifles only so many times. He searched the stone floor and found his Thompson. He clicked his last clip against the trigger guard. To his right, he caught a glimpse of Cavell, crawling across the floor with what looked to be a Japanese satchel charge. A leg and an arm stuck out stiffly from his body. His hair was plastered to his forehead.

Joe Canlon pulled a spent clip from his grease gun. He glanced out the window and noticed that a woolly, gray dawn was trying to break. It struck him as odd that dawn—and everything else—would go on as usual after he was gone. He understood in that microsecond that everything else wasn't important. He was important. There had to be something after this. Hawk had been right. Life wasn't important. For a few minutes, Joe was unafraid.

Hawk stayed on one knee, rattling bursts into the enfilade in the corner. Hocker dropped beside him. He, too, was firing. He pulled repeatedly on the trigger of his M1, shooting it from the hip. He had no need to aim. Every bullet would hit at least one man amidst the mob in the corner. "They got us," Hocker groaned between clenched teeth. "You got a grenade on your belt. Use it, Hawk."

Hawk reached down, slipped the pin from the bomb and lobbed it over the heads of the men struggling in the center of the room. Men stood on top of men, alive and dead, in their efforts to hit or stab one another. The grenade landed along the front of Kawamoto's men, killing a few and scattering all of them in a wild panic. Hocker sat down heavily. Blood saturated his shirt from mid-chest to navel. His glasses fell off. "Sons of bitches got me," he growled. His hands moved in slow motion as he inserted another clip of .30 caliber shells into his rifle.

Hawk stood. The sudden dispersion of Kawamoto's men troubled him. He feared the general would escape in the confusion. It dawned on him that Kawamoto was working his way toward the stairway. He ran around the few men still fighting in the center of the room. Rackaby came from out of nowhere and ran beside him. Bullets sang past their ears. They didn't realize that the shots were coming from outside on the mezzanine. Rackaby had defied the odds for far too long. His head jerked to a forty-five-degree angle and his helmet flew off. Blood and brains erupted upward. His body collapsed in front of Hawk, tripping him. When the sergeant hit the floor, his Thompson still rattled mercilessly, slashing the legs from under the men trying to reassemble in the corner. Two or three grenades struck the cornered men of Kawamoto. The general was still in there somewhere, lying among the dead, hoping it would all go away. His men knew they had lost the fight by now. Losing meant nothing to the Japanese. The fight was far from over.

Lyles crawled beside Hawk. "What's the plan?" he shouted.

Hawk looked over toward the mezzanine. "Cover the windows! Get some shit goin' that way or them other ones is gonna come in on us!" Lyles nodded, seemingly satisfied to have a purpose in this nightmare. He crouched and scampered to the windows, stopping only long enough to absorb a .303 in his already injured arm.

The men outside were not as rabid as those on the inside. They were behaving more civilized. They advanced cautiously and methodically. When Lyles engaged them with a dark enthusiasm, they were content to seek cover and fire back at him only when sure that he wouldn't pick one of them off.

Hawk saw that the enfilade had been neutralized. Now was his chance. He thought of Joe Canlon and quickly dismissed the thought. "Get 'em!" he screamed. He was up and running for the disorganized enemy troops in the corner. He didn't know who was left or who would follow. He was aware of very little as he and some others crossed the floor and once again crashed into the Japanese defenses. Angry warriors surrounded him. He brushed a bayonet aside with a wriggle of his body. Hands dug into his flesh. Then he and all of the mass of men holding onto him were knocked to the ground by an explosion. He saw other marines jump over him as he lay face up and dazed on the floor. A shredded Japanese arm lay between his legs.

The marines had charged headlong into the remaining defenders, intent on beating them and clubbing them into oblivion as they had done the men in the center of the room. Their larger statures were no small factor in this design.

Three men unimpressed with stature chased Spence back to where two walls met in the corner. Two carried rifles with bayonets, a third carried his bayonet in his hand. Spence's face contorted like that of an anxious baby. He flailed futilely at them. The three blades interwove and clattered on one another as they slid into the huge chest.

A muzzle was jammed into Tolliver's back. The muzzle spat the bullet directly into his body. Tolliver winced and turned around. The muzzle spat again. Tolliver grinned wildly as the blood spewed from his chest. He took the gun barrel and rammed the butt into the teeth of its owner. He swung the rifle at another man, and another. A black bullet hole appeared between his heart and the top of his shoulder. A man leapt on his back and hacked at his neck with a knife. It took yet another bullet to knock him off his feet. His dead face continued to smile.

Joe Canlon was in the middle of all of it. He stood beside Chevron swinging his Ml for a club. His M3 was slung over one arm. He caught a glimpse of the stairway that he had come into the room upon. His fear returned. There was a way out—but he wasn't taking it, he was here. He looked over at the stairs again.

Hawk rolled on his side. His hearing slowly returned. His eyes focused well only on closer objects. A hazy world of lightning fast activity buzzed on the outer limits of his vision. He pushed the severed arm from between his legs. The explosion had thrown it forcefully into his groin. He got up on an elbow and shook his head. He looked up groggily and saw him.

Kawamoto stood over him. Hawk blinked with difficulty. The general looked taller than he had ever looked before. It came into focus. Kawamoto was standing over him with a samurai sword poised high above his head. He heard him shriek, *"Kami tatewari!"*

Coming out of a curled position, Hawk dove at the general's knees with a poor imitation of his former vigor. He managed to bowl Kawamoto over. He felt his opponent fall down around him. The sergeant summoned all of his strength and managed to lift his head. What he saw this time was worse than a descending sword. Kawamoto was running away. Hawk saw him hop over Cavell and scamper his jiggling bulk up the stairs.

The sergeant got to his feet. He felt as if a mule had kicked him. Dragging a leg, he ran across the floor to the stairs. He leaned against the wall there to catch his breath. He watched what was left of the fight like a disinterested visitor from the spirit world. His thoughts ran together and congealed like water turning to ice. He didn't have the slightest idea of where he was. He had only the dimmest feeling that he was somehow a part of this brutal display. The wild, vicious eyes were vacant. A hot brand seared through the icy thoughts. Kawamoto was getting away.

"Nah," he told himself. He heard his own voice. It

brought him back a little. His mind touched lightly on solid ground. He looked up the stairs and back across the room. The fury pent up in the thick stone walls had played havoc with flesh, blood, and bones. Smoke, shouting, and gunfire still roared across the cramped Hades. Strange brown light weaved its way from the windows and through the layered curls of smoke. Sulphur and cordite and the odor of spent ammunition filled his nostrils in a brassy fusion. The smell revived him a bit more. "Nah," he repeated.

He lifted his leg onto the first step. He dragged himself to the second. His mind demanded that his body move. Come on, you're not hurt that bad. He made it to the third and fourth and by the time he got to the first landing, he was beginning to believe that his mind was right.

The prolonged search that he was steeling himself for did not develop. He found the general standing on the floor above him. The sword was again poised. The general was either surprised to see Hawk, or his extraordinary expression was one of a terror so deep that it had been petrified on his ugly features. The expression stayed the same, like a hideous aborigine mask. The face was a frightful thing, closer to resembling a Satan that any deranged artist could conjure. Hawk pulled his knife out and took another step up. He could have run away and found any weapon more suitable. Kawamoto held his stance. Hawk threw the knife at him. The speed with which Kawamoto wielded the sword was beyond belief. He batted the knife aside in midair. Once again he held the sword above his head. Blood dripped from its blade. The long jeweled handle provided plenty of room for the general to use a firm two-handed grip. Hawk took another step up. Kawamoto looked into the clear eyes beneath the brooding scowl. A dark shadow was over the marine's face. But the eyes burned through it. Hawk took another step. He was now easily within the range of the upraised sword.

Kawamoto's lifelong fear of a violent death, the fear that finally maddened him, was coming to a fateful conclusion. All of his precautions, all of his skills and practice would now be put to the test. The hour of his contest with death had arrived. His prime reason for being, the central motivating force of his life took over —kill.

Hawk jumped back like a well man as the sword fell. It struck the vacant step. Hawk stepped on the blade, but it wouldn't break and Kawamoto would not release it. The general pulled it free. Before he could use it again, Hawk was on him, knocking him down and sitting on his chest. He marveled at the weakness of Kawamoto. His mighty hands closed on the oily throat. The general pulled at the thick wrists. They didn't budge. A moment before Kawamoto's consciousness was squeezed into a black eternity, he poked at the marine's eye with a sharp fingernail. Normally Hawk might have accepted such punishment and gone ahead and finished the task. But this would have taken some small amount of reasonable thinking. He operated on instinct alone now, and both hands released the choking grip and went up to protect his eyes. When they did, a knifing chop lashed up beneath his adam's apple.

A black curtain fell over Hawk's brain. He toppled backward, with the sharp, crushing pressure in his throat seeming to ride him down the stairs. He couldn't feel the steps bouncing against the back of his head, only the pain in his throat registered. He skidded to the bottom, somersaulted and righted himself. He was as ready as he could force himself to be for his attacker. The attacker wasn't there. Kawamoto was still struggling to his feet. He was crawling upward, away from Hawk and toward escape. Slowly, but more quickly than Kawamoto, Hawk again ascended the steps.

Kawamoto heard him crawling up the steps behind him. The general began to cry. "Jap..." Hawk rasped like a ghost. "Jap..." he called after him. Kawamoto sobbed, his sphincter muscle flared open and he crapped all over himself. He slipped and rolled back to the landing. He got to his feet in time to face his pursuer.

Hawk weakly raised his fists to the level of his narrow hips. Kawamoto turned his big butt toward Hawk, raised his leg and snapped a well-directed sidekick at the marine's groin. "Why you son of a bitch!" Hawk snarled through his injured throat. Even locked in honorless combat, the cowardly effeminateness of a kick aroused him. The edge of the general's boot dug into his thigh. A new and invigorating rage made Hawk move with a speed that blinded the aging expert of the martial arts. His large boot was driven into Kawamoto's groin with ferocious might. It went unblocked, unchecked, and with a power that the general only dreamed of in his younger days. The blow nearly killed Kawamoto. Unfortunately, it didn't. Kawamoto spun around in agony.

As Hawk dragged himself after him, the wall crumbled at his side. An explosion of some sort had shaken the other side of the wall. He found himself looking at men on the mezzanine below. A gaping hole exposed part of the stairway to the outside. The soldiers on the outside raised their rifles and fired at the bizarre figure above them. Hawk looked down, enchanted by the scene. Kawamoto formed his hand into an open claw at Hawk's eyes. It missed and ripped down his face. Bullets twanged around them. The marine grabbed Kawamoto's neck again and swung him away from the opening. The general's strength was gone. He let himself be pulled toward the wall. Operating on sheer rage, Hawk banged the head repeatedly against the wall.

Kawamoto hadn't the strength to voice the slightest outcry. The only sound was of his head ramming into the stone.

Hawk smiled at the mangled head dangling from the neck in his fist. "Did that hurt?" he asked it. He threw back his head and roared an insane laugh.

He could have been judged harshly at that vile moment, even by his own rough peers. His emotions had overcome him. He had to do something to equal what Kawamoto had done to his people. He had to have revenge. And now it was over. But it wasn't enough. It just wasn't enough. He felt stronger now. He looked up the steps. His eyes shined. "Come on, Jap." He labored to breathe. For Belva, for Ivania, for Jordan, and for Company D, one stinking corpse wasn't enough.

Boots pounded up the steps. He turned and prepared to throw Kawamoto into those climbing after him. The ghost-white, blood-streaked face of Joe Canlon appeared. Joe paused at the grisly sight. "Hawk, they're comin' through the windows. Every Jap in the world. Nobody's left, how do we get out?" Joe begged.

Cavell was struggling up the steps below, still carrying the satchel charge.

Hawk ducked beneath the hole in the wall. Men on the mezzanine continued to fire through it. He picked up his fallen jungle knife. "This way," Hawk pointed up. "This way, Joe."

"No, Hawk, we gotta go down. We gotta get out."

"Take off, you two," Cavell gasped. He held the satchel charge with his knees and adjusted it with his good hand. Hawk climbed the stairs, taking his prize with him. He didn't look back.

"Hawk!" Joe called out. "Please!"

Hawk went to the next floor and dragged the body across it and to the chimney. He climbed out into the well and onto the ladder, clinging to the heavy impediment that had been General Kawamoto. He climbed with one hand, teeth clenched and straining his muscles to their limit. Joe climbed below him, tears falling like a child's. Blood rained on Joe in a deluge. They heard the reverberating blast of the satchel charge as Cavell blew himself and a dozen pursuers to hell.

Hawk climbed on, maddened by revenge, and Joe Canlon, maddened by the horror of it, followed him. Without his reasoning processes, Joe was still only a follower. When they got to the top of the smokestack, Hawk ripped his shirt off and tied it around the corpse's neck. He tied the other end of the shirt to the topmost rung of the ladder. With a superhuman effort he hoisted the massive body over the top and let it fall outside. It hung loosely from the top of the chimney.

Hawk climbed out into the grotesque gray dawn. "You wanted war! I'll give you war!" He screamed into the opaque fog that enshrouded the island. But no one could see his prize, the fog was too thick. He stepped back down. His chest heaved.

Joe reached up and put a hand on his boot. "Please, Hawk. Please."

"The punks...all the punks...war...by God Almighty...I gave them war." Hawk hung limply onto a rung with both arms. The pain in his loins made him retch dryly. He dropped his head and it banged like a piece of metal on the ladder. "...war."

"No point to this," Joe cried. "Hawk..."

"No point." He breathed heavily for a few minutes. His mind raced with the thought of all of the lesser, ignorant, incompetent, incapable, and frightened little men that made war. The sight of Joe Canlon crossed his vision. Joe Canlon was alive. That's all that was left of his platoon, his company, his world. Joe Canlon was his country now, his universe. They took it all. In their weak, scared little way, they took everyone.

"Oh..." Joe gasped. His eyes and mouth were wide open. "Oh, my heart..." Joe clutched at his chest. "I—I'm gonna..."

Hawk looked down into the distended eyes. He frowned, bent over, and jammed a thumb into Joe's throat. "Knock that shit off, you dumb bastard." Joe gagged and clung more tightly to the ladder. "Come on, I'm takin' you outa here." They both hung against the ladder with their heads hanging loosely. Finally, Hawk caught his breath. "Well, get movin'. You gonna roost on this thing forever?"

* * *

General Rowchetti struck a tense pose on the bridge of the flagship. The rising sun burned steadily at the fog. A gentle wind pushed at the enveloping cloud. He raised his field glasses toward Verhangen. "Gentlemen," he said, "I don't know about you, but that's good enough for me. Give the order to jump off."

12

JOE WAS QUIET NOW AS HE CLIMBED DOWN THE CHIMNEY. He had more than one reason for his silence. He was troubled by more than just the obvious. He had seen Ivania Broeder alive. He had glimpsed her yellow hair and tall slender form being moved across the mezzanine. He couldn't bring himself to tell Hawk. He knew that they couldn't possibly save her. She was alive and under guard—that's what she came to Verhangen for. Considering the fates of the other participants in the holocaust, she was fortunate. She was, in fact, better off than Joe Canlon. If Joe mentioned her presence to the sergeant, he would likely revert to his irrational state and go after her. Joe didn't want to risk that, not after all of this. Not after seeing the bared soul of James Hawk.

They descended the ladder for as far as they dared. Hawk gestured for Joe to enter an open door leading to one of the floors under the tower. The base of the well, down in the sewer, would be well guarded. They had to have an alternate route to the ground. Hawk was quiet, too. He displayed the caution of a mortal man now. He was settling into an emotional hardening, into a singleness of purpose that would allow him to bull his way off of this island. He would outsmart all of the obstacles. He would show them—whoever they were: the Japanese; Hulmore; MacArthur; FDR; the 4Fs; all of them. He would get off Verhangen, and he'd bring Joe Canlon with him. It was better for everyone that he didn't know about Ivania.

The floor that he had chosen proved to be deserted. Hawk took Joe's M3. Joe carried his Ml. Hawk craned his neck hopefully around every corner. Finally his eyes widened.

"What are you lookin' for?" Joe whispered.

"This. I s'pose this is it." They walked into a little closet-sized guard's office, long abandoned. "See here, the thing you shit in is gone. We can climb down the hole," Hawk explained. He lifted the heavy planking from the floor, exposing a dark shaft.

"Are you sure?" Joe looked skeptically at the narrow shaft.

"I've done it. Give me a hand with these boards." It took both of them to move the two-by-twelve-planked trap door. Hawk had easily maneuvered one like it on his trip into the prison. The aching in his lower abdomen had subsided, but it left him with an unshakable weakness. He sat down heavily with his legs in the hole.

"What's wrong?" Joe asked.

"Shit. I'm tired." Joe waited patiently. Being tired in the midst of this life-threatening turmoil never occurred to him. Finally, Hawk took a deep breath and lowered himself into the tunnel. Joe slid in after him. Canlon tried to close the trap door. The points of the twenty-penny nails on the reverse side of the planking dug into the stone, resisting his effort to slide the door. He gave up.

Hawk let himself drop rapidly down the chute, slowing himself only enough to prevent an injury. Joe came down quickly, slowing only enough to keep from hitting the man below. In a short while, they were standing in the sewer, at a point that was dark and unprotected. "We're gonna make it," Joe gasped, "I know we are." They were already beyond the guarded well bottom.

"Shit yeah. Them goons is too busy fightin' each other now. Let's go this way. I don't want to try that goddamn grill again."

They took the route toward the side of the prison opposite the one they entered upon. Hawk knew the rubber rafts were gone. All he could hope to do was reach the sea and grab some sort of floating object. He didn't know that no man had ever escaped Verhangen Prison. For decades, hundreds of men had tried. Some were excellent swimmers—seafaring men. None made it. Hawk didn't know that, but he had seen the stretch of water between Verhangen and Rechnung. He hadn't had many hopes in the last twenty-four hours, this was really no time to start. If the opportunity arose where he could divert the enemy and Joe could escape, he would take it. Joe was a good swimmer. He wasn't. The ocean, however, was a long way off.

* * *

TANIGUCHI WAS among the first of the men to burst through the windows of the tower's mezzanine-level floor.

He paused at the sight of the shocking scene he found inside. He saw smoking remnants of humanity, their frail interiors splattered everywhere, as if the room was a giant mixing bowl into which they had inadvertently fallen. The fury of the battle was marked all along the walls and the floor. Taniguchi motioned for his corporal—his oldest and most loyal assistant—to check the stairway. Taniguchi joined in the checking of the bodies. While ostensibly looking for Kawamoto, his only concern was Hawk. He hoped against hope that Hawk lay alive among all the dead, still gasping for breath, so that Taniguchi might be the one to kill him. It seemed only just that this should be the case, and the *hancho* looked seriously, with a conviction that he would find the American.

But he didn't find him. Of course, many faces were gone completely. It was difficult to tell the nationality of the deceased in some cases. Taniguchi knew at least that he wasn't there. The cowardly animal had escaped again. Taniguchi knew such men well. Their avoidance of responsibility and morality was matched only by their physical slipperiness. They were the criminals turned soldiers. When the *hancho* heard the explosion on the stairs, he knew that Sergeant Hawk had once again eluded him.

Taniguchi's corporal was killed. The *hancho* charged up the stairs in anger. But he caught himself. Why would they go up? No, they had rigged the explosion in such a way to make it look as if they were going that way. If Hawk wanted out, he would have to go down. The *hancho* organized his men. He sent a small party to guard the chimney. He didn't expect his American fox to try that simple route. Were he that foolish, he deserved to die out of the presence of Taniguchi. The *hancho* proceeded to the ground below. He expected to intercept Hawk as the marine tried to reach the sea. He would probably go back for the rubber rafts. There were too many places to hide in the prison itself, but when Hawk came out, Taniguchi would catch him. The American had this time chosen the wrong party to match wits with.

* * *

WHEN HAWK and Canlon reached the end of the tunnel they found three soldiers sitting at its mouth. They were silhouetted against the gray wooliness of the fog outside. The sergeant stopped Joe with a hand.

"We gotta get these bastards with our knives," he said in a low and urgent voice.

"That's risky. A couple bursts will take 'em out," Joe replied.

Hawk shook his head. "There's got to be more right outside. No sense tippin' 'em off if we ain't got to." Hawk pulled out his knife.

"Jesus, Hawk, I don't think I can do that knife business."

"Why? I think I can get two of them. Just get one. Get all over him. Get mad and go for the heart. If we move fast enough, you can get him from behind." Hawk slapped his back, where the heart was located.

Joe put a hand on Hawk's arm. "Is it...hard to stick one in 'em?"

"Nah. Unless you hit a goddamn bone. Don't hesitate—that's the whole thing. You act silly and that son of a bitch'll kill you right here. Just remember that. It's the only way out of this."

"All right."

The two Americans moved soundlessly along the dark protection of the tunnel wall. Hawk's eyes were glued to the prey. Two had their backs to the sewer, the other his profile. The sergeant pointed to the two he intended to attack. "Don't hesitate. Follow through —hard."

The enemy soldiers were talking. Hawk waited for them to laugh. When you jump a man, he always seemed to have about a six-foot radius of natural radar around him. Dimwits call it a sixth sense. It's actually a combination of expectation, hearing, and peripheral vision. Sentries who counted on the alarm bell of a sixth sense eventually wound up dead. If a man laughed or was otherwise self-distracted, you could neutralize that radar. These fellows were pretty solemn. They spoke in low tones. There would be no laughter. Hawk inched closer, his long knife held in front of his bare chest. He didn't look back at Joe. If Joe choked on this one, he wanted to be moving fast enough to get all three. That would be virtually impossible.

They were close enough to be seen by the enemy now. The gloomy light that flooded the tunnel opening etched a stark, arcing line along the sewer's interior. Hawk stepped from the protecting shadow and into this light. Joe was beside him, close enough to touch him. Joe wanted to rush them, to get it over with. But he trusted Hawk and felt confident with him. Had he been alone, he would have dropped the knife and his rifle and ran the other way. Hawk moved a centimeter at a time, poised for action, but still waiting for the vital distraction.

One of the men sneezed. As he snorted to sneeze again, seven inches of steel went through his back and lanced his heart. Joe had done his job. Hawk couldn't afford such deep thrusts. He had to get two of them. He dashed out and stood between the two startled men with his legs spread wide apart. He lashed his knife across one man's throat and as the other clambered awkwardly to his feet, whipped a well-aimed backlash to the exposed carotid area under the jaw line. He pounded the blade vigorously into both of them to finish them off. Joe put a boot on his victim's back and pulled the knife out. He slumped against the tunnel wall.

"Good job, Joe," Hawk said quietly.

"Yeah. It was," he answered. Hawk stepped to the tunnel edge. Peering out he saw a ditch similar to the one on the opposite side of the prison.

"Don't see nobody," Hawk reported. He turned around to see Joe vomiting on himself. Hawk clenched his teeth and shook his head. He ran his arm across his grimy forehead. He batted his eye, trying to rid himself of a case of double vision bestowed upon him by General Kawamoto.

"Something about...stickin' a knife in a guy..." Joe gagged.

"For chrissake, come on. We'll crawl along here to the water. Keep that knife handy."

Hawk had had the help of Major Keizo and Taniguchi getting into Verhangen. It wouldn't be there this time. They crawled beneath a strand of barbed wire and crossed the intersecting ditch of the enemy lines before they were spotted. Shouting Japanese voices threw an icy dam across Hawk's racing blood. He looked up. They were within the view of one of the bamboo guard towers. The fog was no longer thick enough to protect them. He could see machine gunners, in a panic to move their weapon from its location on the opposite side of the tower. Other shouts came from the ground. They came from all sides.

"Well, shit," Hawk growled. That was that. It had already hit the fan. He climbed to the top of the ditch. He could see men running in a dozen directions. He didn't know where they were going, but he knew they would all wind up in his lap. He turned his grease gun skyward and pounded a long burst into the guard tower. A bullet hit one of the machine gunners there in the hand. He stumbled and fell over the railing, plummeting headfirst to the sand. Cries from above indicated someone else had been hit.

Hawk ducked beneath the top of the ditch. He folded his upper lip against his teeth. "Goddamn, Joe, let's run for it."

They got up and ran. A grenade hit their erstwhile position. Other grenades exploded along the ditch, following closely along their fleeing path. It sounded to Joe as if the shrapnel were blowing just over his stooped shoulders. A concussion grenade finally did knock him off his feet. Hawk stopped, reached down, and snatched his shirt. He pulled him to his feet. The skin of Joe's face was imbedded with sand and stone. The little red whelps were his only injury.

"Come on, we can make it to the water!" Hawk shouted into Joe's deafened ear. He knew that they would be shot down along the beach. James Hawk wasn't going to sit here and wait for them.

* * *

TANIGUCHI JUMPED into the passenger's side of a truck. He shouted orders to the driver. He had received a second-hand report that the marines were escaping along the other side of the island. They thought that they had fooled the old master, and they had—once. Once wouldn't be enough to get off Verhangen. The truck roared into gear, spewing sand from under its tires. The heads of the four occupants jerked with the sudden start. Taniguchi nodded approval at the breakneck speed of the driver. The truck careened around the corner of the prison and headed toward the shore of Verhangen that faced Rechnung.

The *hancho* had no fear of losing them. There was no vegetation. The fog was dissipating. The intricate trenches teemed with thousands of Japanese. They had no place to hide. Two observation planes and a Zeke fighter were already taking off for the beach. Taniguchi had alerted the airfield. The marines were dead. Taniguchi's only fear was that he wouldn't be the man to kill them, or failing that, he wouldn't be there to see it.

The driver hit the brakes. Two figures dashed in front of the truck. Bullets lanced through the windshield. The driver slumped over the steering wheel. A hand reached in and threw his body out onto the sand. Taniguchi saw the merciless face through the open door. He reached for his sidearm. The *hancho's* door was torn open. Joe Canlon was at his elbow. Joe motioned him out at rifle point. The men on the other side of the truck were not so lucky. They faced Hawk. Joe thumped Taniguchi's head with the rifle butt. Hawk left his two men bleeding to death on the sand. The sergeant jumped into the truck. Joe dove beside him.

Hawk gunned the motor and popped the clutch. Taniguchi sat up slowly. As they sped away, bullets thunked into the thin body of the truck. One whistled through it.

"Ahhh sh..." Joe jumped, bumping his head on the low roof. His arm spurted a fountain of red. He grabbed it with his other hand. Hawk floored the accelerator. The vehicle lurched wildly on the irregular ground. Mortar shells crashed in front of him. Sand flew in a dozen violent spirals. Hawk whipped the wheel to the right and left, trying to avoid being bracketed. Mortars fall straight out of the sky. They are hard to avoid. All of his maneuvering was just as likely to lead into as away from one of the black explosions.

"I...see...the water," Joe choked.

"Yeah." They flew off a high embankment. The terrific shock of hitting the ground caused Joe's head to ram through the windshield, shattering the already bullet-pocked glass. Blood streamed from his forehead. He rocked back in his seat, somewhere on the edge of consciousness. The motor stalled. Hawk stomped the starter pedal. Submachine gun bullets traced a pattern in the sand by his door.

Two imperial soldiers, no more than thirty feet from his door, were charging him. Hawk poked his M3 through the window. He managed to drag a short burst across the legs of the foolhardy men. They dropped and Hawk turned back to trying to start the truck. No luck.

"Come on," he snapped. Joe made no response. Hawk cursed violently as he jumped out, hopped the hood, and pulled Joe out. Two little planes whined overhead like moths around a flame. They showed the way for the pursuers. Hawk lashed an arm around Joe's waist. With clumsy, weak steps, he made his way toward the sea.

Taniguchi led a party of howling warriors down to the beach. They leapt off the seawall that had stalled Hawk's truck. Some were firing their weapons. All were screaming for blood. The old *hancho* ran faster than any of them. If he hadn't, they would have buried him beneath their boots.

Hawk felt the heavy impact as another bullet hit Joe. "Jesus," he heard Joe say. The sea lapped at his boots. Hawk trudged wearily into it, somehow satisfied that he had made it this far. A Zeke fighter blazed along the water line, some forty feet from the ground. One second it was the size of a dime, the next it was the size of a mountain. It got louder and louder until it seemed there was no limit to how loud *loud* could be. A line of twenty millimeter cannon fire ripped mud on one side of them and water spouts in the water on the other side. "Christ," Hawk grunted as the crushing noise vibrated over him. The Zero was again the size of a dime.

He heard shouts behind him as the airplane droned away to bank. He decided to die facing them. He dropped Joe, unslung his MC and lay in the surf. A few hundred yards away, it looked as if the entire width of the island was covered with Japanese soldiers. Coming from the other direction, the Zero again soared along the beach, this time thirty feet from the ground. Before it could open fire again, there was an audible rattling along its fuselage. It bled flames. The massive hurtling missile struck the ground and cartwheeled into the attacking Japanese, scything through them in a brilliant multihued fireball.

Other planes streaked overhead toward Verhangen Prison. They came from the sea. They were U.S. Navy fighters. A dozen of them dropped out of the fog and strafed the crowded beach. The Japanese dispersed in terror. Looking over his shoulder, toward Rechnung, Hawk saw that he had more help. A line of LSTs, LCI gunboats, and LCVPs pushed the fog before them. Verhangen Prison began to crumble under a rocket barrage. The LCIs brought the gray-beige stones toppling to the sand.

Hawk accepted this as a matter of course, stood, and picked Joe up again. He backed into the water, keeping his grease gun aimed at the beach.

Taniguchi did not flee the surprise attack. He seized a rifle from a retreating private and raced across the beach. No amount of hardware, of men, or of money could save Hawk from him. The marine was waist deep in the water before he saw a lone Japanese coming after him. It would be an easy shot. He raised the M3 with one hand. Out of bullets. He dropped Joe again.

Taniguchi flung himself to one knee and aimed carefully. The eye of Taniguchi was sure. Years of war hadn't dimmed it. Hawk ducked reflexively and searched Joe for a handgun. Joe had lost it. Taniguchi's rifle clicked. He looked angrily at the insubordinate weapon. It had no magazine. "Fool!" Taniguchi cursed. He stood and waded into the surf. Wave after wave of U.S. planes thundered over the top of his head. Thousands of battle-tried U.S. Marines approached from the ocean. Thousands of Japanese began scrambling for the beach to defend their positions. But in the middle of these two behemoths were only Hawk and Taniguchi.

Taniguchi had lost his detached pragmatism. Hawk was exhausted. They were both reduced to what they feared the most. Taniguchi knew that he could not leave the beach a victor. The American landing parties were too close now. He could kill Hawk, but he couldn't escape with his life. He waded up to the American. They studied one another only briefly. Taniguchi swung his rifle and Hawk backed away to dodge it. The *hancho* swung again. Hawk swung back with the M3, holding the wire stock in one hand. The rifle clattered against the machine pistol. The cheap little grease gun would never fire again. Hawk's hand was numbed by the collision. He continued to stagger away, clutching the wire stock of the pitiful little tin-can bodied M3. Taniguchi pursued, stalked. He kept coming, swinging again and again at his hated foe. Hawk swung back as a defense, slamming the pressed metal of the submachine gun into the invincible hardwood stock of the Arisaka rifle. His last blow bent the cylindrical body of the M3 into an L.

Taniguchi no longer saw the youthful rage of his opponent. The cruel face was now pale and white. It was lined as badly as Taniguchi's. The movements of the American were like those of a man asleep. He reared back, and with all the strength of his broad shoulders, aimed the point of the rifle butt at Hawk's head. Hawk slapped at the stock, somehow, once again fending off the death blow. Taniguchi tried again, and again another weak slap barely diverted the blow. The M3 was a shredded ball of metal on the end of its wire stock. Hawk stared defiantly into the *hancho's* flinty eyes.

A spout of water blooped to Taniguchi's right. Another blooped to his left. Marine sharpshooters were targeting him from the bouncing landing crafts. Twenty years of rationalism overcame his momentary rage. He cursed Hawk in Japanese and slung the rifle at him with a vengeance. It shot through the air, hit Hawk's shoulder and fell into the green surf. The *hancho* screamed more passionately when he saw that he had done no damage. Then, Taniguchi turned and with an unhurried stride, walked back to the beach.

More than satisfied with the stalemate, Hawk managed to sneer a smile and fall down into the cold water. He sat there for a moment. Then he roared at Taniguchi's rigid back: "Go to hell, Jap!"

13

Hawk hardly recognized Stocken Bay. It had become the second front that it was supposed to be. The Japanese forces on Rechnung were on the verge of collapse. Across the strait, Verhangen Island was under heavy attack. It was difficult for Hawk to comprehend that all of this had happened in a day's time. He had been given first aid and was allowed to wander around the bay on his own.

He was called in to see a Lieutenant Murphy not long after his return. Murphy was located in Jordan's old CP, though what his official title or function was escaped the sergeant. Hawk was in the process of hitching a ride over to the sick bay on the other side of Rechnung when he got the news. He was going to pay Joe a visit.

Hawk entered Murphy's hut without asking permission. The officer ignored the indiscretion and returned Hawk's salute. He remained seated. Hawk stood. "Sergeant Hawk, I've been asked to give you a little debriefing on the situation here. You won't have a unit to rejoin. You'll be reassigned. Company D was destroyed last night in the gas attack. There is some evidence that Captain Jordan escaped. We just don't know yet."

Hawk looked into the twinkling young eyes of the lieutenant. "Yessir." He cleared his throat and looked down. The officer noticed that he was having trouble blinking his eyes simultaneously. "I can report that Captain Jordan was killed on Verhangen Island, sir. A Jap general killed him and I witnessed it. You can tell his family that he killed the general, too."

Murphy made no comment. He reached into his desk and brought out a stack of brightly colored shoulder patches. "These came. For your company. I guess since you're the only effective, you're the only man authorized to wear one." The lieutenant took a patch off the top and handed it to Hawk. He swept the rest into his wastepaper basket. Hawk stared for a moment at the inside of the garbage can. He blinked his left eye. The white of the eye was red and it stung.

Hawk reached out slowly and took the embroidery. Chevron's hideous skull grinned up at him. Hawk snorted at it. "Yeah..." Hawk finally said, "...real sharp."

"You'll be the only man in the world with one of those. That's something to be proud of." Hawk glanced up quickly at him. For some reason a cold chill ran up Murphy's spine. "What was it like in Verhangen?" Murphy asked quietly.

Hawk looked thoughtfully over the top of the patch. "Bad." He shrugged. "Thanks, Lieutenant." He turned and left.

He made it to the hospital later in the day. Joe didn't look so good. He was thinking of Ivania Broeder. It was still too soon to mention it to Hawk. He still felt like they were in Verhangen. And a dark part of them always would be.

"How you doin', Joe?" Joe had a sheet up to his neck.

"Not too goddamn hot. They're talkin' about sendin' me home."

"Shit. Can't beat that."

Joe had tears in his eyes. "What am I gonna do at home? Turn out ball bearings in a factory ten hours a day? I belong here with you guys."

"There ain't no guys. Just me." Hawk sighed. He looked out the window.

"I...wish we had somethin' to show for what we done," Joe said in an odd voice. He was trying to work Ivania into the conversation. It was hard. "All we went through...all that everybody went through...and nobody left..."

"Ah," Hawk said, "Oh, yeah. I brought you something." He took the patch out and handed it to him. "This'll give you a kick in the ass."

Joe smiled broadly. "Damn! My patch." Joe sat up. He studied the picture. "Kinda spooky-lookin', ain't it?" he asked. Hawk batted one of his eyes. He saw the fear in Joe's face.

"Yeah. Real sharp, Joe. Just like you said."

Joe looked away from it. "It's...bad luck. I couldn't wear it. All them men..."

Hawk smiled encouragingly. "Ain't no such thing as luck. What do you mean you ain't gonna wear it? You been talking about it for a month."

"Nah, I couldn't wear it. Here, you keep it. I'd like to look at it every now and then. If...I come back, you'll be wearin' it and I can see it. If...you ain't afraid of it, I mean."

Hawk's expression grew serious. "You'll be okay. Just don't give the doctors no shit."

"I can't give nobody no shit." A nurse stuck her head in and told Hawk he'd have to go. "Not even her," Joe added. She was pretty.

"Them nurses," Hawk smiled. They both got quiet. "Well. I'll be back around. I'll see you tomorrow or something." Hawk stood. Joe picked the patch up off the sheet. "Here, take it. Sew it on. For good luck, Hawk."

"Okay, Joe." Hawk waved and left. Joe stared at the door.

Later that day, Hawk stole a sewing kit and put it on his shoulder.

* * *

ON A FAR BEACH OF VERHANGEN, where the vicious fighting had not spread, the *hancho* Taniguchi buried the remains of his friend Keizo. Taniguchi dropped a flower on the grave, the grave of Keizo, the soldier who loved the flowers. Keizo, whose family waited in vain for their saintly patriarch. Keizo, whose unborn grand-babies would never know his kind smile, or his even kinder soul. Taniguchi turned his hard features toward the ocean. As hard as he was, he couldn't stop a tear from falling. All the world was a harder place now without his major. Another tear fell. Taniguchi bowed his head. His broad shoulders shrank with the pain in his breast.

Only a few miles away, on a secluded Rechnung